A SHORT HISTORY OF THE GIRL NEXT DOOR

A SHORT
HISTORY
OF THE
GIRL
NEXT
DOOR

JARED RECK

ALFRED A. KNOPF · NEW YORK

Text copyright © 2017 by Jared Reck
Jacket art copyright © 2017 by Jeff Hinchee

"Sentimental Moment or Why Did the Baguette Cross the Road?" reprinted from *Calls from the Outside World* copyright © 2006 by Robert Hershon, with permission from Hanging Loose Press.

Visit us on the Web! randomhouseteens.com

Educators and librarians, for a variety of teaching tools, visit us at RHTeachersLibrarians.com

Library of Congress Cataloging-in-Publication Data
Names: Reck, Jared, author.
Title: A short history of the girl next door / Jared Reck.
Description: First edition. | New York: Alfred A. Knopf, 2017. | Summary: After years of pining for the girl next door, fifteen-year-old Matthew Wainwright must deal with Tabby dating a popular senior just when he needs her most.
Identifiers: LCCN 2017017965 (print) | LCCN 2016038358 (ebook) | ISBN 978-0-5247-1609-7 (ebook) | ISBN 978-1-5247-1607-3 (trade) | ISBN 978-1-5247-1608-0 (lib. bdg.)
Subjects: | CYAC: Best friends—Fiction. | Friendship—Fiction. | Dating (Social customs)—Fiction. | Basketball—Fiction. | High schools—Fiction. | Schools—Fiction.
Classification: LCC PZ7.1.R398 (print) | LCC PZ7.1.R398 Sho 2017 (ebook) | DDC [Fic]—dc23

The text of this book is set in 10.6-point Aldine 721 BT.

Printed in the United States of America
September 2017
10 9 8 7 6 5 4 3 2 1

First Edition

FOR MOM AND DAD.

Maybe I'll even pay for breakfast one morning.

CHAPTER ONE

THE MOMENT I KNOW IT'S OVER

I know it's over when Liam Branson's black Accord pulls in front of Tabby's house before school.

I'm shooting free throws in my driveway, like I do every morning, waiting for the bus to deliver me to another memorable day as a freshman at Franklin High. It's late October, which means the weather is perfect for my before-school shootaround ritual. Warm enough that I don't have to shove my fingers into my armpits, panini-style, after every few shots to prevent frostbite, and cold enough that I'm not a sweaty mess when the bus pulls up.

I'm about fifty free throws in when Branson's car rolls into our circle, going around and stopping in front of Tabby's house, straight across from mine. I try not to stare too much between shots. But what is a senior guy—one of *the* senior guys, varsity starter on our Black Bears football and basketball teams—doing picking up a freshman girl before school?

He beeps his horn, and an instant later Tabby's front door flies open. Tabby throws her book bag over her shoulder and jogs across her front lawn, beaming, looking amazing in that not-even-trying way that Tabby has—worn jeans and a T-shirt, her red hair pulled back into a sloppy bun. It's perfect.

When Tabby reaches the car, she opens the back door—I didn't notice Liam's sister sitting in the front seat—and throws her bag inside. She looks at me over the top of Branson's car and waves.

"Hi, Matty! See you at school!"

I give a weak smile and wave back as she hops into the car. Naturally, I brick my next shot off the side of the rim and have to chase the ball to the end of my driveway. I grab it just before it bounces into the circle as Liam Branson drives by, giving me a lame peace sign with the hand resting on top of his steering wheel.

Shit.

What's my move here? Mirror back his peace sign? Smile and wave like a little kid? Stare him down so he loses focus and crashes into a mailbox? In my head, I give him a little nod as I turn and trot in for a casual power dunk, *everyone* in that car knowing who the man is.

Of course, I manage none of these. I stand there, holding my ball, staring like an idiot as Branson—with Tabby—pulls away.

When Branson's car is out of sight, I dribble back and sink my next ten in a row before I hear my bus pulling up at the end of the street.

Shit.

CHAPTER TWO

A SHORT HISTORY
OF THE GIRL NEXT DOOR

Okay, so technically she lives across the street, but whatever. And really, since we live on a cul-de-sac, it's kind of across the street *and* next door. See how that works?

Right.

"No Tabby today?" Miss Edna asks as I climb the steps to board the bus.

"I guess not," I say with a fake smile, heading down the aisle to my seat. Let her think that Tabby's just absent.

Out of habit, I slide in against the window of seat eighteen and prop my knees up on the seat back in front of me. Then, feeling stupid, I set my book bag on the empty space next to me.

It's not that I have anything against riding the bus. I really don't, other than that, at my height, I don't really fit into the seats anymore. I can't drive yet, and I don't see how I improve my image in high school by having my mom drop me off.

Honestly, I've always kind of loved riding the bus. There are no delinquent assholes on my route, so it's usually pretty peaceful, especially in the mornings. Plus, we've had the same bus driver, Miss Edna, from the time my mom helped me climb the steps on my first day of kindergarten. Miss Edna's gotten drinks and snacks for us every Friday since then—even the high schoolers, who should be too cool for Goldfish and Little Hugs—and she always has the radio tuned to her classic-hits station. When I get my license next year, I think I'm actually going to miss it.

And the best part, up until today at least, is Tabby.

The school bus has always meant twenty minutes, before and after school, of uninterrupted Tabby time. Time that, until today, I've always taken for granted.

When my mom helped me climb those steps on my first day of school over nine years ago, Tabby was right there next to me, her Hello Kitty backpack nearly as big as her entire body. She flopped down beside me in the first seat behind Miss Edna, chattering away about what our teacher would be like, and what kind of toys would be in the classroom, and what the snack might be, and what the other kids would be like.

And that's how it's always been.

With Tabby's mom already gone—she disappeared from Tabby's life barely after it began—my mom started babysitting Tabby when she was a few months old. And since my mom stayed home with me until I started school, Tabby was at our house nearly every day. She's part of our family. Hell, she was at the hospital when Murray was born four years ago, crying right along with my dad when they let us in the delivery room to see Murray for the first time. Tabby and I were both only-children up until that point, and it was like we both got a new little brother with Murray.

When we were younger, my parents used to laugh at how I would follow Tabby around, trailing after her like a giant puppy. Little Tabby would decide what we were going to play—her squeaky, high-pitched chef's voice shouting out orders for our fancy restaurant, or the doctor instructing me how to take care of the stuffed-animal patients in our doctor's office—and I'd follow right along, happily doing my best to please her, weaving in my own ideas as we went.

Following her lead.

In fact, it was Tabby who got me my first "girlfriend" in fifth grade. She'd decided one day after school that November that it was time for me to have a girlfriend, to which I thought, *Okay. Cool.*

"What do you think of Rebecca Gaskins?" she asked while we fixed a snack in my kitchen.

"Who's Rebecca Gaskins?" I asked, a knot already forming in my stomach.

"She's the tall girl with curly brown hair in my homeroom. She's nice. She sits at my table at lunch."

"Wait, did she say she likes me or something?" I was confused, starting to panic. I was only vaguely aware of who this girl was, and part of me could tell where this was going. Tabby's plan was already in place, and, as usual, I was going to follow along, provided I didn't wet my pants or pass out. And even then, really . . .

"Of course she did, Matt. So do you like her?" Tabby grinned, leaning across the bar in our kitchen while I pulled the bag of popcorn from the microwave.

"I . . . I mean, I guess." My heart was beating faster now.

"Would you want to go out with her?" Tabby's grin widened, like the hungry cat grins at the mouse in cartoons. What the hell was I dealing with here?

"Hold on, did she ask you to ask me out for her?"

"Don't worry about that yet, Matt," she said, brushing off my concern. "Would *you* want to go out with *her*?"

The simple answer was *Yes, absolutely*. Even though I had never talked to Rebecca Gaskins before, and the thought of talking to her now was nearly causing me to go into cardiac arrest, I did like the idea of having a girlfriend. I really had no clue what that meant, other than that I would get to tell people that, yes, I did in fact have a girlfriend.

"Hey, Matt, you got a girlfriend?"

"Yeah, man, of course I have a girlfriend."

"Awesome. Which one is she?"

"I'm not totally sure."

"Awesome. Play on, playa."

It would be my membership card for this new grown-up world of awesome.

"Sure . . . I guess so," I replied. "So did she ask you to ask me?" I said again.

"Yes! Perfect!" Tabby said, not really in response to my question. She hopped off her stool and pulled out her phone. She started dialing as she walked into the living room without me.

"Wait! Tabby, what are you doing?" I asked, following behind her.

"Hi, Rebecca?" she said into her phone, waving me off. "It's Tabby. You know my friend Matt? Matt Wainwright? He rides my bus." She paused, waiting. Then she laughed and said, "Yeah, that's him." (What the hell did that mean?) "So yeah, Matt's my neighbor, and he wanted me to ask if you'd go out with him."

My whole body went rigid.

"So, is that a yes?" Tabby continued, now looking at me and

smiling, one finger in the air, as though I were about to interrupt her.

And then her final act of sadism.

"Oh, Rebecca, that's great! Hold on, your boyfriend is right here. He wants to talk to you."

My memory gets a little fuzzy at this point, as my brain and the rest of my central nervous system had completely shut down. I may or may not have shit my pants. It's hard to say.

What I do remember is Tabby, bouncing back and forth on the balls of her feet, a look of twisted glee on her face, forcing her phone into my petrified hand. She lifted my hand up to my ear, like I was some life-size Ken doll, did some weird little dance, and disappeared briefly into the kitchen.

When my body forced me to start breathing again, the air escaping my lungs must have vaguely resembled *Hi, Rebecca,* because somewhere in the distance I heard her say, "Hi, Matt," then giggle nervously.

Much silence ensued.

Tabby returned, popcorn bag in hand.

I think the most my brain could muster over the course of what had to have been twenty excruciating minutes was, "Uhh . . . So . . . do you . . . have any homework tonight?"

"No."

"That's good."

More silence.

Tabby did this to me at least four more times that year, me following blindly each time.

Even through the last couple of years of middle school, when we started getting involved in our own separate activities and hanging out more with our own groups of friends, we had that time on the bus each day, time when Tabby could rant about her day or whatever was going on with her life, and I could just listen and make lame jokes to get her to laugh. Time where we could still be buddies.

At some point, though, Tabby became more than my buddy. At least to me. I mean, she's still my buddy, but every day it feels like more and more of a sham. Because while Tabby's still happy to sit down next to me—where my book bag now sits—and give me daily updates on her new life in high school, I sit here each day, silently hoping for more. I'll watch her lips while she talks, and my brain kicks into romantic-movie mode. She bumps into me, or puts her hand on my arm during one of her stories, and my whole body tingles. Then I overanalyze every little thing she's saying, searching for any hint that she could be harboring similar feelings for me.

But as insane as I feel every day, our time on the bus together has become even more important to me. Now we're in high school, and apparently older guys are taking notice.

Pulling up to the curb in front of Franklin, seeing Branson's car already parked in the senior lot, I imagine the three of them walking in together, laughing, and I feel desperate, out of control.

I am completely in love with my best friend from childhood, she has absolutely no idea, and now she's interested in older, more popular guys.

This sounds like a bad movie already.

CHAPTER THREE

THIS MOVIE SUCKS

So why not just tell Tabby?

Why not follow the script, and in some heart-wrenching scene—preferably under a streetlamp in the rain, where tears and raindrops stream down our faces as one—say something like, "Tabby . . . it's you. It's always been you," and watch as my words take purchase in her consciousness, replaying all the moments I was *there for her* in her mind before she closes both the literal and the figurative gap between us with a kiss so full of longing and passion the camera has to turn away? Story over, right?

Well, it's complicated. Which is why I've organized my rebuttal into three parts:

1. These movies? They're all written *by* the best friend in love, probably while the person longed for is off getting busy with his/her *actual* lover. (Please tell me the universe did not just slip up and give me a glimpse of my future.)

2. How *do* you tell somebody who's been your friend your whole life that your feelings have totally changed? That while you used to share a *Blue's Clues*

coloring book after school, and have burping contests until one of you threw up orange soda in your mouth, and argue over what names to give to your legion of Play-Doh creatures, you are now apeshit bonkers for her and can't walk by her in the hallway without feeling sick?

"Hey, remember how we used to spend hours playing together in your sandbox? Wasn't that so great? Well, now I really wanna go make out in your sandbox."

"Wait, where are you going?"

"It doesn't have to be in your sandbox!"

3. Even if we eliminate number one and number two—say the best-friend-in-love movies are actually based on reality, and I find a copy of *Telling-Your-Best-Friend-You're-Really-in-Love-with-Her for Dummies* in the library—there's still the overwhelming problem of *me*.

Let me attempt to illustrate:

When we were in fifth grade, Mr. Holowitz had this hand-made laminated sign hanging next to his whiteboard. All it had was OTM ≠ OTM. He waited for a kid to ask about it before he explained—that kid was Tabby.

"On the mind *does not equal* out the mouth."

After smiling at our blank expressions for a moment, he then explained to us how fifth graders—as we started to mature and learn things that younger students could not—sometimes suffered from what's called *diarrhea of the mouth*.

"As you get older, you learn that not every little thing that flits through your brain throughout the day needs to be shared with the rest of us."

It was kind of an advanced way of saying to shut your mouth during class, but I liked it.

And whenever he caught Tabby whispering to me during class—which was usually at least twice a day—he'd tap his pointer on the sign and raise his eyebrows at her. Tabby would smile, and Mr. Holowitz would smile, not insincerely, back.

Mr. Holowitz never once pointed to the sign while looking at me.

For Tabby, OTM ≠ OTM was a gentle reminder—a swig of Pepto to quell her constant diarrhea of the mouth.

For me, OTM ≠ OTM was my default setting: nothing in my brain ever came out—and if it did, it was never how it sounded when it was floating through my head.

If Tabby had diarrhea of the mouth, then I suffered from verbal constipation.

Perfectly clear now, right?

I'm an idiot.

CHAPTER FOUR

IT'S NOTE-TAKING MONDAY. JOY.

"Too cool to ride the cheese now, huh?"

"Too cool to still call it *the cheese*," Tabby replies, smiling, suddenly interested in her book bag hanging over the back of her chair.

I slide into my seat at the lab table right behind her a few minutes before the bell for third period. Science is the only class we have together this year. Not coincidentally, it's the class I'm earliest to.

"So who was that who picked you up this morning?" I ask, knowing full well who it was.

"Lily Branson's older brother. Liam. He's a senior. Do you know Lily?" she asks quickly.

"I think I know who she is. She's a sophomore, right?" I reply, again knowing full well who Lily Branson is. During eighth-period study hall in the library the first week of school, I paged through last year's yearbook, and I started making a mental list of the top-five hottest girls by grade level. Lily Branson landed the #1 ranking on my list.

"I guess everyone knows who the Bransons are. Aren't you on the basketball team with Liam?" Tabby continues before I can note how much older Liam is, that we've *never* played together before this year. "Lily's my math partner. People say she's all stuck-up, but she's actually really nice. I think people just say stuff because she's pretty, you know?"

"Oh yeah, I know. She seems really nice," I say, feeling like a complete ass. I'd made that comment—and worse—more than once, about Lily Branson and any number of other attractive girls. Probably every girl on my top-five lists. Because, you know, if a hot girl doesn't want to mate with you, she's obviously stuck-up.

"She asked if I'd want a ride to school, and I said sure. Thought I'd mix it up after a decade of riding the bus next to *you*." She gives me a wicked smile as she pulls her notebook from her book bag.

In the old days, I would have given her the boogie gun after a zing like that and laughed it off. But now? Well, okay, I still give her the boogie gun—thumb in nostril, forefinger extended, other hand cranking like an old-school-gangster tommy gun—but I can barely breathe, hiding the sting behind my barrage of imaginary boogies.

At the bell, Mrs. Shepler collects her notes from behind her lab table to start class. (Joy!) Tabby turns around one last time and whispers, "Don't worry, Matt. Her brother's got football, so you'll still get to see this lovely face on the bus after school." She looks forward again.

I swear, there are times when I'm convinced Tabby has some kind of secret connection to my brain, like she's bugged the lines of my inner monologue. Very disconcerting.

"Okay, welcome back, folks," Mrs. Shepler says, papers in hand. "We've got a busy week ahead of us, so let's get started."

It's Note-Taking Monday, which, despite her claims of

busyness, means we copy directly from her PowerPoint slides as she reads through them, lecturing for an extra ten minutes on each slide, so that we never actually finish the notes on Note-Taking Monday. Painful. While Mrs. Shepler digs through piles of papers on her lab desk to find her new PowerPoint clicker, I pull out my notebook and flip it open, glancing at week one's notes on . . . note taking. Awesome.

Okay, so to be totally honest, Note-Taking Monday isn't so bad. Since note taking in the Sheplervian sense really consists of copying word for word directly from a PowerPoint slide, I don't have to do any actual thinking. I don't have to pay attention to her lecture to know what's important to write down. I don't have to do any of that forced-interaction bullshit teachers use to try to keep us engaged—*now turn to your partner and try to summarize the concept we've just discussed.* I hate that. I have enough awkward conversations on my own, thank you.

So while Mrs. Shepler spends all of Monday—and usually Tuesday—talking through her slides, my mind is free to wander for forty-five minutes. Much of that time I end up staring at Tabby while she writes in her notebook or whispers to the girl next to her at her lab table (Rebecca Gaskins, of all people), noting everything from how Tabby holds her pencil—the same way she used to hold her crayons, hunched over our coloring books as kids, oddly similar to a kung fu grip—to how she taps the eraser on her notebook when she's not writing, to how she brushes the same strand of red hair behind her ear every few seconds, just to have it fall in front of her face again.

And once, almost every class, usually when my brain has taken a much-needed Tabby break and has moved on to the lunch menu or chauvinistic rankings or working through game scenarios for basketball, Tabby does this thing where she stretches both arms above her head, then leans back over her chair. And every single time, when she gets to the point where her hands are right over my lab table, she pretends like she's trying to grab my notebook or my pencil. We both know it's coming, and when she finds I've already got my things secured, she tilts her head back and gives me this goofy, upside-down smile.

And my brain is fucked.

Seriously, how can you see a person nearly every day of your life and never think a thing of it, then all of a sudden, one day, it's different? You see that goofy grin a thousand times and just laugh, but goofy grin number 1,001 nearly stops your heart?

I know. Rein it in, M-Dub.

When the bell rings, we're only on the third slide of notes (out of eleven). Mrs. Shepler sighs and shakes her head at the clock. "We'll have to finish these notes tomorrow," she says, not really to anyone in particular, as we shove our notebooks into our bags and head out the door.

"So you're still riding the bus home in the afternoons?" I ask Tabby once we're in the hallway, trying my best to sound casual.

"Aww, Matty, did you miss me this morning?" she replies, bumping into me with her hip—which, at barely five foot, catches me mid-thigh.

"Actually," I say, "a lot of girls were asking about the empty seat next to me. Prime real estate, it seems."

Tabby laughs. "And did you tell them that Miss Edna doesn't let sixth graders sit in the back?"

"Touché."

"Don't worry, Matt, I'll be there this afternoon to help fend off the ravening hordes."

"Very kind of you, Tabby. Thank you."

I know Tabby has geometry next—because I just know these things—and when we turn down the math hallway, I see a group of students clustered outside her room. Lily Branson with some other über-popular sophomores talking to her brother, leaning against a locker. Lily smiles and waves as we approach, the whole group of them turning to smile, including Liam Branson. I can *feel* Tabby beaming next to me, and I know our ridiculous conversation is over.

Obviously not a single one of them is smiling at me. In fact, while I'm probably the tallest person in the hallway, a head floating above a sea of bodies, it's like they don't even notice that I'm there, practically arm in arm with Tabby.

Now, a competent social being would smile right back at all of them—maybe give a little nod to Liam. Stand there and pretend to be part of their conversation for a minute before touching Tabby on the arm and saying, "I gotta get to class, I'll see you later," which really says, "Sorry to interrupt, kids. I'd love to stay and chat, but this guy's got shit to do." Give Branson another little nod—maybe even give his sister a wink—and head off down the hall.

But I am not a competent social being.

Instead, while they're having their cool-kid smile-fest with Tabby, I stare straight ahead, down the hallway, and check the watch that I'm not wearing. *I'm* pretending that I don't notice *them*, you see. Even as they start talking to the girl I'm clearly walking with.

Nope, I am fully focused on what awaits me at the end of this hallway (absolutely nothing, maybe a pee stop before English) even as Lily Branson says, "Are you gonna make it to our Halloween party this weekend? Liam promised to wear a costume!"

I can't focus on Tabby's response, I'm trying so hard—and apparently succeeding—to remain invisible, but I notice Liam smile sheepishly at Tabby. "I gotta get to class; I'll see you later," he says, before heading off in the other direction.

Awesome.

CHAPTER FIVE

EAGLES DO NOT ENJOY TWIZZLERS OR THE COMPANY OF TROLLS

"Matty, I finished your tail feathers! Come take a look!"

I find Mom in the dining room after washing the grime off my hands from shooting around in the driveway. The table and floor are covered with craft supplies. After years of staying home with me and now again with Murray, Mom is an arts-and-crafts Jedi. She can do things with a hot-glue gun that would make Martha Stewart envious. But as I stand next to her to take a look at her creation, I immediately start to panic.

"Mom. No, Mom. Mom, I cannot wear that."

She has the full costume laid out across the table. She ignores me and pulls a tight white beanie down over my head.

"You agreed to go trick-or-treating with Murray tonight. He begged me to let you take him. Instead of me. Do you have any idea how hard that is for me?"

"Can't I wear the old troll mask or something? An old bed-sheet for each of us?"

"Yes, Matthew, even though Murray's had this exact idea picked out for the past six months—never once wavering, no matter how many great ideas I've tried to put out there—I think you should go ahead and wear a ratty old mask that your brother hates. That would be awesome of you."

I start to respond, but Mom's just getting warmed up. The line between playful sarcasm and pissed can get blurry.

"And, you know, it's not like I've been working on this costume for the past week or anything. I know you've been really busy playing in the driveway and not doing your math homework on this beautiful Saturday, so you probably haven't had time to notice."

"Hey, hey, I don't think the sarcasm is necessary. I'm the one who's going to be humiliated here, Mom."

The complete costume: bald eagle mama and chick.

Me: white beanie cap, which Mom crocheted herself; rubber beak; one of Dad's old, gigantic brown wool sweaters, with feathers sewn into the sleeves for wings; and the final piece—bright yellow skinny jeans that Mom probably found on the clearance rack at Sears, possibly in the juniors' department, with horizontal stripes drawn in black Sharpie down the legs and long brown tail feathers hot-glued to the butt.

Like I said: arts-and-crafts Jedi.

"Seriously? Those pants? Can't I wear my own jeans? Nobody's going to care what I'm wearing anyway."

"Murray cares. He'll notice right away that you don't have the right bird legs."

"Do you see these things?" I say, holding the yellow skinny jeans up to me. I'm getting desperate. "Do you know how tight they're going to be? Where am I supposed to keep my nuts in these things?"

Mom turns and grips the edge of the table. That line between playful and pissed is less blurry now that I'm clearly on the other side of it.

"They're *bird* legs, Matthew," she says through gritted teeth. "It's a *costume*."

"But—"

"And if you like," she continues, clutching the hot-glue gun, "I'm sure we can find *some*where to put your *nuts*."

"Mom—"

"Since they're clearly big enough for you to talk that way to your *mother*."

She looks me in the eye as she says that last part, her nostrils flared.

"You're right," she says finally, but I have a feeling she's not suddenly understanding my side of things. "Nobody out there is going to care how you look. But your little brother *does*. So try to get over yourself, Matthew. This night isn't about you anymore."

"Ugh," I say, my final statement of resistance, throwing the skinny jeans back on the table in front of her. I mutter an f-bomb to myself as I turn to leave the room. I know she hears it, but she doesn't say anything else, just lets me storm into the living room to flop onto the couch and turn on the TV. She's probably saying the same things under her breath—I can hear her throwing stuff back into craft bins and slamming drawers.

Mom and I don't do this often. We both tend to try to defuse tension with humor—sometimes inappropriate—but that doesn't always work when you're the cause of each other's tension.

Twenty minutes later, Mom comes back in the living room and sits down next to me on the couch. We stare at *Sports-Center* in silence, neither of us really watching. The strain from our little episode is gone, but my stomach still churns at the thought of knocking on every door in the neighborhood in full mama-bald-eagle regalia. I know no one really cares what some fifteen-year-old kid is wearing to take his little brother trick-or-treating, but that doesn't mean I can just roll with looking like an idiot when inevitably some hot high school girl answers the door to hand out candy between make-out sessions with her leering boyfriend.

"Dude, nice pants."

"Ha, yeah, thanks. They're supposed to be bird legs."

"No, yeah, I see. Love the yellow. They girls'?"

"No, no, pretty sure they're just old skater jeans . . . Not mine . . . My mom bought them . . . uh . . ."

"Yeah. Here's a Twizzler. Have fun trick-or-treating, douche."

Mom takes the remote from my hand and clicks off the TV. She gives my leg a gentle squeeze as she stands.

"Come here a minute," she says, walking up the stairs. I don't know where this is headed. She sees me hesitate, unsure about her change in tactics. "Come on, Matt. I want you to see something."

I stand and follow Mom to the top of the steps, where she silently pushes open the door to Murray's room.

"He's been wearing it all day," she whispers, and stands aside so I can see into his room. Murray sits on the floor in front of his bed in his bald-eagle-chick costume. Stuffed animals are arranged all around him: he's immersed in his favorite imaginary game, *Animals! Animals! Animals!*

Murray's costume: matching homemade beanie with little tufts of white feathers sewn in, matching beak, tan fleece sweatshirt, and the bottom half of a papier-mâché egg attached by suspenders, made to look like he's in the process of hatching. I notice his costume does not include yellow skinny jeans.

Murray's light brown curls jut out from beneath his cap, his beak hanging loose from his neck so he can give voices to his animals.

"Murray," Mom says softly, "you wanna show Matty how you look in your costume?"

Murray is immediately on his feet, beaming, as though he's been sitting there waiting for this moment all day. Which I suspect he has.

"Matty! Look at my baby-bald-eagle costume!" Murray puts the beak back over his nose and starts flapping his arms and screeching, running around in circles on his town rug before crashing into my legs and laughing.

"You look awesome, buddy. Very nice." I smile and noogie his white-capped head.

"Where's *your* costume, Matty? Aren't you gonna get dressed as the mommy bald eagle for trick-or-treating?" Without waiting for my response, Murray bounces over to Mom's legs and latches on. "Is it time to go trick-or-treating now, Mommy? Is it? Is it?"

"Soon, Murray, soon. I told you, after dinner, once it starts to get dark out."

Murray gives a high-pitched *woo-hoo!* and flaps back to the scene on his rug. Just like that, he's in his own world again, which I now notice involves two stuffed animals trick-or-treating through the town on his rug. What I thought was a random explosion of stuffed animals, action figures, and play food is really an intricately organized system.

Mom and I watch in silence for a minute before she looks up at me, eyebrows raised, with a hint of a smirk on her face.

"Dirty move, Mom. Dirty move."

Mom's smirk blooms into a wicked smile. She kisses me on the cheek and smacks me on the butt on her way out the door. When I reach to wipe my cheek, she calls from halfway down the steps, "You're just rubbing it in!"

Freaking Mom.

The doorbell rings while I'm still lingering in Murray's doorway, and I think it must be some way-early trick-or-treaters.

"Matt, Tabby's here!"

Oh sweet mother of shit.

"Tabby!" Murray bolts past me and flies down the steps to find her, little tufts of white trailing in his wake.

Holy fucking fuck.

When I reach the bottom of the steps, Tabby is already gushing over my mom's costumes in the dining room, the two of them shoulder to shoulder.

"Oh my gosh, those skinny jeans look perfect!"

"I know, right? Can you believe Matt's not going to wear them? He's just going to pull out that old troll mask again, probably scare poor Murray to death."

Tabby whirls, her eyes finding me at the bottom of the steps, where I give a weak smile and wave.

"Matthew Wainwright. You are wearing this costume."

She's not smiling.

Murray, whose winged arms are now wrapped around Tabby's legs, looks up first to Tabby's face, to Mom's, and finally across the room to mine.

"Matty, why are you wearing the troll mask?" he asks, his voice rising in panic. "I thought you were gonna be bald eagles with me." The corners of his mouth are dipping downward, his cheeks turning that blotchy red they always do right before he loses it.

"No, no, no, I didn't say that, Murray!" I look to Mom, avoiding Tabby's stare. "Mom, I did not say that!"

Mom again chooses to remain silent, shrugging and raising

her eyebrows behind Tabby's shoulder, as though this dramatic turn of events is just as surprising to her. At which point, up against these three impossible creatures, I give in to the fact that there's no way out—I'm going to be rocking some seriously tight yellow skinny jeans tonight.

"C'mon, Murray, of course we're going to be bald eagles together."

When Murray decides that I'm telling him the truth, I finally look at Tabby and give another weak smile.

"Tabby, why don't you give me a hand in here," my mom says. "Mark will be home from work any minute. You can stick around for dinner."

"Ohh, it's baked ziti night, isn't it?" Tabby's voice is friendly, but her eyes narrow. She gives me an almost imperceptible shake of her head before following Mom into the kitchen.

Dad retreated to his downstairs office immediately after dinner, nabbing a handful of Milky Ways from the trick-or-treat bowl on the way. He's the main tech guy at a neighboring school district, and he *does* work a lot from his computer downstairs, but I have a feeling he's hiding from the barrage of tiny strangers who will be on his porch over the next few hours. He's not the most social of creatures. I have him to thank for my general awkwardness in any and all social situations. No idea how he won over Mom. I've always assumed that Mom chose him—walked up to him somewhere, said, "I'll take you," to which my dad just shrugged and followed her home.

He's always had a special spot for Tabby, though. When Mom asked if he was heading down to do more work as he was rummaging through the candy bowl, he winked at her (smooth, Dad), then lobbed a Milky Way to Tabby. "Keep the birds out of trouble tonight," he said before retreating down the steps.

Tabby smiled without looking up and said, "Will do," while tearing open her Milky Way. Which answered *that* question—the eagles, it seemed, would not be flying alone this evening. Awesome.

So now I'm standing in the bathroom, wondering what's going on with Branson's party, trying to make sure this itchy-ass sweater is long enough to cover the top of a pair of jeans that were apparently designed for a young lad or lass whose butt crack measures only an inch and a half from stem to stern. I thought the skaters just pulled their pants down really low, but seriously, *where are the rest of these fucking pants?!*

Mom calls for me to hurry up, that trick-or-treating starts soon. I take a deep breath and step out for them all to see.

"Oh, Matty," Mom says, "you look great!" She puts a hand over her mouth. I stare at her. I think for a moment she's forgotten that I'm a six-foot-three high school freshman, and that this is, in fact, not in any way adorable.

Tabby is able to smile and nod for all of twenty seconds, her lips pursed tight and trembling, before bursting out laughing. She can't even look me in the eye, her body convulsing, doubled over. Mom starts laughing then, too, throwing her arm around Tabby's shoulders, and Murray joins the action, dancing around me screeching, "MAMA! MAMA! CHEEP CHEEP! MAMA! MAMA! CHEEP CHEEP!" in his most enthusiastic baby-bald-eagle voice. When Tabby looks up between convulsions, there are tears running down her cheeks.

"You guys suck."

■ ■ ■

A few minutes before the official start time, Murray's still running circles around me, out on the driveway now, while Mom and Tabby take pictures, Mom with her mega-camera, Tabby with her phone. Which is also the moment my grandparents' giant white land-yacht pulls up in front of the house.

Fuck me.

Murray pauses midflight around his mama bird and makes a beeline for the car. Gramma scoops him up into a hug as soon as she steps out of the passenger seat, careful not to crush his papier-mâchéd bottom.

Grampa climbs out of the driver's side, beaming. He's a big man. Tall—taller than me—and athletic-looking, save for the magnificent, third-trimester belly that hangs off the front of him. He has a thick head of white hair, a blinding smile, and a deep, booming voice. He'd look like a senator if he weren't always wearing sweatpants. He's a long-retired school principal, and Dad claims he hasn't seen him in dress clothes since the day he retired.

"Grampa! We're going trick-or-treating!"

"Hey, how 'bout that?" he says, pulling out one of Murray's arms to inspect his wing. "How's my Murray?" he says, bending down to kiss the top of Murray's head, his eggshell still at Gramma's shoulder. Gramma's tiny. The Wainwright men's infatuation with pocket-size women is apparently genetic.

"We had to come see the mama bird and the baby bird take flight!" Gramma says to Murray, then smiles at me.

Grampa looks me up and down, a sympathetic look on his face.

"Sweet Jesus," he says, shaking his head.

Help me, I mouth.

"You're a good man, Matthew." He places a hand on my shoulder, then looks over my shoulder and booms, "All right, Tabby's here!"

Tabby's standing next to Mom, that huge, goofy grin plastered to her face. She only has one real grandparent left—her dad's mom, who lives in a nursing home over an hour away, and who really isn't all that nice.

"Hi, Grampa Wainwright," she says.

"What's shaking, T-Bone? How's high school?" he says, ambling up to them, and Tabby's smile grows somehow wider. I watch her face as they small-talk. It's like she turns into a little kid around my grandpa. I swear, he could pull a quarter from her ear, and she'd jump up and down with glee, begging him to do it again.

They chat with Mom, Grampa's arm around Tabby's shoulder, while Gramma takes more pictures of the eagles. When Gramma pauses between shots, Grampa, without a word, gently shoves Tabby over to us, so that she's in the pictures, too.

They can pretend like they're surprised to see her, but there are three Halloween goodie bags poking out of Gramma's purse.

Once we get started, it's not so bad.

Mr. Hodgson's house is tough: "Dear Lord, Matthew. What did that woman do to you?" But other than that, most people laugh—in a nice way, mainly—and swoon over Murray. At every single door, after a muffled "Trick or treat!" from behind his beak, Murray says to the person, "This is my big brother, Matt!

He's a mama bald eagle, and I'm a baby bald eagle!" which, from at least half of the houses we stop at, earns him an extra fun-size candy bar. With Tabby's dad, who's sitting on his front step in an authentic Ghostbusters uniform, it gets Murray an extra *full*-size bar. Because that's just the kind of badass Tabby's dad is.

And once I get laughed at the first few times, I start to relax. Yeah, Tabby is here to witness it all, and yeah, people are laughing because I look utterly ridiculous—all justifiable reasons to be mortified—but shit, it *is* funny. After a while, I laugh when people open the door and get a look at us, too.

And every single time Murray and I step off the porch and head back down to the sidewalk, Tabby is standing there smiling.

Every single time.

When we get back to our house nearly two hours later, Grampa's land-yacht is gone. The eagle chick is about to crash, delirious from exhaustion. I've been carrying his pillowcase for him for the last hour, which is so stuffed full of candy I can't even twist the top closed to throw it over my shoulder.

Murray runs to Mom as soon as we walk in the door. When Mom swoops him up in her arms, Murray's whole body deflates into hers. Mom takes him immediately to his room to get ready for bed, smiling at Tabby and me as she heads up the steps— loving-Mom smile this time, not wicked-and-manipulative-Mom smile. We don't hear a single protest or plea for candy. Murray's wiped.

Without even thinking, Tabby and I head downstairs to the den and settle in on the floor in front of the sofa, just like we've done after trick-or-treating together every year since we were Murray's age. I dump all of Murray's candy into a pile on the floor.

"Damn," I say, in reverence to the mountain of treats before us.

"I'm not sure we ever got this much candy *combined* back in the day."

And—just like we've done every year—Tabby and I set about organizing all the candy according to a strict hierarchy: at the top, candy bars and all things chocolate; next, anything gummy and/or fruity, liberally including items like SweeTARTS, Sprees, and Bottle Caps; next go all lollipops and Tootsie Rolls; and finally, all the crap that will get eaten only out of desperation—unidentifiable hard candies, homemade treats of various origins, raisins, and the like. And off to the side, existing outside the candy hierarchy, in a pile closely guarded on the other side of Tabby's legs, lie the Nerds. Because Tabby is a Nerds fiend.

It is a glorious sight when it's all organized, displayed before us. It's almost too beautiful to eat. It stings a little, knowing that this is all Murray's, though I suspect most of the Nerds will be smuggled out of here when Tabby leaves.

She absently runs her hand through the pile of Nerds boxes, like she's stroking a beloved pet.

"You know those are Murray's, right?" I say, trying to give her the same hard look she used on me earlier.

"What?" she says, almost startled. "Of course I do," she says then. "I'm not going to eat Murray's candy."

I stare at her, down at her hand still swimming through the pile of Nerds, then back up to her eyes again.

She narrows her eyes and tears open the first little box. "Like you weren't planning to scarf down like six of those Kit Kats?"

Actually, I eat eight of them. Tabby's polishing off her fourth box of Nerds when her phone buzzes. She pulls it from her pocket and immediately busts out laughing.

"Oh my gosh!" she says, fighting to keep the Nerds in her mouth.

"What?"

"It's from Lily," Tabby says, a hand over the wide grin on her face.

She reaches over to show me her phone. There on the screen is Liam Branson, decked out in a lame-ass pirate costume, a sheepish grin on his eye-patched face, looking into the camera, like he knew where this picture was going. Beneath it, I catch a glimpse of Lily's text: *chk out ur boy* ;)

"That's pretty funny," I say, forcing out a laugh and pulling the bald eagle cap from my head, running a hand through my matted hair. The Kit Kats in my stomach turn to lead.

Tabby types something to Lily that I can't see, before shoving her phone back in her pocket. She's still smiling as she goes for another box of Nerds.

"So what's with the 'ur boy' thing?" I ask, trying to sound innocent, like the interested, inquisitive friend I'm supposed to be. "Are you guys, like, together or something?"

"No." Tabby laughs. "Lily's acting like her brother won't stop talking about me and stuff. It's stupid." The color rises in Tabby's cheeks as she rubs her hands on her lap. "Besides, he's a senior."

After a minute of awkward silence, she picks up another box of Nerds. "I could eat these things all night."

"So I've noticed," I say, and wait until she's tipped the rest of the box into her mouth before asking what's been at the back of my mind all night, pretending that I've suddenly realized it. "Weren't you supposed to be at their Halloween party tonight?"

Tabby shrugs without looking up from her empty box of Nerds.

"Lily really wanted me to. But it's no big deal. It's all upper-classmen anyway."

Exactly, I say in my head. *Very sensible. Older guys, never good.*

"And besides, I couldn't miss trick-or-treating with you and Murray! It'd be the first time we ever missed going together!"

"That's true," I say, smiling.

My heart swells and sinks at the same time. She chose trick-or-treating with me over going to Branson's party, a party I know he specifically wanted Tabby to attend, whether Tabby's willing to admit it or not. Granted, she also picked Murray over him, and I'm not sure if that makes it better or worse.

But her words stick in my brain: *It'd be the first time we ever missed going together.* And it kills me because there will be a first time. This miraculous streak will end. And there's a damn good chance it ended when we walked back into the house tonight.

Tabby takes out her phone, looks at it again, and types something in before putting it away. She stretches her legs out in front of her and yawns.

Dad walks in then from his office and finds us surrounded by spent wrappers, an impressive display of candy still before us. He rubs us both on the head as he steps between us, plucking a Snickers from the pile.

"I love trick or treat."

CHAPTER SIX

THE DRIVEWAY IS MY DOMAIN

I hit the driveway early the next morning. Sunday. It's early enough that everything is still a shade of gray. I can see my breath as I grab my ball from the tattered box in the corner of the garage.

I'm sure Mr. Hodgson is overjoyed to hear the rattle of our garage door and my ball echoing across the circle as I go in for my first layup at quarter after seven. By the time my ball settles through the stiff net and my feet touch the ground, though, that thought is gone.

My routine: Ten shots in a row, one hand only, three feet in front of the rim; take a step back and repeat, ten in a row, until I make it to the foul line, usually my fourth set of ten. Then I move to the right block and repeat, ten in a row, one-handed, before taking a step back at a diagonal from the foul line. When I've made it through four rounds, I move to the left block and repeat, then finally along the right and left baselines.

If I'm perfect, that's two hundred made shots before I allow myself to just play around and work on my moves. I've never been even close to perfect, and because I make myself go back to zero at each spot after a miss, it's probably closer to four or five hundred buckets before I make it through the circuit.

I don't like to miss.

I know it sounds crazy, but there's something about the rhythm, the routine of it, the perfect, delicate sound of ball only touching net—the feeling of being good and still working to be better—that frees my mind. It allows my brain to sink down a level, to see things how they really are.

This morning, though, my brain keeps wandering back to Liam Branson, smiling in that picture for Tabby. At seven in a row from the foul line, I can hear her phone buzzing in her pocket. At eight, I see her beaming at the screen, her hand at her mouth. At nine, she remembers I'm still there and looks up, says something I can't make out, and goes back to her phone. At ten, I feel the pang of inadequacy, and my shot clangs high off the back of the rim.

I do this to myself four more times—choking number ten while some movie of Tabby and Branson rolls in my head. Shit that hasn't happened yet: Tabby, wearing his oversize varsity jacket, cheering him on from the student section of the gym; waiting for him in the lobby after a game and leaving together, his arm draped over her shoulders; and the worst, Branson draining jumper after jumper over me in a scrimmage during practice while Tabby watches from the baseline, telling me "Good job, Matt!" and "Keep trying!" even though she can't take her eyes off Branson after each basket, which really doesn't even make any fucking sense.

Actually, that last image hits when I'm only up to six, and when my shot bounces back to me off the front of the rim, I scoop it up and overarm it as hard as I can into the backboard.

Not part of my routine.

All right, Matt. Time to get a grip here, buddy.

I decide to forgo the rest of my shooting routine for once and practice some moves, try to work out some of the weightless pinpricks that come with blinding frustration. At least before I break another garage-door window. Or Mr. Hodgson comes out and decides to go retired army ranger on my ass—he's got to put up with this ball bouncing way early in the morning *a lot*.

And what good does it do me to agonize over Liam Branson? It's not like he really knows who I am, anyway. Just another gangly, awkward freshman. Basketball season starts in a couple of weeks, and my other best friend, Trip, and I are going to be playing up on JV as freshmen, but even then, I'm not sure Branson's going to care who I am. And I'm not sure why I suddenly need him to.

I'm not out here freezing my nuts off at 7:00 a.m. on the first day of November for Liam Branson. Fuck that. This time next year, Branson will be gone—hopefully putting on forty pounds of beer fat in a dorm at some state college—and it'll be my turn to step into the varsity light as a sophomore. In fact, I want him to have the best season of his career, if only because he has to work his ass off in practice to keep me in my place.

And even though I might fantasize about Tabby watching *me* dominate a game, wearing *my* jacket in the stands, waiting for *me* in the lobby after the game, I'm not out here for her, either.

I just love this game.

I love knowing exactly where to stand on help defense, collapsing on some kid who thinks he's got an easy drive to the basket and swatting his shot out of bounds. I love knowing what Trip's going to do, where he's going to be on the court, know exactly when his scrappy ass is going to dive at a lazy point guard who forgets to protect the ball and be sprinting up the court as it happens. I love when a defender thinks I'm too tall to shoot from the outside and swears at himself after the first unchallenged three, his coach or his teammates on his case as we come back the other way—and again when I blow by him after he charges out to get a hand in my face the next time.

Perfect.

These are the two things I want more than anything: to play at the highest level—to start varsity; and, well, for Tabby to choose me. The first, I'm willing to be patient, to keep working my ass off. But the second. The second is already slipping away.

Even though I can still see my breath, and my hands go numb every fifteen minutes, I've got a pretty good sweat going when Tabby comes shuffling across the circle in sweats and the black-and-sky-blue-striped earflap hat Mom crocheted for me a few months ago. They're Franklin Black Bear colors. It's even got the pom-pom thingy on the top and braided tassels that hang from the earflaps. Mom thought it'd be a big hit at football games and stuff. Which it was. Just not on me.

"Hey, Matty," she says, yawning and sitting cross-legged at the edge of the driveway.

"Back for more of Murray's Nerds?" I say, slowing down to lazy jump shots.

"Jerk." She yawns again and rubs the sleep from her eyes. Then, "Does he have any left?"

I laugh but don't reply. This is my favorite version of Tabby. She's clearly rolled out of bed, and it's like I'm the only one who ever gets to see her this way. Can you be in love with a yawn?

Just ignore that one.

"What are you doing up already?" I ask.

"That's an excellent question, Matthew. Because you would think any normal human teenager *would* still be asleep at eight-thirty on a dreary Sunday morning, wouldn't you?"

I smile and go in for one last layup.

"But there's been this incessant, annoying bouncing noise for the past hour, and no matter what I do, I can't seem to block it out."

"Sorry about that," I say, tossing her the ball and sitting down next to her on the driveway. Steam rises off my arms, and, I gotta admit, it looks pretty cool. At least in my head it does. Like I'm in a Gatorade commercial, or something.

"I'm kidding. It's not my first time at the rodeo, Matty." Tabby attempts to spin the ball on her finger, fails, and lets it rest in her lap. "It'd be weird not to hear it. I can't figure out *why* you're up this early."

"Sorry," I say again. "Just up."

And because my brain is a masochistic piece of shit, I ask, "Did you get any more pics from Branson's party last night?"

Because why would I want to just enjoy my moment with her?

Tabby shakes her head, looking down at the ball in her lap, and smiles briefly before looking up.

"Okay, serious question," she says.

"Yes, Tabby, I pulled the rest of the Nerds for you."

"No, for real." But I see her pause for the tiniest moment—this girl truly is a Nerds fiend. "You don't really think Liam likes me, do you? Like, *likes me* likes me?" She looks down again. "I mean, I know he's a senior and everything, and . . . it's stupid . . ." She trails off.

My heart is breaking. It makes no sense, but I want the answer to be no and yes with the same ferocity. And I can't commit to a side to give her a response.

I mean, I can't wish against Tabby's happiness—not seeing her like this—even if it is killing me. Now, that doesn't mean I'm not wishing some horrendous venereal disease on Branson right now. Something oozing and smelly and highly conspicuous. Because that would be marvelous.

Tabby nudges me with her shoulder after a minute, raises her eyebrows at me, waiting for my response. The most I can manage is a weak laugh and a lame "Why are you asking me?"

"I don't know. I know you don't really know him at all." She pauses and grins. "But, you know, you're kind of a guy."

"Hey, watch it there, asshole."

"Hey!" Tabby says, and punches me in the shoulder, hard. "You watch it, dingleberry!"

"Dingleberry?"

"You heard me. Dingleberry."

I throw a sweaty arm over her shoulder. "This is why we're so close, Tab. I'm the dingleberry to your asshole."

Tabby throws my arm off and punches the same spot, harder. "Dingleberry to a horse's asshole, maybe."

"Well," I say, rubbing my shoulder. "It's hard to imagine how he couldn't like you." Then, when she raises her fist again, "Seriously, Tabby. I don't know him at all, but he'd have to be an asshole not to like you." And I can barely get the next words out: "*Like you* like you."

Tabby smiles and leans in next to me, puts her head on my still-tender shoulder. We stay like that for a few minutes, quiet, watching our breaths. How the hell can I feel like I'm getting closer to Tabby and farther away at the same time?

When she lifts her head again—way too soon—I stand and reach to help her up. "Let's go find some Nerds."

CHAPTER SEVEN

THE DAY I FELL IN LOVE WITH TABBY, PART 1

I was about fifty foul shots in when Trip showed up that morning, dropping his bike on the curb in front of our yard. Trip lives only a few neighborhoods over—maybe a mile or so—and he used to show up all the time on his bike, especially in the summer. Given how small he is, I liked to imagine the dialogue inside the cars he passed along the way. *Look at that little bastard go! He doesn't even need training wheels!* Which I also liked to yell as he pedaled away in the evenings, to which he'd either flip me off or swing around and attempt to run me over. Good times.

It was only about a month into the school year—we were big seventh graders now—so it didn't take long for us to fall back into the rhythms of summer.

Trip headed straight for our garage, putting his hand up in front of my face as he passed—a token shot-block attempt that was more of a hello than a challenge to play—and stopped in the middle where Mom's car usually sat. He stood, hands on his hips, staring at the pile of toys and sports equipment we kept in the corner.

"Dude, we should cork a bat."

Trip's dad had told us once about this baseball player from the seventies and eighties named Graig Nettles, who had been caught using a corked bat in a game. He played for the Yankees at the time—figures, filthy cheaters—and during a game against the Tigers, Nettles's bat exploded, rubber Super Balls spilling out the end of the broken barrel.

"I don't get it," Trip had said to his dad, who sat on the Fogles' gargantuan sofa watching a Phillies game, his legs stretched out in front of him, a beer resting on his stomach. "What's the point of corking it—or stuffing it with Super Balls or whatever?"

Trip's dad took a swig from his beer without looking away from the screen. "Makes the bat lighter. More bat speed, more power. Plus, the Super Balls add more bounce-back. Hit that sucker a mile."

Nettles—who happened to crush twenty-two homers that year and later held the American League record for career home runs by a third baseman—was automatically called out on the play and ejected from the game for cheating. To Trip and me, the message was clear: we needed to cork some bats.

Trip and I corked four different Wiffle ball bats that day, though our understanding of the physics behind bat-corking was at best spotty. We sawed the tops off of skinny, hollow, bright yellow Wiffle ball bats and stuffing them with anything we could find: rocks, acorns, balled-up newspaper—we even squeezed three bottles of Elmer's glue into one of them to try to fill in all the gaps. After duct-taping the tops back onto the bats, we ended up with what were more of twenty-pound death clubs than functional bats. Within a half hour we had cracked every Wiffle ball we had, forcing us to move on to acorns. Tabby's dad even joined us for a few hacks, hopping out of his truck before he backed out of his driveway. "Beautiful craftsmanship," he told us after launching an acorn halfway to the bus stop at the end of the street.

The four corked bats now stood leaning in the back corner of the garage—monuments to our genius in the field of sports science. But Trip . . . well, Trip pushed boundaries. He still stood staring, but not at the mess of sports equipment in the corner. Instead, I followed his gaze to the sandbox tools and little-kid toys heaped in a box close by. Resting on top of the pile was another bat. One of those giant red Wiffle ball bats with an enormous barrel that are modeled more after caveman clubs than baseball bats, so that even the tiniest slugger can crank a few—the tiniest slugger in this case being Murray.

"Dude, that's Murray's bat. We can't cork Murray's bat."

Trip's eyes locked onto mine, a smile playing on his lips. I looked back at the bat, imagining the finished product and the incredible damage it could do.

"He is only two, I guess."

Trip cocked an eyebrow.

"I'll go get my dad's duct tape."

It took us nearly two hours to construct our masterpiece, most of that time spent arguing over what to cork it with. With the top of the red plastic bat and Dad's hacksaw on the garage floor next to us—like the discarded remains of some gruesome experimental lobotomy—Trip and I regarded the sheer volume of the bat. In scientific terms, this was one big-ass bat.

"You could fit all four of those yellow bats into the barrel of this one," I said, staring into the opening. Trip, pondering this for a second, picked up all four yellow bats at once, his fingers straining around the shifting handles, and attempted a few practice swings.

"Dude, we're not gonna be able to swing that thing. It'll be like trying to swing a Buick." Trip dropped the bats in frustration, the debris-filled barrels thudding to the floor around him. "Are you sure you don't have any Super Balls anywhere?"

"We already looked when we made the first ones," I said, shaking my head, pointing to the yellow bats around his feet. "And besides, even if we find some, we'd need like a thousand of them to fill this thing up."

And that's when I remembered Dad's golf stuff collecting dust in the basement.

"Hold on, I'll be right back."

Dad got it in his head one summer that—as a responsible grown man—he should take up golf. After spending a ton of money on custom clubs—"I'm six four," Dad reasoned as Mom stared at the receipt in disbelief. "The guy at Dick's said I'd be wasting my money on clubs that weren't fitted for my height!"—he found that he enjoyed scavenging lost golf balls from the woods and the water hazards more than he liked endlessly hitting his own balls into them. By the end of that summer, he'd filled two five-gallon buckets with golf balls. I'm not even sure he was paying to play anymore, instead just walking out onto the course and pretending to search for a ball he'd shanked.

When I returned to the garage with a full bucket, the handle straining with the weight of the golf balls, Trip's eyes lit up.

"Oh, shit yeah."

"Graig Nettles, baby," I said, smiling.

"Graig Nettles."

. . .

The very first swing broke our only Wiffle ball—presumably the one that came with Murray's bat—clean in half. Trip, who stood on our makeshift mound in the center of the circle—*All right, Matty, let's see you hit the knuckleball!*—swore and flailed in self-defense. On contact, the top half of the Wiffle ball flew a couple of feet before taking a nasty hook to the right, while the bottom half sliced toward Trip's head like a ninja star.

"Dude, that was awesome!" Trip said after checking himself for marks.

"Yeah. Looks like we're back to acorns, though."

After scouring my yard for acorns, Trip and I fell into a nice rhythm, reviving our endless summertime home run derbies, each of us taking turns sending acorns across the circle, over the fence into the Hodgsons' yard (I'm pretty sure they weren't home).

Not long after Tabby's dad gave our newest creation an appreciative nod as his truck pulled away, Tabby emerged from her house, barefoot with soccer shorts on and a tie-dyed T-shirt, her red hair pulled back in a ponytail. She sat down cross-legged in the sun at the edge of her yard to watch us, her phone resting in her lap.

Just like that. Perfect summer day again.

At some point, though, after sending two acorns nearly to the Hodgsons' porch, I looked over at Tabby—head down, laughing to herself, texting away on her phone, completely oblivious to my power display. Which, you know, who cares? I'd never been worried about impressing Tabby before. She was just Tabby. My buddy. Part of the neighborhood. But for some reason, it killed me that she wasn't watching. That she wasn't impressed.

Now, in hindsight, I understand that the scene was probably not that awe-inspiring: gangly twelve-year-old holding a ridiculous red plastic bat that's twice as wide (okay, three times as wide) as his arms, pretending to be a real-live big-league ballplayer while swatting acorns tossed by a pigeon-toed half-pint with a penchant for swearing. Okay.

But in the moment—*in that moment*—I was a fucking hero. I mean, you should have *seen* some of those shots.

Tabby wasn't impressed. She was perfectly happy doing what we always did, hanging out, being kids. But, for the first time, that wasn't good enough for me. I couldn't explain it or understand why it mattered. It just did.

In my mind, if I could hit the acorns *even harder*, Tabby would have to notice, would have to put that stupid phone down to witness the awesome spectacle that was me.

So I swung harder. I gritted my teeth, crouched down in my big-league stance, spit—why the hell did I spit?—and bore down, waiting for Trip's windup. I could almost hear the movie sound track playing in the background, building up to my big moment. I could see the slow-motion end of that movie *The Natural,* where this baseball player actually hits the cover off the ball as it explodes into the stadium lights beyond the outfield wall. Only it's me, my acorn sailing like a comet, smashing through the Hodgsons' upstairs window, Trip and Tabby watching in stunned silence.

And I swung *hard,* already watching the Hodgsons' window.

I barely nicked the acorn. While I nearly fell over with the force of my swing, the acorn went straight down, bouncing once and skittering off to the side.

"Wow, dude, maybe you should swing harder." Trip chuckled, but I made no reply. Just got back into my stance as Trip scooped another acorn out of the bucket and went into his windup. I stole a glance at Tabby, still engrossed in her phone.

And I did swing harder, again barely nicking the top of the acorn and sending it bouncing harmlessly to the curb.

Four more times I swung with everything I had; four more times the acorn bounced no more than a few feet, the image from *The Natural* fading from my mind. My shoulders and the sides of my ribs were starting to ache from the strain, and I could feel blisters forming inside the sweaty death grip I held on the handle of the bat.

"All right, slugger, my turn," Trip said, heading toward me.

"Hold on, one more. I gotta end on a good one," I said, breathing heavily.

Trip dropped his arms and rolled his eyes. "One more pitch," he said, backing up to the bucket again. "Then it's my turn. I'm giving you cantaloupes here."

I focused like a laser on the acorn coming out of Trip's hand and swung with all I had. But my arms were tired, and even though I did actually hit it this time, it was nothing more than a hard grounder down what would be the first-base line, zipping past where Tabby sat a few yards to my right.

She finally looked up, taking in the scene as she stretched her painted toenails out in front of her. She smiled and went back to texting.

"*Now* it's my turn. Let me show you how it's done."

I dropped the bat to the ground and walked past Trip to the bucket, hoping the blood pounding in my face looked more like exhaustion than embarrassment.

■ ■ ■

"All right, Matty baby, put one right here," Trip said, pointing with the duct-taped head of the bat to a spot three feet out in front of him, just above his knees. "It's Big Papi time."

I picked a fat, round acorn out of the bucket and tried to nonchalantly toss it up in the air to myself. But home run derby wasn't much fun anymore. Trip was still playing around, while I had crossed over into something much more serious. I don't know what made me crazier: looking stupid in front of Tabby, or Tabby not looking at all.

I started in on my windup and said, "All right, Papi, let's see you hit this one," trying my best to sound playful. Trip grinned, waggling the bat in his stance, the tip of his tongue poking out of the corner of his mouth. I threw it as hard as I could, and— though I don't think I meant to—struck Trip in the left temple.

"Ooooooowwwwwww! Fucking shit, that hurt!" Trip crouched to the ground, head down, his left hand covering the side of his face.

"Oh, shit! I'm sorry, man," I said, walking toward him, if possible feeling even worse than before. As I got close, Trip took a blind swing at me with the hand still holding the bat, mumbling unintelligible swear words to himself.

Tabby, *now* finally watching, walked over to us, laughing.

"Trip, are you okay?"

"Son of a bitch, I think he popped my eyeball out of its socket," he replied, still holding his face, checking for blood and, presumably, his eyeball.

Tabby laughed harder, bending over Trip with her hands on his shoulders before helping him to his feet. "Still beautiful, Trip. I think you'll live."

"I didn't mean to hit him," I said, shaking my head, unable to look her in the face. "I just wanted to see if Big Papi here could handle the heater."

"Dude, your heater fucking sucks," Trip replied, rubbing his eye and checking one last time for blood.

"I know, I know. No more heaters."

"Cantaloupes, man. It's home run derby. Papi gets cantaloupes like everyone else."

"How 'bout I pitch to Papi?" Tabby stepped gingerly with her bare feet to the acorn bucket in the center of the circle. "Man, I should've taken a video of that."

Tabby took over lobbing cantaloupe after cantaloupe to Trip, who sent one after another over the Hodgsons' fence, while I sat there on the grass like an idiot. Which, whatever—my arms were shaky and my brain was a scrambled mess. I couldn't have lobbed one into Trip's wheelhouse to save my life.

But after every pitch, I looked back at Tabby, totally comfortable with us, happily oblivious to me, and I felt . . . desperate.

What the hell was wrong with me?

CHAPTER EIGHT

ENGLISH HONORS NINE IS SERIOUS SHIT

"Guys, this is the single greatest fart scene in all of literature."

Mr. Ellis. I'm not sure if he's joking, or if he's being sincere, or if it's a strange mix of both. But I don't really care. This is maybe the single greatest class I've ever had. And it's the one I was dreading the most coming into high school.

Official course title: English Honors Nine—Introduction to Literature and Composition. Which sounds freaking brutal— like the name of some ancient, pictureless English textbook. Which, in fact, it is.

At least a hundred of them are stacked on the low book-shelves beneath the windows, their cracked and faded red bindings lined up like an exposed brick foundation. Ellis calls them Ilca, as though the collection itself is a living organism—in his mind, a cranky old teacher. And he regularly talks to her during class.

And sometimes, oddly enough, Ilca responds, Ellis's voice dropping to that of a woman who's spent the better part of her forty-year career puffing two packs a day in the faculty room.

I'm pretty sure Ilca is just a rough acronym of the title printed along each of the tattered spines—*Introduction to Literature & Composition*—with an *A* thrown on the end for a more feminine-sounding name, as opposed to just Ilc or Ilco or whatever. But when anyone asks what kind of name Ilca is, Mr. Ellis claims it's a common nickname for Ilcagene.

Ilcagene Hephaestus McDougal, her full name.

The rumor is that Ellis made a deal with his English colleagues that he'd take all the freshmen if they left him alone to teach whatever the hell he wants. So he kept the course title and liberally interprets it as "Reading Awesome Books and Writing Crap That Matters to Us." His words.

We've just finished reading *The Absolutely True Diary of a Part-Time Indian* by Sherman Alexie, an amazing book about basketball, and masturbation, and feeling shitty and alone, and how Indians are perpetually screwed. And also farting.

"Seriously, guys. Most beautiful fart lines in all of written history. I went and saw Alexie give a performance a couple of years ago, and he was amazing. Did you know that all this really happened to him? From the hydrocephalus when he was born and the giant freaking glasses, the leaving the rez school for the all-white town school, the basketball, the heartbreaking lives of his family and fellow Indians on the rez. All of it."

We're completely hooked. Mr. Ellis goes off on these rants, usually about books he wants us to read and love as much as he does. This one may run to the end of the period, but no one minds.

"You know, I got to meet him for a minute afterward to get my book signed, and I told him I was hoping he'd read the fart-in-the-tree scene. And he said—in all seriousness—that he can't get through it. That there's a few scenes he can't read out loud without choking up . . . and the fart scene is one of them!"

Trip and I have been quoting the fart line ever since we read the book. It's given us a whole new appreciation for farts, especially Trip, who's taken to ambushing me ninja-style, letting loose when I least expect it. All in the name of literary appreciation.

I glance over at Trip, sitting next to me, and he's just staring at me, an evil little grin dancing at the corners of his mouth. I shake my head.

"Other people," I whisper, indicating the innocent classmates surrounding us. I try to focus on Mr. Ellis. Engaging Trip only serves to egg him on.

"What?" he says quietly, feigning innocence. "I'm making a text connection."

"Text connections do not leave visible evidence in your underpants," I say without looking at him.

Trip puts his head down as Mr. Ellis continues his point. "Seriously, guys, if your fart scene is too emotionally charged to read out loud, you know you've nailed it. Alexie ripped my guts out *and* made me laugh out loud, and that's another level of brilliance. There's a fine line between laughter and pain. And I think, sometimes, it's the only thing you *can* do with your pain. Sometimes things suck so bad that you have to laugh at it."

Mr. Ellis may have lost it, here, at some point, and I'm not clear if he's talking about the book anymore. But something definitely feels true about what he's saying.

"You know, when I read this scene," he says, "I actually had to put the book down, I was laughing so hard. That's awesome.

"Quick side note: three books I've read in the past year that have made me stop reading and put the book down because I was laughing. Ilca," he says toward the bookshelves, "you may want to write these down."

"I hate you," Ilca replies, the growl from the corner of Ellis's mouth getting a chuckle from the class.

After class, Trip hangs a left to head to geometry, but I stop when I see Tabby at her locker to the right, outside of Mr. Ellis's door. She looks like she's in a hurry, shoving books into her bag and looking down the hall, away from me. Branson leans against the wall at the end of the hallway, waiting. No Lily in sight. Shit.

Tabby hasn't been on the bus at all the past week or so. Not since football season officially ended. So I've been riding home on the bus by myself, my iPod cranked, trying to convince myself that I really like the solitude, the chance to zone out to my music each day.

Luckily, basketball practice starts Monday, so I won't be on the bus in the afternoons, either. And Branson's afternoon schedule will be full again, as well.

I catch up to Trip and take my seat in geometry a few minutes before class starts, Trip in the desk directly in front of mine.

"Shit. Trip, did you finish all the homework?"

Trip laughs to himself without turning around. "I'm laughing at your pain."

"Dude, I don't think that's what Mr. Ellis meant."

"And I just farted."

"I hate you."

CHAPTER NINE

WINNER STAYS IN Y-BALL

On Sunday evening, Trip and I hit the Y. It's our final chance to run before practice starts Monday and we're back to a straight week of drills and fundamentals. And running until we puke.

We step into the gym and find multiple games going already, which is what we were hoping for—we can shoot around on an empty basket at home. Trip immediately gets the scoop on who's got next while I head to one of the side courts to get some shots in. It's fun to watch the look on older guys' faces when Trip asks if they've got five guys together yet—like, they don't want to hurt a little kid's feelings, but they didn't come to babysit someone's middle schooler, either. Then they see the little bastard play.

We have to wait out two full games before we take our turn on the center court. The Y gym is really one regulation-size court, split into three full courts by these giant hanging vinyl dividers. So the courts are short and fast, like street ball on hardwood. I recognize most of the guys on the center court as we step on to play. Some are varsity guys from Eastern Adams, a neighboring school district. Their team's not very good, but they're still varsity, and they're nice guys. Some are older gym rats who can't necessarily sprint up and down the floor, but who have mastered the art of short-court Y-ball. They can and will make you look stupid if you play careless against them.

I love these games, because it's one of the few times I can play without thinking. No coaches watching. No parents in the stands. No peers in the student section who have no idea that you practice all the time, shooting for hours by yourself. I know I shouldn't need them to care how good I am, but I can't handle having people think I'm *not* good, that I don't belong out there. One of the joys of having my brain, I guess.

None of that comes with me to the Y, though.

Six games in, Trip and I have yet to leave the court. Winner stays in Y-ball: games to eleven, ones and twos, win by two. I'm draining long twos and short turnarounds at will, and Trip is slashing through the lanes like a fucking madman. We don't speak during the hour and a half we're on the court. Communication travels through occasional fist bumps, nods, and simply knowing where the other's going to be at any given moment, our other three teammates along for the ride.

Damn, it feels good. You don't get tired when you're winning.

About a half hour before closing, three of our own varsity guys walk into the gym: Branson, point guard Elijah Leppo, and Trevor Lighty, an absolute behemoth. I've never seen any of them in here before. All three play football, and it looks as though they've just wandered in after lifting, planning on a quick tune-up before basketball season starts tomorrow.

They grab two guys standing against the wall behind a basket and saunter out onto the floor, right after Trip's drive ends our seventh straight win. Branson and crew take a few lazy jumpers, swinging their arms between shots, trying to get loose, while

Trip and I grab a quick drink from the fountain in the hall outside the gym.

Trip looks up after a long drink and lets out a long breath. "Fuck."

"Yeah," I say, and we bump weak fists before heading back onto the court.

Leppo's at the top of the key, ready to start. "What do we play to?" he asks. One of our teammates, equally drenched and exhausted, but still smiling, gives him the rundown.

It's not at all what I expect. The three of them are slow and stiff, their moves almost mechanical, like they're trying to figure out their bodies again in this new arena. Lighty still puts each of us on our ass when we try to box him out, and they're all damn good athletes, so they're by far the toughest competition we've had all night. But they just aren't in sync the way we are.

Trip and Leppo are evenly matched, Trip's intelligence and ultracompetitiveness making up for what he lacks in size and strength. Lighty bashes through everybody, but luckily a few of the older guys on our team are bigger than I am, so I'm not stuck trying to guard him. Despite his advantage in size, he's really rusty, missing more easy shots than he makes, and the other guys are able to score a few cheapies on him just by being in better position.

Branson's clearly the best player on the court, and it's hard as shit to stay with him on defense, especially after seven straight games, but I'm still locked in on offense and stick a couple of long-range jumpers over his outstretched hand. And he gives me props after each one, like he's coaching me or something. It takes everything I have to ignore the fact that this means absolutely everything to me and absolutely nothing to him.

So when I float a turnaround fadeaway over a lunging Trevor Lighty for the game-winning point, it's hard to contain my glee. I can tell Trip is beside himself, too, when he comes over and gives me a hand slap that numbs my fingertips. In my head, I've ripped my soaking shirt off and I'm airplaning around the court. On the outside, I'm hanging on to my shorts, giving everyone on the court the obligatory high five and "good game"—except for Lighty, who immediately slammed through the doors to the lobby.

Trip and I are sitting against the wall, cooling off and packing up our stuff for the night, when Branson and Leppo sit down on the floor in front of us.

"You guys looked good out there," Branson says, pulling off his shoes.

"Thanks," I say. "I think you guys are just still in football mode."

Lighty returns, his bag over his shoulder, and stands behind Branson and Leppo, looking down at us. "You got that right," he says. "That weak shit's not gonna work this week."

Leppo laughs to himself and shakes his head. But Branson says, "Shit, Light, I'll take shooting like that any day." He gets to his feet and reaches down to help me up. Leppo does the same for Trip. This is weird.

"You're Matt, right?" Branson says as we walk out through the lobby toward the parking lot. "Tabby's neighbor."

"Yeah," I say, which is all I can think of to say, so I say "yeah" again.

"I thought so. That girl's pretty cool," he says, and for whatever reason, it seems unnatural coming out of his mouth.

"Yeah," I say yet again. "We've been friends since we were little kids."

He doesn't say anything to that. Just lets it hang there before turning back to Trip, walking behind us. "What's your name again, man?"

"Trip."

"Trip?" Lighty booms from behind him. "What the fuck is that?"

"Uhh, it's a nickname," Trip replies, looking back at Lighty like he's the biggest dumbass on the planet. Which, well. Trip does not get intimidated by many people. When everyone's bigger than you, I guess you don't really give a shit how much bigger they are.

I smile and point to Trip's feet as he walks. I've never seen anyone as severely pigeon-toed as my boy Trip. "His mom started calling him that when he was little," I explain, more to Branson and Leppo than to the giant douche bag in the back. "Every time he'd take off, she'd think he was going to trip over his feet and bite it."

"No shit." Lighty laughs. "I keep waiting for you to fall on your face."

"Thus the name," Trip replies, not bothering to look at him this time.

When we get outside, Lighty heads straight to his pickup without saying goodbye.

"See ya, Light," Branson calls from the curb. Lighty flips us off without turning around and hops into his truck.

"Douche," Branson says under his breath, and Leppo laughs and shakes his head. Branson turns to us and asks, "You guys need a ride?"

"No, my mom will be here in a minute," I say, feeling like a little kid. "Thanks, though."

"No problem," he says as he and Leppo head for his black Accord. "See you guys at practice tomorrow." When he gets to his car door, he looks back and says, "Tell Tabby I said hi."

"You bet," I say. He waves and climbs into his car, and all I can think is how he's probably going to see her before I do.

We get the hand-on-the-steering-wheel peace sign as they drive by us out of the parking lot.

"Lighty's a total dick. But those guys are all right," Trip says after they pull away.

I nod, watching Branson's taillights disappear down the street as Mom's car pulls up in front of us.

"Branson seems really cool," Trip adds, staring at me a little longer than I appreciate before climbing into the backseat.

Yes. Yes, he definitely does. The bastard.

CHAPTER TEN

I'M LIKE THE DOMINIQUE WILKINS OF JV. YEAH.

After three days of nothing but practice drills and conditioning, Coach Langley finally turns us loose for a light scrimmage. Not an all-out run-and-gun open-gym-style pickup game, but a chance for the varsity team to knock some of the rust off against our lowly JV squad. Coach blows his whistle every other minute and steps into the action to smooth some kinks out of the varsity's offense or to correct their positioning on defense. It gets annoying, really, because anytime we get something going on JV—a turnover fast break or an open jumper coming off a screen—it usually means that the varsity squad didn't do something right, and Coach blows his whistle, stopping the play before we get to the good part. Coach Wise, our JV coach, stands idly behind him with his clipboard. It kinda sucks: on JV, you're allowed to keep playing only if things aren't working for you—if you're getting your ass kicked properly by the big team.

So when DeAndre Miller, a massive junior without enough coordination or experience to play varsity, sets a huge screen for me down low, leaving Trevor Lighty trailing me across the lane, I expect Coach to blow his whistle, to squash my first chance to get an open look on the block so he can show Lighty the proper way to slip the screen and keep his massive forearm planted into my sternum.

But for whatever reason, Coach lets us play, and Trip gets me the ball right off the block with my back to the basket. Trevor is a step behind, his hand on my back as soon as the ball is in my hands. I glance up at Coach Langley on the sideline, still half expecting him to stop the play, but he stands watching us, arms crossed, his whistle hanging around his neck. And I know this is it, my chance to show the varsity coach that my scrawny freshman ass has the post moves to play with the big boys.

Because, dammit, I know I can get him on the duck-under.

I've been working on this move in the driveway for forever. I saw it on this old *NBA Superstars* show they were running on ESPN Classic a few years ago. I'd stopped on what I thought was a Gatorade commercial, because it was that slow-motion clip of Michael Jordan dunking from the foul line. I get a basketball boner every time I see that clip and have to head straight up to the Nerf rim in my room for the replay, which always comes just before Mom yells at me to go outside.

But it wasn't a commercial. Right after the Jordan clip was a guy named Dominique Wilkins, a star for the Atlanta Hawks in the eighties, nicknamed the "Human Highlight Reel" because of these ridiculous power dunks he'd do. I swear, it was like he was jumping over people. He'd fake his defender out of his tiny 1980s short-shorts. Then he'd go *up*.

I was literally sitting on the edge of my dad's chair, my cereal bowl frozen in midair. I remember the announcer calling it a duck-under, and instead of going up to the Nerf rim for flight school, I went straight back out to the driveway to work on my new signature move.

It took me all of two tries to get a feel for it out on the drive-way that morning. Two tries before I was ducking under imaginary defenders with ease.

And I've been playing this scenario in my head all week—I *know* I can get Lighty to bite on the duck-under, make one of the varsity studs look like an idiot, getting burned by some freshman on the first scrimmage of the year.

And right here is why I truly hate my brain.

Instead of my brain going on cruise control through the move I've done a thousand times—acted out in almost this exact scenario—making Coach really have to consider the feasibility of a 160-pound freshman forward on varsity, my brain flashes to all the ways I can possibly screw this up, all the ways that would prove that I don't belong here with these guys at all, that I'm a junior high player who showed up at the wrong practice time. It's this instantaneous montage of me looking like an ass in front of Coach and the entire JV and varsity team: Trevor not biting on the fake and me slamming into his chest, bouncing backward onto the floor like a little kid; Trevor going for the fake, but me botching the layup, shooting it into the bottom of the rim; me power-dribbling off my foot like I've never touched a basketball before today.

As soon as I start my pivot toward the foul line, it's as if everything goes into fast-forward. I'm so hyped up and over-anxious that I go into the duck-under unnaturally fast. It probably looks more like I took a hot poker in the ass than pivoting for a smooth fadeaway in the lane.

Had my brain not intervened, it would have worked beautifully. Trevor *does* bite on the fake, just as I imagined, but because I jerk through the move so fast, he doesn't fully commit to going up to swat my shot. So instead of flying past me, he only half jumps, trying to stay on his feet in position between me and the basket. He's off-balance, and it's enough for me to get by him with my power dribble. But as I start going up for the layup (*power* layup, mind you), my inside foot catches Lighty's, and I sprawl forward, landing nuts-first on the ball before rolling onto my face out of bounds.

Not what I pictured.

I immediately hop back to my feet and bounce the ball to Coach before he can blow his whistle, as though everything is fine and that didn't hurt at all and I am more than ready to shake it off and play some serious lockdown defense.

But I can't breathe as I jog back down to the other end of the court, hunched over like Quasimodo.

"Dude, you all right?" DeAndre asks. "That looked like it hurt."

I nod and give a thumbs-up without looking at him, trying to get a few deep breaths in without puking before play resumes.

Trip looks at me and laughs—the sign of a true friend. "Don't worry, Matt, I'm sure the trainers will find your balls in there somewhere." Then he turns and yells, "All right, D it up!" as Leppo brings the ball up the floor.

When Lighty makes it back down the court, he says, "I told you, none of that weak shit."

Luckily, that is the last possession of the scrimmage, and I somehow make it through the last ten minutes of suicides without blacking out.

On the way back to the locker room, Coach Langley stops me and says, "Matt, that was a good move in the post. When you get stronger and can finish it, that's gonna be a really effective move.

Keep working." He slaps me on the butt and turns back to the other coaches.

Okay. So, the take-home message: awesome move, and you're weak like a little kid. I've never felt so shitty after a compliment before.

Well done, brain. Well done. You win again.

CHAPTER ELEVEN

THE DAY I FELL IN LOVE WITH TABBY, PART 2

After Trip had pedaled off on his bike, meandering up the street toward his house to sit in the air-conditioning and watch the Phillies game with his dad, Tabby and I settled into a more casual home run derby in the circle that afternoon. The September sun still sat above the tree line, baking the street and our shoulders, and the sky was the kind of deep, cloudless blue that made you dizzy to look at for too long.

"Rebecca will not shut up about Michael Martinez. It's driving me crazy." I lobbed another easy one as Tabby talked. "They've been going out for, what, like, a week? She's already sending me pictures of prom dresses. It's ridiculous."

"You can't stand in the way of true love," I said. She ignored me.

"Plus, that kid's a complete perv-ball. Have you seen what he does on his phone at lunch?"

I had. But I didn't say so.

I kept lobbing easy ones to Tabby, who hit them without much effort, gabbing away. We had no classes together that year, for the first time, and I relished the chance to hear her take on new teachers and classmates and drama. I always loved listening to Tabby; it was like she gave me this window into the normal social world.

My moment of machismo had passed, at least for the time being, and I felt almost like my normal self again. I still felt like an idiot, granted—not helped by the fact that every few minutes, Tabby would start giggling again, right before I'd toss her an acorn, and reenact Trip's beaning with uncanny realism.

"Watch it, pal," I said to Tabby after her third reenactment while she sat on the street laughing. "I'm dangerous with these things. I'm not scared to give you the heater, too." I wound up and pretended to go full force at Tabby, easing up at the last second and lobbing the acorn at her where she sat. She squealed mid-laugh, throwing her hands up over her head for protection as though she were swatting at an invisible mosquito. The acorn plunked off her shoulder and onto the ground in front of her.

"You turd." She picked up the acorn and fired it back in my direction from where she still sat.

"That's right, there's more where that came from," I said, reaching for another acorn as Tabby got to her feet.

"Oooooh, can I have some, then?"

Tabby and I both turned at the sound of this new voice as Corey Sheridan coasted into the circle on his BMX, two of his buddies in tow. They rode up a few yards behind me and stopped, Corey leaning forward, his elbows resting on his handlebars. He smiled as Tabby and I watched them in silence.

"How's it going, kids? Playin' a little Wiffle ball?" He kept smiling, a smile that didn't quite reach his eyes.

Now, in an audio recording of this exchange, Corey Sheridan would *sound* friendly and sincere, almost like an uncle dropping by for a visit.

But I should tell you that Corey Sheridan is not a nice person. And by that I mean that Corey Sheridan is a giant fucking asshole.

When Corey and his buddies weren't smoking weed from his parents' stash, they would cruise through neighborhoods on their bikes, loudly telling one another hilarious stories about all the times they'd been giant fucking assholes, all while searching for new opportunities to be giant fucking assholes.

It looked like we were their opportunity that day.

Sadly, Corey Sheridan was also three years older than me—two grades ahead. His buddies I recognized as eighth graders, a year ahead of me, but I didn't know them much beyond that. At fifteen, Corey Sheridan was good-looking and well-built, with shaggy hair and piercings.

Even now, I see older, popular, otherwise intelligent girls fawn over him in the hallways at school, petting his shaggy hair, giggling at his alarmingly honest comments about them and their bodies, squealing—*Ohmigod, Corey, stop!*—when he openly tries to get them to touch his dick at his locker.

Yeah, not a nice guy.

"You aren't going to let us play? Your game looks really awesome."

Corey leaned forward on his handlebars, still smiling, still—to an outside listener—sounding sincere. It's what made him such a *gifted* giant fucking asshole—his ability to look and sound like he really wanted to be buds, to join in and be part of our fun.

And, you know, if I had said, "Sure, Corey, you're up after Tabby. She gets one more good one, and then it's your turn," there's a good chance he would've hopped off his bike and taken a few good hacks and enjoyed it. But I didn't say that, because even if he did join in, it wouldn't be to be a part of our fun. It wouldn't be to shamelessly enjoy imagining himself as a big leaguer crushing a baseball for real, or to enjoy listening to a friend's analysis of the latest drama in the seventh grade. It would be to make us feel stupid. To make a show of really enjoying himself, rounding our imaginary bases and high-fiving his laughing buddies, so that it was clear to everyone in that circle—without ever directly saying the words—that we were still lame-ass little kids.

And I fucking hated that.

So I didn't say, "Sure, Corey," when he smiled and asked to play.

But I didn't do anything awesome, either.

I did what I always do when I am simultaneously pissed off and terrified of confrontation: I turned away and told him to go fuck himself under my breath.

Which was the response Corey was hoping for.

"What was that?" he said, smiling wider, turning his head to the side to hear me better, side-eyeing Tabby still sitting on the curb. When I didn't reply—just looked away, my face burning with shame—he coasted up next to me on his bike.

He was shirtless, and up close I could see the defined lines of his chest and abs, the scabs on his elbows and forearms, the five inches of underwear showing above his worn white skater jeans, his cell phone protruding from his front pocket. He was the complete opposite of me: gangly twelve-year-old limbs like paper towel tubes sticking out of a baggy Franklin Middle School T-shirt and mesh shorts that were probably getting too short for my rapidly growing legs.

"I'm sorry, bro, I missed that. I couldn't hear what you said to me."

I felt weightless, my entire body trembling, like tiny needles were pricking every inch of my body. I swear, it felt like he sat there on his bike for an hour, waiting for me to say something. My ears were ringing, and I couldn't get myself to even look up from his spokes. My throat couldn't take in air, let alone talk; had I opened my mouth, my voice would have caught. I would have choked, and hot tears of humiliation would have spilled down my cheeks—in front of Corey Sheridan, in front of Tabby, in front of the two eighth-grade douche bags who'd now have a reason to remember my face at school.

Tabby stood, the red bat resting on her pink shoulder, her other hand on her hip, clearly unimpressed by Corey Sheridan or his little posse. "Go home and smoke some more weed, loser."

Corey turned his full attention now to Tabby. He smiled that same empty smile, and his eyes moved slowly down over her body, blatantly lingering on what he felt were the important parts, before lazily resting on her face again.

"You know, if you grow some tits, I'll let you suck my dick."

Tabby took one step off the curb, but stopped when his buddies burst out laughing on their bikes behind me. Tabby did her very best to remain unaffected by this, to still appear unimpressed, but I caught her flinch, no more than a couple of extra blinks, her eyes dropping for the briefest moment. Corey caught it, too—he'd spent the better part of his useless life making kids weaker than him feel this way. He knew he'd cut her.

A decade of catching fireflies and filling water balloons, of neighborhood hide-and-go-seek tag and home run derbies, of lying around talking about what we'll do when we're older. And he just rode in and shit on all of it.

Tabby opened her mouth to speak, the corners trembling, and that's when I found my voice again.

"Hey, that's what I said to your mom last night, bro."

It didn't feel as good as I'd hoped. I was out of my depth here. For one, I'd never said *bro* in my life, and it sounded as stupid as it felt coming out of my mouth.

But I didn't want them to just leave, to finish laughing and ride away on their bikes and let Tabby and me get back to our day. I wanted to beat them at their own game. I wanted to match Corey's cutting, shaming insults, and smile as I did it. To have *his* ears burn red and the corners of *his* mouth tip down, watch him pedal away swearing under his breath. And that was my mistake. Because I don't have it in me to be Corey Sheridan, and Corey Sheridan didn't give two shits about me—probably didn't even know my name. I couldn't beat Corey Sheridan at being Corey Sheridan.

He had my shirt in his fist the moment *bro* fumbled out of my mouth.

"You want to talk so we can hear you now, bro?" he said, emphasizing *bro,* pulling me to within inches of his face, where his bloodshot eyes stared right through mine.

Tabby moved closer—I think everyone was assuming she'd beg Corey to stop, and complete the humiliating scene as scripted. But Tabby didn't follow the script.

She said nothing. She swung. Hard.

The bat slammed into Corey's right arm, the dented plastic barrel and duct-taped head finally giving way. And though it probably didn't hurt Corey that much, the effect was awesome:

on impact, golf balls shot out in all directions, bouncing and colliding all around us and ricocheting off their bikes.

She'd gone Graig Nettles on his ass.

Corey fell to the side, tripping over his bike, and had to catch himself with his hands on the street to keep from tumbling, his bike clattering to the pavement.

When he stood back up, he looked around him, breathing heavily, brushing his hands off on the back of his jeans. Half the golf balls were still rolling toward the curb, the only sound in the circle. His eyes locked onto mine for a moment and then onto Tabby's, and in that instant, *Corey* looked like the stupid little kid.

Tabby was a freaking hero.

"Fucking bitch!"

With one fast step, he shoved Tabby to the ground. Tabby flew backward, landing hard on her elbows to keep her head from smacking the pavement. Corey's buddies shook their heads at us and, possibly sensing that this had gone too far, that maybe shoving a twelve-year-old girl to the street was out of bounds even for giant fucking assholes, turned on their bikes and started pedaling up the street. Corey got back on his bike, a sneer on his lips, but didn't look up or say anything else to us and rode up the street after his buddies.

I ran over to Tabby and knelt down beside her, taking in the blood forming on her elbows. "Tabby, that was the most awesome thing I've ever seen."

She laughed, turning her head away from me, her eyes closed, tears and snot now running freely. And I knew she was okay.

"Thanks for saving me, bro." She laughed again.

"Hey! I was about to give him a titty-twister when you went

all apeshit on him with the bat." She was laughing harder now, smiling up at me, squinting into the sky, her face a blotchy mess. So I kept going. "It would've been a good one, too, with no shirt on. I could've ripped that fucker clean off." I pinched the air above Tabby's head and pretended to pluck Corey Sheridan's nipple off his chest. "Pop it in my mouth, chew on it like an eraser, and spit it back in his face."

"Ewww, you're making it worse!" Tabby put her hand over her mouth, eyes squinting back more tears.

"Too far?"

"Too far," she said, sitting up and examining her elbows for the first time.

"Come on," I said, pulling her to her feet. "My mom can clean you up."

"Know what I could use right now?"

"Nerds?"

"Ewoks."

CHAPTER TWELVE

PRACTICE ON THANKSGIVING SHOULD NOT BE ALLOWED

Seven-thirty, Thanksgiving morning. Just plain wrong.

I stop the alarm on my phone and stare at the screen, trying to clear my head of the weird-ass dream that I can't seem to remember. Something with T-ball, my seventh-grade math teacher, and Lily Branson. I don't know who the lucky bastards are who enjoy their dreams every night. I only ever wake up frustrated and confused.

My covers are calling me back to them, but the thought of walking into practice late—to be the one guy standing at the back of the huddle, catching only the tail end of Coach's talk, Coach watching you join the group but never pausing his speech, all the other guys knowing it, too, but unwilling to make eye contact with you—that gets my butt off my bed. That's terrifying. Because the eight thousand suicides I'd have to run by myself wouldn't be the worst part. My body would be past caring by that point, anyway. No, it's the eight thousand suicides the whole team would have to run for my transgressions—JV and varsity—*before* my individual sentence began at the end of practice. And those are on top of the regularly scheduled suicides we run at the end of every practice. Coach calls them "opportunities"—opportunities to ensure that we leave absolutely everything on the floor.

Still, it will not be *this* 160-pound freshman who adds to that torture.

Dad's already in the kitchen making coffee when I make my way downstairs. He's sporting his plaid pajama pants that fall short of his ankles and his ancient Shippensburg sweatshirt, and the hair on the back of his head still stands straight up from his pillow.

"Looking good, Dad," I say, grabbing a Pop-Tart from the cupboard. He grunts without turning around. Since Mom will be doing all the cooking for the family today, Dad volunteered to wake up early and drive me to practice.

I munch my Pop-Tart in silence. Dad reads the news on his tablet across the table. Mornings with Dad are kind of nice—there's no pressure for conversation, and the sound of Dad's coffee brewing is almost hypnotic. And even though it tastes like boiled mulch, I love the smell of it in the kitchen in the morning.

"You ready?" he says, bringing me back from wherever my mind drifted. Dad steps into his man-slippers and pulls on his long winter coat to complete the look.

"You're going out like that?"

"I'm not planning on getting out of the car," he says, pouring himself a cup of coffee for the road.

"Right."

The ten-minute ride to school is equally peaceful, Dad sipping his coffee and jamming out to an old Dave Matthews CD of his. Most of the leaves are down now, and the sun is starting to shine through the bare branches of the trees in the neighborhood.

As we pull up in front of the school, the sun disappears behind the gym.

"Happy Thanksgiving."

"Yeah, thanks, Dad. See you later."

Practice is brutal. Everyone else is as sluggish as me, including Coach, which makes him even more irritated by our sloppy, lethargic play. I don't know how many times he stops a drill and yells, "Baseline!" for a quick, painful opportunity to redeem ourselves.

The only exceptions are Trip and Elijah Leppo, who've formed an interesting relationship when we square off for JV-varsity scrimmages during practice. Trip simply will not be out-hustled. And even though Leppo is about as laid-back as any human on earth, he's a pure athlete, and he loves the competition. They feed off each other: the better Leppo plays, the more Trip dials up the intensity. Leppo usually gets the best of him in the end, partly by being surrounded by a better supporting cast, but there's no animosity, each one expecting the other to bring his best every time.

It's how I imagined I'd be with Branson, making him work his ass off in practice, being the reason he takes his game to another level during real games. But because of my height, I'm automatically put down low at power forward, where I'm awkwardly matched with Trevor Lighty, which can be summarized with this quick graphic representation: │ vs. ■.

│ cannot box out ■. │ cannot muscle through ■. │ can only try to dance around ■. And coaches are not particularly impressed by │ dancing around ■. So yeah. I stick a few turnarounds over him—more of that "weak shit" from the Y—which pisses him off. When I miss, I have zero chance of a rebound because he's already boxed me to the floor. It's awesome.

Branson plays out on the wing at small forward, where he routinely annihilates Devin Heiner, one of the few juniors on the JV team. It's like Branson's on autopilot, which pisses *me* off, because it's like his whole damn life is on autopilot.

After two-plus hours topped off by at least a dozen suicides, Coach calls an end to the suffering.

"All right, bring it in, gentlemen." Coach goes on for a while about our focus and overcoming adversity and says some stuff about our opponents in next week's tip-off tournament, but I'm not sure any of us hear it over our desperate gasping for oxygen and the visions of turkey and stuffing and pie-baking grannies that dance in our heads.

"Try not to eat too much today. Seven-thirty again tomorrow. If you come in the way you did today, you're really going to be hurting." He laughs a soulless laugh to himself. "All right, hands in. One, two, three—"

We all give a halfhearted "Black Bears" and disband. Trip and I stay behind to collect all the balls and put the racks back in the closet. One of the perks of being freshmen.

When we trudge down to the locker room a few minutes later, half the varsity guys are doubled over about something, but I don't think anything of it. They've found a little more energy now that they get to go home. I'm sitting on the bench in front of my locker, pulling out my sweats, when I hear Lighty's voice above the others.

"What's the deal with the freshman, B? She sucking your dick yet?"

My body freezes. The other guys keep laughing.

"Dude, shut up," Branson replies casually.

"She's a cockmonster, isn't she?"

I'm still frozen to my bench, one leg through my sweats, unable to raise my eyes from the crack in the mildewed floor tile in front of my foot.

The varsity guys are still laughing, including Branson. "Light, you're an asshole," he says. "This is why you never have a girlfriend."

To which Lighty starts singing *cockmonster* in falsetto.

I manage to look up for a second, my hands trembling while I finish pulling my sweatpants on over my shorts.

Branson's smiling—there's not a hint of anger on his face, like this is all no big deal. He snaps Lighty, hard, with his towel, Lighty howling with glee.

When Branson turns back to his stuff, he sees me staring. I have no idea how the look on my face reads. I look down at my bag, yank the zipper closed, and sling it over my shoulder.

"Ignore him, Wainwright. He's an asshole."

I fake a laugh as best I can, manage some noise that resembles *yeah* as I walk by them out the door.

Trip comes out behind me and hustles to catch up.

"Were they talking about Tabby?"

"Yeah," I say. I can barely get it out, and I can't look Trip in the eye when I do.

"Tabby and Branson?"

I nod.

"Tabby's a freshman."

I nod again.

"He's a senior."

"I'm aware."

"Whoa."

"Yeah."

Luckily, Dad's car is parked along the curb, so I don't have to wait while Branson and crew come out. I still feel like I'm consciously forcing my lungs to breathe, and I'm not sure I can continue this deep discussion with Trip.

The same Dave Matthews CD is playing when I open the car door. Dad's combed his hair, but the slippers and pajama pants remain, and he's sipping on what is likely his eighth cup of coffee.

"How was practice, bud?"

"Good."

"Good."

And back into the cocoon. Bless this man.

It starts snowing on the ride home—flurries that swirl up and over the car, never landing on the windshield to be wiped away. It's like riding inside a snow globe that's been shaken.

I stare out the window, the usual landmarks blurred by these unusual snowflakes, as my mind runs awful, ridiculous movies on a loop:

Branson going stone-faced in the locker room, grabbing Lighty by the neck and slamming him back into a locker.

"You don't ever talk about Tabby that way."

"S-s-sorry, dude. It was a joke!"

But that's just stupid.

Or me, walking up behind Lighty as he's singing his song, palming the back of his stubby, lumpy head and slamming his face into his locker, smashing his nose and knocking him unconscious. Then I turn to Branson, Lighty's body laid out on the floor between us.

If you're not going to be man enough to stand up for Tabby, then I will.

And I step over Lighty's body and past Branson's incredulous face, walking out without another word.

But my brain doesn't like to let my fantasies run too far without slapping a little reality on them, rewinding the scene back for editing, so when I put my hand on Lighty's head, it doesn't budge.

"The fuck are you doing, freshman?"

And with one arm, he shoves me backward, sends me crashing over a bench, the whole team howling at the scene.

"Song's not about me, dumbass. I'm not sucking your dick. But check with my man Branson, here. He's into freshmen. He might let you suck his."

More laughter. Including Branson.

And throughout all of these, I see flashes of Tabby—

Wow.

My brain sucks.

As we pull into our neighborhood, I try to focus on the familiar houses, the flurries, the music, Dad's drumming on the steering wheel—anything to keep my brain in the present: It's Thanksgiving. I'm going to eat awesome food till I'm sick, lie around on the couch, and let the drone of football announcers lull me to sleep.

Everything's fine.

CHAPTER THIRTEEN

GRAVY MAKES EVERYTHING BETTER, PART I

When I step into the kitchen from the garage, I am hit by a wave of delicious. The air is thick and humid, as if savory, microscopic turkey particles are fighting nitrogen for dominance in the atmosphere. It's intoxicating. My salivary glands are going bonkers.

"Sweet mother," Dad murmurs, walking in behind me and pulling in a deep breath through his nose. His expression is borderline inappropriate.

"Hey, guys!" Mom says, looking over her shoulder from the potatoes she's scrubbing in the sink. She's got her favorite apron on—one Dad got for her that's bright pink and covered in a pattern of Maryland blue crabs. And she looks equal parts frazzled and ecstatic—she frets and complains for at least a week leading up to today, but once she starts, she's like a machine.

"Smells amazing, Mom."

"Thank you. Don't touch anything. How was practice?"

"Good," I say, lingering a moment longer before retreating from the kitchen.

When I step into the living room, I find Tabby sitting on the floor with Murray, watching the Thanksgiving Day Parade on TV.

"Hey," I say, trying to look completely normal, like everything's the same as it always is, which it's not, which probably means I look like a complete idiot.

"Hey, Matty," she says, looking back and smiling from where she sits in front of the TV, cross-legged, with Murray in her lap.

Murray jumps up then and bolts toward me, clutching what appears to be a large, pointy carrot in his tiny hand.

"Matty! Matty! It's snowing!"

"Hey, Murray B.," I say, noogying his head when he crashes into my legs. "It *is* snowing. What's with the carrot?"

"He jacked it from your mom," Tabby says. "Snowman nose."

"It's not sticking to the ground yet. You're a little early."

Murray runs to the front window and looks out, hands and carrot pressed to the glass.

"Can we go play outside?" he asks, entranced by the swirling flakes outside the window.

"Not right now," Mom calls from the kitchen. I'm guessing by the way she says it that this is not the first time Murray's made this request.

"Okay," he says. His shoulders slump, but he remains at the window. A moment later, he turns to walk back to Tabby and sits down in her lap. Just like that, he's back into the parade, transfixed by a Snoopy balloon bobbing high above a Manhattan avenue.

"Your dad working again?" I ask Tabby.

"Yeah. They offered him triple time. I told him to do it; we could blow it all on sushi over the weekend."

"Good call."

"And this way I get your mom's Thanksgiving, too."

"Double whammy."

I'm still working hard to keep my mind in the present. Seeing

Tabby with Murray—Tabby the way she's always been—helps. It's still a struggle, though. The projector lights flicker on in my head, flashes of still shots I don't want to be seeing.

Mom pokes her head in the room. "I don't know if you know this, but you smell. Go wash the stink off before Gramma and Grampa get here."

"Love you, too, Mom."

"You guys doing okay?" she says to Tabby and Murray.

Murray turns. "Yeah, but can we go outside?"

Mom lowers her chin and looks at him.

"Okay," Murray says, defeated again.

I know those guys were just being assholes. The rational part of me gets that it was guys BSing in the locker room, teammates ragging on one another, because that's just what we do. And right now, Branson's the obvious target, sniffing around a freshman.

I get that.

But what's killing me is that when they walk out of that locker room, it becomes more than BS. They're automatically going to see Tabby differently. Even if it's just a dumb joke. Every time one of them sees her, that thought is going to pop into his head. And he's going to *wonder*. Fuck, I'm doing it right now, and I hate myself for it. I know better. I know Tabby. The reality of Tabby hanging out with Murray down there should patch over the twisted images in my brain.

Meanwhile, the flawless perception of Branson goes unchanged.

What is he doing? This guy could have any girl he wants. Why a freshman? Why Tabby?

I step out of the shower, the bathroom filled with steam. I was in there longer than I thought. I wipe the steam from the mirror with my towel.

Well, if you could have any girl you wanted, who would you *pick?*

"In here, Matty," I hear Tabby say when I come out of my room, decked out in a fresh pair of sweats in preparation for the day. I find Tabby in Murray's room. The stuffed animals are out in full force, lined up along the main boulevard of Murray's town rug.

"We're having a parade!" Murray says, beaming up at me from behind his wall of animals.

"We've got one all picked out for you," Tabby says with a grin, patting the head of a stuffed giraffe sporting a polka-dot ribbon tied around his neck like a giant bow tie.

One time. One time I called the giraffe Bernard and gave him this awful British accent, and ever since, Bernard has been my permanent role. There's no version of *Animals! Animals! Animals!* that doesn't include Bernard the British Giraffe. Not that I'm lobbying for new roles. But it's not a good British accent: all Bernard ever says is "'Ello, guv-nah!" and asks if we've got whatever weird food I can remember from the Harry Potter movies. Awful.

"Come on, Matty!" Murray says, grabbing Bernard and holding him out for me to assume my role.

"Hold on a minute," I say. "I need to go steal some food first. I'll be right back."

"Make it shnappy, mishter," Tabby says through the gap-toothed beaver puppet on her hand, waving a furry little fist in my direction as I grin and retreat down the steps.

I find Mom and Dad both in the kitchen, Mom feeding Dad a hunk of stuffing and kissing him.

"Mmmmm. Hottest kiss ever," Dad says.

"Gross," I say, heading to the refrigerator.

"Go away," he says. Mom slaps him playfully on the chest and turns back to the stove. Dad's changed out of pajamas into jeans, though he's still wearing his old Ship sweatshirt and slippers.

"Nice pants upgrade, Dad."

"Likewise," he replies, nodding at my sweats. Holidays are casual in the Wainwright house.

"I made you a sandwich, sweetie," Mom says, pointing to a plate on the counter next to me. "I know you're probably hungry. You can't have any stuffing yet, though."

"Yeah, I don't think I can ever eat stuffing again."

Which is a total lie, of course. Besides being an arts-and-crafts Jedi, Mom is also an unparalleled stuffing Jedi. Like, the Yoda of stuffing making. None of that Stove Top garbage or those lame, prepackaged bread cubes that turn to mush. No, Mom uses some crusty sourdough she gets from the bakery and mixes in sausage and apples and some other crazy stuff, and then makes her ridiculous homemade gravy to go on top. We force her to make triple batches so we have plenty for leftovers. I think Dad and I both get stuffing boners at the mention of it.

Well.

Let's add *Dad boner* to the list of things I now need to scrub from my memory. Thank you, brain. Big day for you.

I inhale my sandwich in a few bites and leave Mom and Dad in the kitchen. Bernard is waiting for me when I sit down on

Murray's floor, set apart from the line of animals he and Tabby have arranged.

Murray holds back a smile, waiting.

"'Ello, guv-nah!" Bernard yells to Murray and the parade line in general. "Have you got any bangers and mash?"

As always, one of the animals happens to have whatever Bernard asks for on hand. "This is for Bernard," Murray says through an old stuffed bear to Tabby's beaver puppet, which now has a tiny T-shirt pulled over its head, its face poking out of the neck hole.

"Here'sh your bangersh and mash!"

"Right-o, guv-nah!" Then in my own voice, "What's with the T-shirt?"

"He's into Ewok cosplay."

"Right."

A few minutes later, when the parade animals start asking each other if they're allowed to play outside in the snow, and if they've ever made a snowman, and whether they've ever made snow angels or had a snowball fight, we give in to Murray.

"You wanna go outside, Murray?" Tabby asks, smiling and shaking her head.

"Okay!" Murray replies, as though this was Tabby's un-prompted suggestion, and takes off out of his room and down the steps.

"He's a persistent little bugger," Tabby says, sliding the beaver-wok off her hand and getting to her feet. I stand, too. "You were never like that," she says, nudging me with her elbow as we follow Murray out the door.

I smile. I have no idea if that was a compliment or a quick

point-of-fact memory. And before my filter can catch it, I say, "I was just happy to follow your lead."

Good gracious.

My inner romantic-movie screenwriter applauds and waves his little beret in the air, just as my inner realist punches him in the wiener. How the hell did that one slip through?

Tabby glances back at me on the steps, eyebrows raised. "Ish that sho?"

"Mom, we're going to take Murray out front to play!" I call, a little too loud.

Mom pokes her head in again, giving the stink eye to Murray, who's refusing to look up at her: he remains focused solely on Tabby as she pulls a hat down over his head and helps him zip his coat. This is a smart little dude we're dealing with here.

Mom sighs and shakes her head.

"Are you guys sure you're okay with that turkey?" she says to Tabby and me.

"We're good," I say.

"All right. Gramma and Grampa will be here soon, anyway."

I shoot baskets with half-numb fingers—actively restraining myself from digging them into my pits in front of Tabby—while Murray alternates between running around in circles, cheering on the snow, and standing still with his head up and his mouth open, letting the snowflakes land on his tongue. The fact that none of it is sticking to the ground has not dampened his enthusiasm. I don't have the heart to tell him that we don't get real snow in south-central Pennsylvania until January. Murray's got that carrot on standby. And honestly, his excitement is infectious. I can't help but cheer on the snow with him. You know, in my head.

Tabby stands in the middle of the driveway in the crocheted Franklin hat and her old gymnastics team jacket, the gravitational center of Murray's orbit. She rubs her hands for warmth, smiling at Murray's routine, and opens her mouth to the sky along with him.

When I block out the locker room from this morning, this is another perfect Tabby day—the kind of lazy, no-worries, just-hanging-out days I've enjoyed with her my entire life. But it feels numbered now, and I hate that I have to pretend part of this day didn't happen for it to feel how it used to feel.

"Matt, you look like you're in pain."

"What? No, sorry. I was spacing out, trying to warm up my hands. It's freezing out here."

"Why don't you stick them in your armpits, like you usually do?"

"Right."

Right then, the land-yacht pulls up to the curb in front of the house, and, just like every time, Murray makes a beeline for the car for Gramma to scoop him up in a hug. Though this time she has to avoid getting her eyeball impaled by Murray's carrot.

Grampa steps onto the driveway, decked out in his standard uniform, grinning at Murray. I don't know where he finds sweats that big.

"Grampa! It's snowing!"

"Hey, how 'bout that?" he says, holding out his palms and looking up to the sky, as though he's just now noticing. "How's my Murray?" He kisses the top of his head, then pretends to take a chomp of Murray's carrot.

Tabby leans into my arm, watching them. I don't think she realizes she's doing it. But I know she's waiting for her turn.

"All right, Tabby's here!" Grampa booms on cue, and I swear, I can *feel* her face break open into that huge grin.

"Hi, Grampa Wainwright," she says as he walks up to us.

"What's shaking, T-Bone? Keeping my boys here out of trouble?"

"Doing my best."

Grampa tugs the strings of her earflaps, turns to me, and grins.

"I've got my turkey-eatin' pants on," he says, hooking his thumbs inside the elastic waistband of his sweatpants and stretching it out in front of him.

"Right there with you, Grampa," I say, mirroring his move with my own waistband.

Grampa will use this line at least forty-seven more times today.

Tabby will laugh every time.

Naturally, Grampa adores her, too.

Later that evening, after all the dishes have been cleaned and the leftovers are brought back out for turkey sandwiches and more stuffing—allowing Grampa to work in a few last references to his turkey-eatin' pants—Tabby decides to head home. Mom loads her down with food for her dad whenever he finally gets home from work, which Tabby tells her should be pretty soon.

"Matty, why don't you walk Tabby over?" Mom calls from the kitchen, where she stacks Tupperware containers in a grocery bag for Tabby's dad. "It's dark out there."

I roll off the couch, decide not to mention that Tabby lives right across the street and that we live in a cul-de-sac. Tabby hands me the overstuffed bag of leftovers, nudges my arm, and opens the door. "Following my lead?" she says, grinning, and steps outside.

"Just to the curb," I say, trying to hide my embarrassment. "Then it's gravy-mugging time."

"Try it, buddy. I will record your death and rewatch it over leftover stuffing."

I smile and follow her into the dark.

The flurries have picked up again, and I can see a light dusting of snow covering Grampa's car. As we make our way across the circle, Tabby checks her phone and looks up the street, but doesn't say anything.

"Hot date tonight?"

Oh.

"Wouldn't you like to know?"

Shit.

"So your dad will be home soon?"

"Yeah, he should be," she says. Maybe she's battling turkey coma, too, but she seems a little off. Nervous maybe. And the morning comes flooding back into my brain.

When we get to her door, she slides her key into the lock, and again glances up the street.

"I can get those," she says, holding her door open with her foot and reaching for the bag of leftovers. She looks up and smiles. "Thanks for today, Matty. Tell your mom thanks again. Happy Thanksgiving."

I so badly want to keep dragging this day out, to find some excuse to stand here on this dark stoop with her and watch the snow fall. Instead, I return her smile and hold the door as she takes the bag inside.

"See ya, Tabby. Happy Thanksgiving."

When I'm partway across the circle, I look back. I can still see Tabby inside the front door, looking down at her phone, the glow from the screen highlighting the profile of her face. Wherever she is has nothing to do with me.

I trail my fingers across the hood of Grampa's car, a light skiff of snow falling to the curb when it runs off the edge. On the driveway, I reach up and swat the net of my basketball hoop as I pass underneath. I look up into the dark sky, watch the flakes disappear in my breath, and head back inside.

When Gramma and Grampa leave a little while later, I look out across the circle. The black Accord is parked across the street.

CHAPTER FOURTEEN

IT'S BLACK FRIDAY

I climb back into bed as soon as I get home from practice the next morning. I didn't sleep very well last night.

Coach wasn't lying, either. We came in even more sluggish than the day before, our turkey hangovers making it seem like we were wearing ankle weights. It's like we were two steps slower on every drill. Coach refused to let up, determined to run it out of us, as though it's possible to sweat gravy.

Devin Heiner actually puked into one of the water fountains during a break, which I think aptly sums up the entire experience. Branson was especially off, which had my brain going haywire, since I never saw what time his car was finally gone last night. I wanted to enjoy watching him struggle, but it left me overanalyzing why he might be struggling this morning, which took my brain places I didn't want it to go. I couldn't even look him in the face.

Painful.

And that was before the suicides at the end of practice.

I sleep until late in the afternoon. When I make my way downstairs, the whole house feels gloomy, the only light coming from the den downstairs. Sometime over the night, the snow gave way to rain, dashing Murray's dreams of a white Black

Friday. No snowmen. No scooping fresh snow off the ground and eating it.

Mom and Murray are in the den, Mom sorting through Christmas decorations, Murray on the floor in front of the TV watching some nature documentary Mom's queued up for him. He's wearing a Santa hat and has a few of his favorite tree ornaments around him, but he's mesmerized by the footage of the giant squid on the screen. Despite having seen this video about a bajillion times already.

"Hey, look who's awake," Mom says.

"Putting the tree up today?" I ask, pulling an ornament from the box on the couch. It's some kind of dog made out of Model Magic, colored brown with scribbly marker. I made it before I was even in kindergarten. Tabby's got one in here somewhere, too. A turtle with purple toenails. I set mine back in the box.

"Probably not till this weekend," Mom says. "I wanted to get everything out of the basement, give your father a chance to come to terms with the fact that he'll be hanging lights this weekend."

Dad would be perfectly happy slapping a wreath on the door and making sure the tree is near a front window, but Mom's not having it. The Wainwright house will have Christmas lights, and it is his job to put them up. End of story.

"You can heat up some leftovers, if you're hungry," Mom says. "It's kind of a lazy day. I'm not planning on making dinner or anything."

"Sounds good."

I head to the kitchen. After the misery of practice this morning, I'm not sure if I can do any more stuffing and gravy. Which means I stop at two bowls.

I'm back in near coma state on the living room couch when there's a knock at the front door. It's Tabby, clutching an armful of empty Tupperware, shifting from foot to foot in the rain.

"You didn't have to bring those back in the rain. We're not that desperate for Tupperware," I say, taking the stack of containers from her and setting them on the counter in the kitchen. She's still standing inside the door when I come back, looking around like she's never been here before.

"You okay?"

"Yeah. Yeah." She presses the string from her hoodie to her lips, a tic I haven't seen her do in years. "I need to show you something. Can we go up to your room?"

"Yeah. Of course."

"What's going on?" I ask after closing my door behind me. She doesn't respond, just goes straight to my desk chair and pulls out her phone. She opens Instagram and starts scrolling. I sit at the foot of my bed next to her and see her pull up Liam's profile.

I'm still not totally following. Did he trash her on Instagram? That doesn't seem likely.

Tabby sits back so I can lean in and read. It starts with a photo of the three of them—Branson, Tabby, and Lily—taken from the driver's seat of his car. His face is cheek-to-cheek with Tabby's, leaning in from the backseat, with Lily's wide smile filling out the other side of the frame. It's hard to breathe, looking at how fucking happy they all are. Especially compared to how miserable real-time Tabby looks right now next to me.

Then, the comments.

emma_b: really, Liam? a freshman?

bri_easton: freshman? is she skanky?

chaseblevins: skanktastic!!!

tylerp: I'd do her—GINGERZ RULE!!!

It goes on from there. It seems like maybe the same four or five assholes doing most of the posting, but some of the nastier comments get ugly.

Tabby's eyes are wide and red-rimmed, her mouth paralyzed in a perfect upside-down U, trembling at the corners—what she and I used to call Muppet mouth when Murray did it because of how much he resembled Beaker from the Muppets. But there's nothing funny about this.

I reach past her to my laptop and turn on music, buying a moment to think.

What do I do with this? My first thought is to bash Branson, to call him out for not saying anything, for not shutting these assholes down. To spill what happened in the locker room, and bash him for not making more of a fight there, either. Because I would have.

But at the same time, I know it's easy for me to say that, to claim how honorably I'd act if it were me, because it's *not* me. And no one would give a shit if it *were* me. I can fantasize about going ballistic on an overgrown prick like Lighty, because I'll never really have to do it.

Which leads my brain to other incredibly unhelpful, selfish, and ultimately unappealing suggestions for Tabby.

See, if you were with me, you wouldn't have these problems! Because no one would care! Isn't that great? What do you say?

"Matt?" Tabby croaks, waiting for me to say something. Waiting for her best friend to pull his head out of his ass and be a friend.

"It's gonna be fine," I finally say. I force myself to look her in the eyes. "This will all blow over quick."

"But I didn't do anything," she says, her mouth trembling and the red splotches growing around her cheeks and eyes. "I don't even know those people!"

"Listen," I say, and it feels crazy—this is the first time I've ever been on this side of the conversation with Tabby, me having to explain how things work to her. I am guaranteed to fuck this up. "Liam's a senior, and—"

"But I didn't do anything!" she says again, pleading.

"Tabby, I know. But he's *the* senior. There's gotta be like a hundred girls who flirt with him every day. And like another two hundred who don't but secretly wish they could.

"And beyond that," I continue when Tabby doesn't cut in— she actually seems to be listening to this drivel—"there's gotta be at least a couple of ex-girlfriends floating around. And here you are, this little innocent freshman girl," I say, reaching over and patting her on top of her head, which brings a tiny smile, "and he's paying attention to you. You don't think there's at least a *few* girls," I say, gesturing toward her phone, "out of three whole grades above us who might be jealous and catty enough to post dumb shit on Instagram? It'll blow over."

Tabby pulls her feet up onto my desk chair, hugging her arms around her legs and resting her chin on her knees. That same strand of light hair falls loose from her hair tie and hangs down over her knee. I so badly want to reach over and brush it behind her ear. She's smiling again and the blotches are starting to fade. And since I'm clearly such a fucking genius, I continue.

"I mean, he's athletic, he's good-looking, he's actually nice to people, even underclassmen. . . . He's perfect. I think I hate you now, too."

Tabby laughs, finally, a short burst. She rubs her eyes, then her whole face with her hands. She takes a deep breath and looks up at me again, her eyes still red and glassy.

"We aren't even going out yet or anything," she says.

Yet catches me like a thorn. "It's pretty obvious he likes you. He's around you all the time now."

"Not all the time," she says. She tries to sound defensive, but it's clear she's holding back a smile—the corners of her mouth twitch, and now she's not looking me in the eye.

"Really, Tabby? The hallways, the rides to and from school," and before I can hold it in, "showing up at your house at night?"

"What?"

Shit.

That one slipped through the filter. I hope it didn't sound as accusatory as it felt.

"What the hell? Are you stalking my house?"

"No! I mean, I just saw his car last night after you left."

"What's that have to do with these people?" she asks, shaking her phone at me, as though I'm the one attacking her.

"What? Nothing. I was just saying he must really like you."

"We weren't doing anything, Matt."

"I know, but—"

"But what?"

"Tabby, I know—"

"He came over to drop off *whoopie pies*," she says, almost snarling at me now.

How the hell did I get here? How do I get back to where I had her laughing? Where she was looking to me for help?

"He had Thanksgiving at his grandma's house. Pumpkin whoopie pies are her specialty. He wanted to give some to me and my dad. We hung out and talked until my dad got home. Is that all okay with you?"

Her eyes burn holes through mine.

"Tabby. Hold up. Why are you getting pissed at me? I didn't do anything! You know I don't think any of that stuff." When she keeps glaring, I say, "You know that, right? I would never think that about you."

I feel like I'm groveling now. And like I'm losing it. Part of me is desperate for her to understand, to get how I feel about her, how I've felt for a long time. And the other part is just getting pissed: How the hell have I gotten thrown in with these assholes trashing her online? After she came crying to me about them? Is it because I mentioned seeing Branson's car last night? Because, oh yeah, you live across the street—if I walk by a window, *I can see your house.* That's not an accusation. That's fucking geographical proximity.

Neither of us speaks. The song that pops on—a version of "The Wheels on the Bus" that I downloaded for Murray one day—makes this moment even more absurd, doubled by the fact that neither of us acknowledges it. But it's at least filling the heavy silence between us. I keep hoping she'll notice it, and we can both laugh and break this tension.

Tabby doesn't seem to notice.

"I'm sorry, Matt," she finally says, turning away. It's hard to tell if she really is sorry, or if she's sick of the moment—sick of me—and moving on, which only intensifies the conflict between desperation and anger. "I do know that. I'm sorry," she says again, without looking at me. "I think—" She stops, starts over. "You know, I've never had anyone say stuff about me before." She pulls up her phone, scrolling as she continues. "I've never talked to these people before. I don't even know who some of them are. How am I supposed to deal with it?"

"I know," I say, leaning back against my wall, the tension finally starting to drain out of me. "It'll blow over, Tabby. They're just jealous, and it's just Instagram."

"You're right," she says, and she sits up straighter, slaps her hands down on my desk, decidedly ready to move on. She takes a deep breath, forces a smile, and looks around my room. "So what's new with you?" It's meant to be friendly, but it sounds more like a great-aunt asking about a little kid's day, artificially sweet and with insincere interest. But I'm glad to be at the end of this roller coaster, at least. "Nice song, by the way," she adds as the last *all through the town* fades out. She picks up the eighth-grade yearbook sitting next to my laptop and glances down at the open notebook underneath, and—

Oh.

Oh. Oh. Oh. Oh. Oh.

Oh, shit. No.

I was in a really bad place last night—

"'Do List'?"

Tabby turns in her chair to face me but doesn't look up. She scans the sheet filled with my writing, brow furrowed, while I try to sink into the wall and disappear. She doesn't ask what it is, just reads aloud:

"'Girls I would do if there were no consequences—social, emotional, or physical: freshman class.'"

Fuck me and my thoroughness with ranking parameters.

Tabby looks up, face frozen, equal parts horrified and confused. I'm paralyzed. She keeps going:

"'Number one: Hannah Marchetta. Number two: Megan Landis. Number three: Abby Brendemann.'"

She keeps scanning. Then flips the page.

"One hundred and seventeen?"

"It was just something stupid I was— It's just a joke," I say, knowing how stupid that sounds.

But what else do I say? That after a near-perfect day yesterday, it all fell to shit when I saw Branson's car? That it felt like it wiped out everything good—that every moment I loved really wasn't that special? That it was more a convenient habit? Do I explain that it made me want to be shallow and destructive and as far from emotionally sensitive as I could get?

I was awake for hours last night putting those rankings together. Paging through the yearbook and judging each face, blatantly disregarding that each was a real person—a person I knew—with her own story. Her own thoughts and feelings.

I wanted to play the senior, scoping out the fresh meat.

And it felt good.

At the time.

"Are you kidding me with this?" She meets my eyes. "Who are you?"

"No, Tabby, it's just—" And I stop, squeezing my eyes closed, shaking my head. This isn't supposed to be happening. I'm about to actually try to explain how, really, no one would know and no one would be hurt. That the rankings factor out those elements of reality. That the list is for rhetorical purposes—you know, rhetorically doing someone.

You see, I almost try to get her to *see the science* behind the rankings. As though that will clear up this whole silly misunderstanding. Luckily—if we can still use that term—I can hear how awful and moronic it sounds in my head before it comes out of my mouth.

"It's just stupid," I finally say. "Just a stupid joke."

"You're better than that," she says, tossing the notebook back on my desk in disgust. "And if you share your *joke* with anyone, Matthew, I will kill you."

The shame is unbearable, and I can't move from my spot on my bed, pressed into the wall, my eyes glued to the tiny hole in my covers I pick at with my fingers. For the moment, I'm thankful she didn't look at the list long enough to notice, because I have no idea how she would have taken it.

"So where am I on this list?" she asks a moment later, grabbing the notebook again. Guess I *am* going to find out how she takes this.

"Uh."

There are two columns of names, front and back. I watch her eyes scan through each one.

"Wait, I'm not even on the list?"

Of course Tabby's not on the list. Even at my worst, my darkest, most destructive moments, I wouldn't put Tabby on the list—wouldn't subject her to my ugliness. Tabby's not rhetorical.

"Do you want to be on the list?" I say, cocking an eyebrow, a desperate attempt to make light of the situation.

"Oh really, Matt? Could I?" Obviously not funny. Opposite of funny. "Would you be so gracious as to expand your do list to one hundred and *eighteen*, so I can make the cut?"

"Tabby, just—"

"Let me know when you've *done* the first hundred on the list, Matt. So I can spread my legs and wait my turn."

"Stop! Tabby, just stop. You don't understand."

I'm on my feet now. It's the ugliest thing I've ever heard come out of Tabby's mouth. And it's directed at me. I can't look at her. I pace the room, running my hands over my head.

"You exist outside the rankings," I mumble.

"Yeah, I got that, Matt. Outside of the top one hundred and seventeen. Thank you."

"No." I don't know how to get this out so that it makes sense, so that she sees that this awful, terrible thing is really a *good* thing. "You're not part of the rankings. You're . . . you're too good for my stupid, asshole list. There's, like, *you*," I say, holding out my left hand, "then there's, like, everybody else," indicating with a wave of my right. "Tabby, I—"

I almost say it. Two more tiny words. Seven tiny letters. I don't know if she knows it.

"It's like Nerds."

Tabby stares at me. I can't read her expression, so I keep going.

"You know how every year after Halloween, how we have all our shitload of candy, and we put them in our piles? We make our hierarchy, our candy rankings. And, you know, chocolate bars are clearly at the top of the rankings, and then SweeTARTS, and Tootsie Rolls, and all the way down to raisins—"

"If you call me a raisin, I'm going to punch you in the nuts."

"No, you're not a raisin. Hang on a minute. So we have our rankings, but off to the side, every year, are the Nerds. The Nerds are so good, so amazing, they're not even part of the rankings. They exist totally outside of the hierarchy.

"You're the Nerds."

That's it. That's as close as I can get to saying it without saying it. That's the moment in the movie where everything becomes clear and Tabby falls into my arms, and later, when we are a blissfully happy couple lying in each other's arms, we look back at this moment as *the* moment. Our moment. *You're the Nerds.*

Instead, Tabby raises her eyebrows and smirks, hands on her hips. "Okay, that's the sweetest, weirdest thing I've ever heard," she says, emphasizing *weird*. "But a do list, Matt? We just eat the candy. We don't defile and degrade it."

I am simultaneously crushed and swooning. Did she really not get it? Not care? Think we're like brother and sister Nerds? And she's always, always trying to make me a better human being. I want to reach out and put my hand behind her neck and pull her in, press my lips against that smirk.

She rolls her eyes and turns back to her phone.

"Oh my God." She breaks into a huge smile, her face almost touching the screen, as she reads. Like the last twenty minutes didn't happen.

I step closer and look at the screen over her shoulder.

Branson's finally responded.

liambranson: if you knew her, you'd understand. get over yourself.

And in his bio, he's added today's date. The official start.

"Oh my God," Tabby says again through her hand. Her eyes are glued to the screen. So much for *yet*.

Lily's comment pops up right below her brother's: YAY! Tabby!

Dozens of new comments follow, all positive, even though

Branson's bold declaration has been up for less than five minutes. Tabby's beside herself.

"Over Instagram? Really?" I mutter, mostly to myself. She whirls around in the chair and shoves me away.

"I don't see you asking anyone out, Matt. Here," she says, grabbing the notebook again. "You've got a hundred and seventeen girls you'd be willing to *do*. Why don't you actually *talk* to one of them?" And she tosses the notebook to me.

And I'm done.

I catch the notebook, turn, and fire it across the room as hard as I can. It crashes into my bedroom door, leaving a divot.

Tabby's shocked, her eyes huge, looking past me to my door. She slowly turns back to her phone, trying to continue like normal.

"Did you see what Lily—?"

"Fuck, Tabby," I say, sitting on the edge of my bed, resting my face in my hands. "Don't you have any girlfriends to talk to about this or something?"

She's quiet for a moment.

"Yeah, Matt. I'm sorry. You're probably right."

She walks out of my room, closing the door behind her.

When I pull up the picture again on my phone later that night, Liam and Lily's legion of friends have rallied behind him, showering him and Tabby with encouragements and trashing the original haters. Even Trevor Lighty left a *Do it B!* in his feed.

I guess Tabby's problem's been solved.

■ ■ ■

So to recap:

Matt Wainwright tries to help the girl he loves, ends up a misogynistic pervert who compares girls to Halloween candy and undoubtedly loses the girl forever, even as a friend.

Liam Branson thumbs a nine-word comment into his phone, the girl swoons over him, and everyone else in the free world swoons over their new coupledom.

At what point do I get to start laughing?

CHAPTER FIFTEEN

THE DAY I FELL IN LOVE WITH TABBY, PART 3

"I hope you at least made it to the base," Mom said to Tabby, smiling and shaking her head after we explained how Tabby had fallen playing baseball in the circle. No need to mention Corey Sheridan, not unless we wanted to be thrown in the car to hunt him down and drag him to his front door to have a talk with his parents. And we didn't.

After Mom finished cleaning up the cuts and brush burns on Tabby's elbows, I went into the kitchen and microwaved a bag of popcorn while Tabby went down to the den to cue up some Ewoks.

Tabby sat in the middle of the sofa, her legs curled under a blanket, intently reading the prologue as it scrolled up the screen, lines she'd read thousands of times. I plopped down next to her and put the bowl of popcorn between us, propping my feet up on the coffee table. Like I'd done a thousand times.

My dad—a serious *Star Wars* geek—used to always tease Tabby about her love for the Ewoks. Apparently, to the true *Star Wars* fan, the Ewoks are a joke: George Lucas's biggest mistake before the Jar Jar Binks debacle. But it's why Tabby always picked *Return of the Jedi* over the other five movies. I claimed to love *Jedi* for Jabba the Hutt, but deep down—and I'd never admit this to my dad—I loved the Ewoks, too.

We fell into a steady rhythm as the movie got rolling, taking turns with our hands in the popcorn bowl. And while the movie played on the screen, my mind rewound and replayed the day, over and over, analyzing every painful moment and fantasizing about what I *could* have said. How would Trip have reacted, had he stayed? Would *he* have said something first? Could he have made Corey Sheridan blush with shame? Would he have told him to fuck off the moment Corey rolled into the circle, gotten his ass kicked but gone down swinging? Would it have been Trip's elbows my mom cleaned up while warning him about swearing in her house? Would Tabby be right there, laughing and smiling at him?

And was I one twisted asshole for being glad it went down the way it did, instead?

I glanced over at Tabby every few minutes, and I felt that same twinge of desperation, and I wondered, *What the hell is wrong with my brain?*

When the movie hit a slow part, the popcorn bowl down to unpopped kernels, Tabby sat up and turned to face me.

"Do me a favor," she said, reaching over and wiping a buttery hand on my shoulder.

"Get you a napkin?"

"No, no, I'm good," she said. Her face looked serious for a moment, and she settled back in beside me, shoulder to greasy shoulder, before continuing. "Never talk about people's mothers."

"What?"

"Outside. With Corey. You did that whole *your-mom* thing to him. Don't ever do that." She looked down as she said this, looking neither at the TV nor at me, more like she was addressing the coffee table.

I was stunned for a moment. My fantasies aside, it had taken everything I had to get that out of my mouth, to actually *say* that to Corey Sheridan. And even if it sounded crude and stupid and embarrassingly unnatural—I could still hear him mocking my "bro"—I did it for Tabby. For *Tabby*.

"Tabby, he told you—"

"Yeah, Matt, I heard him," she said, pressing her elbow into my side, letting me know that certain details were not to be re-hashed here. "I just . . . I hate the *your-mom* stuff. It's disgusting and degrading and—"

"I didn't really mean—" I started defensively.

"I know it wasn't a factual statement. I hate the whole idea of it."

I couldn't say anything. Just sat there, looking helpless and defensive. I mean, I knew Tabby's mom hadn't been around since she was a baby. We talked about it sometimes. But still.

"Look, what you did was awesome," she said, and I couldn't help thinking, *No, what* you *did was awesome; what* I *did was weak and lame and—apparently—degrading to women.* "You stood up for your friend, and nothing's more important than that. But just . . . Okay, I think of it like this: the only people who actually say *your-mom* stuff, they're either complete buttholes like Corey Sheridan, or they're people trying too hard to be something they're not."

Like me.

"I don't want you to be either one of those people, Matt."

"But, I'm not—"

"I know you're not, Matt," she said, exhaling and rolling her eyes. "Just no more *your-mom* stuff, okay?"

"Okay. Whatever you say." I huffed.

"Good. Now shut up. This is my favorite part."

And just like that, she turned and settled back in next to me, her focus back on the movie. She laid her head on my shoulder and squeezed my arm as two giant logs smashed an Imperial Walker in the forest of Endor, Ewoks and rebels raising their arms in triumph. Even though nothing made any sense to me at all, I smiled. It was my favorite part, too.

My brain went back to wandering during the rest of the movie, one part wondering why she wasn't noticing me more, while another part was yelling, *Dude! Pay attention! She's on the couch, right now, with you! Her head is on your shoulder! What else do you want here? Is she supposed to gaze at you for the whole movie? For Chrissakes, are we really jealous of Ewoks now?*

I tried to shake the hormones and the stupidity from my head. On the screen, the Death Star exploded into fireworks above the evening Endor sky. A minute later, the theme song blared and the credits started to roll, but Tabby didn't stir. Her breathing was deep and steady. She'd fallen asleep.

Her head rested against the grease spot on my shoulder. Blood was oozing out from beneath the Elmo Band-Aid on her elbow, soaking into the side of my shirt. Her neon-green toenails poked out from the edge of the blanket. I laid my head back and closed my eyes.

That was the day I fell in love with Tabby.

CHAPTER SIXTEEN

IF WE WERE SCIENTISTS BEFORE, WHAT ARE WE NOW?

"Okay, everyone, let's get started. We've still got quite a few plant cell notes to get through, so take your notebooks out and get started on the warm-up on the board."

It's Thursday.

We're not even entertaining the idea of labs anymore. Mrs. Shepler's notes run up through Wednesday. Study guide/review packets on Thursday, check them on Friday and take a quiz.

Repeat on Monday.

It's boring as shit, but at least it's easy.

In front of me, Tabby stretches her arms above her head, and for a moment I hold my breath as she arches her back over her chair. And out of habit—and hope—I put one hand over my books and grip my pencil with the other. But her arms drop to her sides. She leans forward over her notebook.

I look at the stupid death grip I have on my pencil and feel my ears start to burn.

Tabby hasn't done the reach-back in over three weeks. Not since we came back from Thanksgiving. We haven't spoken since that night.

When Mrs. Shepler hands out study guides a few minutes later, Tabby turns partway round in her chair to hand copies to me and my table partner, Evan Walko, without looking up at me.

I reach forward to take them, and I want to keep reaching, grab her wrist and tell her I'm sorry. Sorry for being a jerk, sorry for losing it, sorry for being such a perverted loser. Even if it just got me a Tabby lecture. Fuck, *especially* if it got me a Tabby lecture.

Instead, when her eyes flip up and meet mine, I drop mine to the pages in my hand.

"Oh boy. Another packet."

She gives a weak smile in return and faces forward without a word.

"You may work on your study guides with your partner," Mrs. Shepler says from the front of the room. "And use your notes. I'll be around for help if you need it." At which point she retreats behind her desk and sits down, where she'll likely remain for the rest of the period.

Tabby doesn't turn around again.

The rest of the period goes the way it's gone since Thanksgiving: I work on my study guide in silence, keeping the answers visible for my partner, Evan. I think Evan's got some serious learning disabilities, so this is kind of our unspoken agreement. I give him all the answers on the study guides and review packets, making it look like we're working together. So when Evan invariably tanks the quiz on Friday, he's got enough points from the completed packets to keep him at least passing.

We've never really discussed it, this arrangement of ours. It just kind of happened. After I saw his first two quiz grades at the beginning of the year, I started making sure my packets were in the middle of our lab table and that my arm wasn't blocking his line of vision. One time, he muttered, "Thanks, man," and I nodded, and that's the only time we've spoken of it.

I suppose it's not the best way for him to learn science, but I don't think that's my job to worry about. And really, what's Mrs. Shepler going to do, anyway? Tell him to find the answers in his notes and lecture him to study more? Yeah, sign me up.

At least this way, Evan passes and we both get to feel human.

So as Evan scribbles down my definition for *eukaryotic cells,* I have a moment to torture myself and watch Tabby.

Her thick hair is pulled back in one long red braid that falls over a soft, pale yellow sweater. She taps the back of her pencil absently against her exposed neck just below her ear as she talks quietly and laughs with Rebecca Gaskins.

I watch the two of them work, looking from one to the other, trying to make sense of things. In my head, it's like the side-by-side QB comparison that flashes on the screen during halftime in a football game, their pictures at the top, their running statistics stacked up underneath for easy, objective comparison.

Yeah, Rebecca's not bad-looking. She's way taller than Tabby, and really, now that I'm thinking about it, she's got a pretty fantastic body. She's smart and friendly and all that. Would I be interested if she asked me out, picking up where our tor-rid, three-day relationship left off in fifth grade? (Not going to happen.)

She *was* on my list. Tabby knows it. But that's not really the same thing. That list was stupid and perverted and degrading—all the things Tabby thought about it and all the things I feel so much shame over—but that was kind of the whole point of the rankings, the point of this stupid-ass exercise right now: to ignore the blatant perversion, to ignore the shame. To take the shit that makes no sense, that I can't seem to control, and factor it out.

Isn't that what sports analysts do? Isn't that thinking like a scientist, Mrs. Shepler? I mean, I could have called it Freshman Class Physical Attractiveness Rankings (FC-PAR) and avoided most of this trouble. It might still seem a little degrading, but it doesn't connote the involvement of my dick—*rhetorical* dick—the way *Do List* does.

But what can I say? I was hurt and angry, and Matt's List of Prettiest Girls didn't feel right.

Not that it matters now.

But so what if Rebecca Gaskins did ask me out? She's attractive. She's nice. Say we went to the movies and started making out (putting me in double digits in that category. Minus nine.). Can you just do that with people? I mean, how do you share that kind of closeness with someone—to show her she's the one you want—when deep down you really want someone else? I'd feel like even more of an asshole than I already do.

Yeah, I could make out with Rebecca Gaskins, and it would probably be pretty awesome. But at the end of the night, I'm still going to be wishing it could be Tabby.

As the bell rings and Evan finishes copying the last answer onto his packet, Mrs. Shepler reminds us of tomorrow's quiz.

"Remember to study," she says from behind her desk as we file out her door.

Which leads to the other daily occurrence since we've come back from Thanksgiving break: Liam Branson is waiting for Tabby outside the door. I'm right behind her, like always, and I see his face light up when she steps into the hallway, and even though I can't see it, I know hers is doing the same.

"'Sup, Matt," he says, and gives me a fist bump over Tabby's shoulder, where his arm subsequently lands. He's been extra nice and supportive in practice since Thanksgiving. Awesome.

"'Sup, Liam," I reply, and turn to walk the other way.

Even though we spent the first three months of the year walking the same way—literally arm in arm some days—Tabby never asks why I'm going the other way and never calls for me to walk along with them.

And it hits me, deep in the gut, that I'm Rebecca Gaskins. Well, the hypothetical wanting-to-ask-me-out version.

I could have my moment. I could lean in and kiss Tabby with everything I have—hands on her face, in the rain, sound track rising in the background—and maybe she'd even kiss me back.

But at the end of the night, she'll still be wishing it could be with Liam Branson.

CHAPTER SEVENTEEN

MR. MINT FINALLY SPEAKS HIS MIND

"All right, gang. Welcome back to our Friday Poetry Cafe, sponsored—and hosted—by Ilca's Coffeehouse."

Mr. Ellis claps his hands together at the front of the room as the last person takes her seat. He's wearing his black turtleneck—hopefully his only one—thick-rimmed glasses, and an honest-to-God beret, which he claims Ilca knitted for him. And of course, we can only snap. It's cheesy and over-the-top and goes against everything Mr. Ellis has taught us about poetry—how it's *not* this ridiculous stereotype of puppies and rainbows and rhymes about love—but here we are. I can't help but love it.

"I see some of you remembered your coffee mugs. Awesome. If you didn't, no big deal, I've got Styrofoam cups up here. Though, for the record, the environmental impact goes on your carbon footprint, not mine.

"I've got regular for me, decaf for you, and herbal tea with a hint of lemon for Ilca—"

"At least you do one thing right," Ilca mutters in her raspy voice.

"And water for those of you without gum who are too self-conscious to suffer through the rest of your day with coffee breath. Ladies, come on up first."

Now that science has become a daily masochistic torture session—waiting for Tabby to reach back or turn around, give me some sign that she hasn't written me out of her new life—Mr. Ellis's class has become a sanctuary, the one place during my school day where I can think and laugh and interact like a reasonably intelligent human being. Relatively speaking, given the balding black man in his turtleneck and the talking bookcase.

"Gentlemen, your turn. And while everyone's getting settled, take your persona poems out and read them a few last times to yourself. I am pumped to hear these things."

I head to the front of the room, where Mr. Ellis has the coffee station set up: two desks slid together against the side of his teacher's desk along the front corner of the room, like he's created a bar. He sits on a tall cushioned stool at the end of the bar, where each of us will sit to read our poems. He adjusts his ridiculous beret and strokes his beard, chatting easily with a few of the girls who sit up front. He looks like an idiot. I love how stupid he looks—that he relishes it, even. He's all in.

I pour a cup of decaf into the oversize ceramic mug I brought from home—the one with "I ♥ Mom" and a faded pic of my smiling, semi-toothless, five-year-old face—and load it up with fake, delicious French vanilla creamer so that my mug looks more like tan milk than coffee.

"Wow, Matt, that might actually turn into cake," Mr. Ellis says, watching as I drop my third scoop of sugar into my mug. Dad would be repulsed. Like Mr. Ellis, he drinks his coffee black.

"That's kinda what I'm hoping for," I say, smiling, then taking a sip. Perfect. It's like liquid dessert. "It's the only way this stuff is drinkable."

"Don't worry, you'll be a man one day." He takes an exaggerated sip from his cup of regular black.

"Nice beret, by the way."

"Thank you, Matthew. Ilca says I look like a member of the Black Panthers." He leans forward and stage-whispers, "But she's a little racist."

I laugh and grab a cookie from the tray on Mr. Ellis's desk and carry my mug back to my seat, clinking coffees with Trip before opening my writing folder.

This is the third Poetry Cafe we've done since we started after Thanksgiving, and I've liked it way more than I'm willing to admit. We began the first week with sensory poems, which kinda sucked, though Mr. Ellis seemed to like them. Trip and I both played it safe and went for basketball poems, his zooming in on the feeling of blowing by his defender to the basket, mine on standing at the foul line, late in the game, down by one, going through my foul-line routine—two hard dribbles, back spin, crouch, deep breath, look up, release.

Again, kind of lame, but a safe start. I can share a poem while still letting everyone know I'm a stud.

Which, yeah, I'm sure they all noted.

Stud-poet, bitches.

Last week, our second week, Mr. Ellis introduced us to this guy named Pablo Neruda, who wrote odes to things like artichokes, or tuna fish, or his socks. Really weird. I loved it.

So I wrote my "Ode to a Toilet Brush" and read it last Friday, which allowed me to recite "combing through the fecal smear" to a roomful of people. People actually groaned—Mr. Ellis nodded, grinning, exuding poetic pride.

This week, I've pulled out the big guns. Mr. Ellis started the week by sharing his all-time favorite poem, one called "Maybe Dats Your Pwoblem Too," which is from the point of view of Peter Parker/Spider-Man, who, in the poem, is not only bored to death with being Spider-Man but also, inexplicably, has a speech impediment. Ellis read it perfectly, like Baby Bear from *Sesame Street* or a hyperactive Elmer Fudd. Our job, in turn, was to take on a persona of our own.

It's been a particularly shitty couple of weeks. And on top of everything with Tabby, Murray has rekindled his obsession with Candy Land, which means I've been forced to play at least three rounds a night with him. Normally, Tabby would absorb some of the burden, and the three of us would play together. Obviously that hasn't happened lately, so it's been one-on-one Candy Land every night.

I hate Candy Land.

The little bastard's a shark, too. I don't know how he's doing it, but I only ever win, at most, one out of the three rounds each night. I'll be cruising along, double-oranging my way to King Kandy's castle, when—BAM!—I pull Plumpy from the deck and get sent all the way back to the beginning, Murray squealing with delight, gleeful in my disgust.

The first time it happened, I made my little blue token-dude wave and talk to Mr. Mint on his second pass through the Candy Cane Forest.

Mr. Mint did not appreciate the traffic.

Murray loved the exchange.

So now I have to do it every time, Mr. Mint griping at each of our tokens as we pass, Murray giggling and egging him on.

On Monday, the night after hearing the Spider-Man poem and on my eight thousandth trip back to Plumpy's stupid tree, inspiration struck.

I take a sip from my mug and pull the now-finished poem out of my writing folder. I scan the lines one last time and take a breath, trying to picture Murray sitting at one of the desks; it's a hell of a lot easier to channel my inner-grumpy-old-man voice when he's my only audience.

Trip's leaning over, looking at the title, frowning. "'Mr. Mint'?"

"Candy Land," I say.

"Ahh. Nice." He nods approvingly. "I went with Wolverine. Who secretly wants to be a woman." He pauses, then says, "I may have to skip some parts."

I laugh, and Mr. Ellis clears his throat at the front of the room to get things started.

As usual, he reads his own work first, his poem from the point of view of a cafeteria worker who spends his life rinsing off the lunch trays and utensils of obnoxious high school kids. We laugh and snap our fingers in response, Mr. Ellis smiling and waving us off.

"All right. All right. Thank you. Now who's up first? Ilca baked an extra cookie for our first brave soul of the day."

Hands go up around the room, and our Poetry Cafe begins in earnest. Just about everyone's come up with something impressive. Maya Torres blows everyone away with a poem from the point of view of an ice cream truck driver—equal parts hilarious and deeply, deeply disturbing.

"Holy crap, Maya," Mr. Ellis says when our semi-raucous snapping dies down. "I will never let my kids buy anything from an ice cream truck ever again. You've scarred us all."

Maya beams. That is high praise in here.

We laugh and snap through the class period, pausing intermittently for coffee and cookie refills, until, somehow, our hour is nearly over, and I'm the only one left to share.

"All right, Matt, you're up," Mr. Ellis says, smiling and rubbing his hands together. "Let's hear what you've got."

I take a deep breath and move to the front of the room. I settle onto the stool, careful not to look up at anyone, still trying to picture Murray, cross-legged on the floor in front of me. Everyone's shared and everyone's laughed, so most of the pressure is gone, but tiny beads of sweat pinprick my forehead and the buzz in my ears drowns out any noise in the classroom around me. I heard somewhere that, in a survey of what people fear most, dying comes in second. First is public speaking.

"Okay," I start. "So I went with Mr. Mint, the candy cane lumberjack of Candy Land."

I glance up and see a few smiles, a couple of nods, and I catch Mr. Ellis giving me a fist pump from the back of the room.

I take another deep breath, flip the switch on my cranky-old-man voice, and go for it:

> *Do any of you know*
> *how long it takes to grow*
> *a goddam candy cane?*
>
> *much less a whole*
> *freaking peppermint forest?*
>
> *But they don't care.*
>
> *These punk kids come*
> *trolloping by here every day—*

the red one, the yellow one,
the green and the blue one—
like some dandy eighties pop group

skippin' around stage
singin' about girlfriends
and lollipops
and whatever other lame
crap these kids are into these days.

"Hi, Mr. Mint!
"How are you today?"

You just tramped
on twenty new candy cane sprouts,
you bright little turds.
How do you think I am?

I can hear everyone laughing as I read, which is good, because it goes on for another two pages as Mr. Mint voices his wildly inappropriate opinions on King Kandy, the princess, and most of all, Plumpy, whom Mr. Mint tells to choke on it.

People snap and smile when I'm done, but all I can hear for a moment is the blood pounding in my ears. My legs—I can't even *feel* my legs when I slide off the stool, and I have to concentrate on moving them properly to make it back to my seat.

I hope I never have to do this for something important.

"Wow, Matt," Mr. Ellis says, grin plastered to his face. "I'm torn between giving you a hug and sending you to guidance."

Instead, he gives a double fist pound on the top of my desk as I take my seat and makes his way to the front of the room. Trip reaches over for a fist bump as we start packing up to leave for our next class.

"That was amazing, gang. Thank you. Next week, being the last before holiday break, we're going to look at gifts of writing. So start thinking about whom you may want to write for—who in your life could use the gift of poetry," Mr. Ellis says, grinning at us. "Have a great weekend. Take another cookie on your way out."

My mind immediately jumps to Tabby, my shitty-romantic-movie instinct cranking up the ol' film reel in my brain, confident it can fix all of this. It's a romantic Christmas movie, no less, so the scene is double cheesy, with mistletoe appearing just as Tabby's eyes read down my poem, a single tear pooling at the corner of her eye, threatening to spill over, her breath catching as she takes in my words, words that express gratitude for our irreplaceable friendship while revealing a desire for more. At which point, as I'm apologizing for not getting her a "real" gift, Tabby stops me midsentence, practically jumping into my arms, pressing her lips into mine so hard that that single tear on her cheek bleeds onto mine, and—

"Matt, you okay?" Mr. Ellis asks from the doorway. I'm still at my desk, hunched over, staring into my open book bag. I'm the only one left in the room, save Trip, who's standing next to Mr. Ellis just inside the room, staring at me like I'm a complete moron.

"Yeah, yeah," I say, quickly zipping up my bag. "I was making sure I had my . . . yeah . . ."

Trip continues staring as I make my way up the aisle toward them.

"Awesome job today, guys," Mr. Ellis says. "Who do you play tonight?"

"Eastern Adams," Trip says.

"They any good?"

"No, they're pretty bad. We should be okay."

"Well, good luck, if I'm not there in time for the JV game."

"No big deal," Trip replies. "Nobody usually is."

Mr. Ellis laughs. "Have a great game, guys."

When we're out in the hallway, Trip says, "Did you fall asleep in there or something?"

"No," I say, forcing a laugh and feeling my face grow hot. "I was trying to figure out the opening lines of my gift poem for you."

"Aww, that's sweet of you, pal."

"I couldn't think of a word that rhymes with *bulge*."

Trip laughs, and as we part ways to head for our respective lockers before geometry, Trip stops and turns back, grinning.

"Indulge." He winks and turns back down the hallway toward his locker.

Thank God for Trip.

CHAPTER EIGHTEEN

SEASON HIGH/PERSONAL LOW

Eastern Adams's JV team sucks even worse than I could have imagined. We lead by twenty-four after two quarters—and we're only sitting at thirty-one—and I've scored fourteen myself. Yet I can still feel myself tightening up while we take lazy jump shots during the last few minutes of halftime. Pretty much every game has gone like this, and my brain knows it.

True to Trip's words, the gym was basically empty while we ran through our warm-ups before our JV game started at six. Just parents and varsity guys camped out behind the benches. Grampa chatting with Coach Langley by the door. The stands didn't look a whole lot different at the end of the second quarter, either. I love it. It feels like playing at the Y, only with much cooler jerseys.

Then fans start showing up for the varsity game, and things start to fall to shit.

The buzzer sounds for the end of halftime, and we hustle back to our bench for a quick huddle around Coach Wise.

"Same five we started with. Keep playing hard. No letups, gentlemen. Bring it in, on three."

Despite my brain creeping in, I start the third quarter right where I left off: a quick layup when Trip steals an inbound pass, followed by a quick bucket from the elbow coming off a brutal DeAndre Miller screen.

Barely two minutes into the third quarter and Eastern Adams has to call a time-out, with our lead extended to twenty-eight, Adams still stuck in single digits. It's a bloodbath. A really, really fun bloodbath.

When we take the floor again after the time-out, I see students starting to accumulate outside the gym doors in the lobby. Standing in the doorway about to come in is Lily Branson with a group of friends, their faces painted black and light blue. Arm in arm with Lily stands Tabby, her red hair pulled back from her painted face in a long braid. She and Lily both wear Franklin varsity jackets, though Tabby's is about ten sizes too big. I don't need to be able to read the name embroidered on the chest to know whose it is.

I barely notice Adams's JV point guard bringing the ball up the court, until Trip yells for us to D it up.

Within seconds of their point guard crossing the half-court line, Trip's forced him into making a sloppy pass that I easily intercept, and I take off the other way for what should be an easy layup. And what will be my first ever twenty-point game.

But Lily, Tabby, and crew are watching from the lobby door behind our basket, and as I'm running, my brain is screaming, "FUCKDON'TMISSDON'TMISSPLEASEDON'TMISS!" My central nervous system has gone so haywire I can't feel my legs as I cross the three-point line, and—even though I've taken thirty-eight bajillion layups in my life and have the muscle memory to do this with my eyes closed—my body feels like it's never done this before as my feet leave the floor, and I botch the layup.

"Fucking shit!"

It's supposed to come out under my breath, but it comes out much louder, and—at least in my head—I can hear Lily and company laugh. And Mom gasp.

The ball drops right back to me for the rebound, and, because I'm now in complete panic mode, I go up for the gentlest, easiest, slow-motion two-foot jumper, like I'm trying to place a baby bird back in its nest. I don't notice that my defender, who I've owned all night, has of course caught up to me by this point. And, in what will probably end up as the highlight of his unpromising high school basketball career, he swats my lame follow-up into the wall behind the basket.

"Fuck!" I yell—definitely not under my breath this time—as the whistle blows for out of bounds.

The ref stands right next to me on the baseline holding the ball. "Son, this is your only warning to clean up the language. Got it?"

I can't meet his gaze. Just keep my head down and nod.

They're standing inside the doorway, all of ten feet away. They have to be watching now. I know it. And in the ten seconds they've watched of this game, they've only seen me miss a wide-open layup, have my second easy attempt swatted into the wall next to them, and be scolded by the ref for dropping two temper-tantrum f-bombs.

It shouldn't matter. I know it shouldn't matter. We're on our way to the biggest blowout of the season so far. We've played with relentless intensity as a team. And I've scored eighteen points—my highest ever—in a little more than half a game. It shouldn't matter.

But it matters.

I can't stand the fact that all they've seen is the last ten seconds, that no matter how awesome I've played tonight, I still look—to them—like a blundering jackass who shouldn't be out here. It makes me crazy.

On the inbounds play, I come off a double screen for a wide-open three on the right side. Again, no matter how natural and fluid everything felt in the first half, my brain is now hyperaware of everyone watching, of Tabby and Lily still a few feet away to my right, of the parents in the stands, of the varsity team lounging on the bleachers behind our bench. So instead of catch-pivot-jump-release, my brain's flipped off the autopilot and it becomes catch-pivot-*pleaseGod*-jump-*pleasedon'tfuckingmiss*-release-*oratleastgetfuckingcloseplease!*

As soon as the ball leaves my fingers, I know it's short—way, way short—and I can see them tracking my air-ball three in my periphery. I've had nightmares like this, but this is actually happening right now, and I can't do anything to stop it, to make myself wake up at the worst part, to go back and redo the last thirty seconds.

So what do I do?

Sprint back on defense and try to regain my composure? Take a deep breath and try to see the big picture, that it's a blowout JV basketball game, and no one really cares that much or will ever remember?

Yeah, no.

I swear vehemently at myself, loud enough for everyone to hear, and punch myself hard in the leg. Jog back to half court, fighting back tears and trying to pretend I didn't just charley-horse myself like a motherfucker. Or that I can't hear Branson yelling encouragements from the stands.

When an Eastern Adams guy bricks a jumper on the other

end and DeAndre Miller hauls in the rebound, our coach calls for time. He's seen enough. Even after my pathetic display, we're still up 35–9. It's time to get our bench guys on the court.

I flop down at the end of the bench with the rest of the starters—trying hard not to limp—put my head in my hands, and close my eyes. Coach Wise and the remaining guys tell us all *great game*.

To the outside observer, I probably just look exhausted after a hard run. I keep telling myself that as I slowly try to pull my shit back together.

Eighteen points. Season high.

Easy win.

Over and over.

When I open my eyes again, Tabby and Lily are sitting in the second row of the student section directly across from us, their friends filling in around them. They all laugh and chat, checking their phones, not watching the rest of the JV game. I'm not sure if that makes me feel better or worse, if it even registered how badly I sucked right in front of them. Would it have mattered if I'd made that layup? What, would they all start getting here early for some hot JV action?

Fuck.

At the end of the third quarter, the varsity team gets up from the bleachers behind us to head into the locker room. They cross the court, past the student section, which has to be the coolest feeling in the world.

And I can't stop myself from watching Tabby's face as Branson makes his way across. Their eyes are locked, and Tabby's beaming, this wide smile spread across her face. Her teeth glow in contrast with her face paint. I can't hear what, if anything,

Branson says to her, but she smiles somehow wider and looks down at the varsity jacket she's wearing. She stands and holds her arms out for a moment so he can see the sleeves hanging a good six inches over the ends of her fingers. She laughs, never taking her eyes off his, and sits back down, Lily throwing an arm around her and laughing, too.

It's like they're the only ones in their world. And I just get to stand and watch.

Eastern Adams doesn't fare much better against our second-stringers, and when the buzzer sounds at the end of the fourth quarter, we end up winning 58–22. The final score disappears from the scoreboard before we're through shaking the other team's hands, the numbers all reset for the varsity game.

The varsity team is lined up next to the student-section bleachers, just outside the doors to the home locker room, waiting to jog out into their pregame layup drills.

I could probably use some of those, actually.

The varsity team is huddled together, arms locked over each other's shoulders in a tight circle. They bounce lightly on their feet, shifting their weight back and forth in unison. As we cross the court and head for the locker room, I can hear Elijah Leppo in the center of the circle, leading the chants to get his team fired up for what will likely be another blowout.

Those in the student section crane their necks to see over the side of the bleachers, bouncing right along with the varsity team. This is the only time you'll ever hear Elijah Leppo fired up about anything. I so want to be in that huddle, ready to burst out onto the court for pregame warm-ups in front of a packed house, our pep band blasting out fight songs.

When I glance up at the student section one last time, Tabby's looking directly at me. Not bouncing, not craning over the side like all her new friends. Just watching me. I drop my eyes to the floor, another wave of embarrassment washing over me, but I feel equally stupid avoiding Tabby's eyes. I mean, it's Tabby.

When I look back up, Tabby's still watching me. She gives a tiny wave with her sleeve-covered hand, a small smile, and mouths, *Good game*.

Even though—based on the two minutes Tabby actually saw me on the court—that's a complete lie, this is the best I've felt all night. Maybe the best I've felt since Thanksgiving.

Maybe I haven't totally lost Tabby after all.

"God, I wish we could be out there," Trip says as we watch Elijah Leppo pick up the ball at half court to hold it for the final ten seconds. The student section is on its feet, yelling and stomping the bleachers across from us.

"How many times have we run with those guys at the Y?" Trip says, shaking his head, watching the Eastern Adams starters hunched over in exhaustion. The varsity game ended up much closer than expected. They got sloppy in the second half, playing lazy after leading by fifteen at the half, which means some serious suicides for all of us on Monday. The Eastern Adams guys—guys Trip and I have been holding our own against for two years—went on a crazy run.

We barely pulled away at the end, thanks mostly to Elijah.

"I can't believe it was that close," Trip continues. "No way we would have let that happen."

"I know. Next year."

His competitive juices are flowing again. He looks like he could go out and play another full game. And really, I probably could, too.

It's hard to watch the varsity team struggle against guys you've been beating for years. But at the same time, I can't help but flash back to the thirty seconds I played in front of a handful of students and my parents. To recap: wide-open layup missed, f-bomb, shot swatted, second f-bomb, referee's warning, air-balled three, uncountable stream of profanities likely including more f-bombs, self-inflicted charley horse—all against guys who looked like it was their first time playing.

I hope I get a grip on this before I do get a chance to play varsity.

As the varsity team walks off the court toward the locker room for what I'm sure will be an interesting postgame speech from Coach Langley, I decide I don't need to see this silent exchange taking place between Tabby and Branson. Branson played particularly shitty in the second half, and I imagine Tabby is sending him I-love-you-no-matter-what rays with her eyes, Branson unable to withhold smiling back at her as he walks off the court. Fuck, since I already have this awesome movie playing in my head, I can skip the real thing. Instead, I grab my bag and head to the lobby with Trip.

A few minutes later, after a wave from Grampa on his way

out to the parking lot—he was kind enough to leave without mentioning my swearing—Trip and I stand off to the side of the lobby, devouring lukewarm pizza we scavenged from the concession stand as they were cleaning up.

"Good game, guys," Tabby says from behind us.

We both turn, mouths full of pizza, and Tabby's standing there with Lily Branson. Trip freezes for a moment, taking in the fact that Lily Branson is kind of talking to us, before we both attempt to swallow and say thanks at the same time.

When Trip recovers, he says, "Yeah, my man here had a big game. What'd you end up with, Matt? Eighteen?"

"Really?" Tabby and Lily say at the same time, both looking at me now, eyes wide.

I instantly feel stupid again. I imagine they *are* surprised by this news.

"We didn't get to see you guys much," Lily says. "You came out right after we got there. But you guys were way up."

Trip laughs then, realizing, and I immediately drown him in the training room ice tub in my mind. "So you only caught Matt's air ball," he says, then turns to me. "That sucks."

Lily looks back to me again, with what looks like actual concern. "Did I see you punch yourself?"

"Uh . . . I . . . yeah . . . uh . . ." Which is all I manage before I turn my head away from Trip's laughing and stuff the rest of my crust in my mouth.

After a few more awkward minutes of this, the varsity guys finally start to trickle out into the lobby, hair still dripping from the locker room.

"How we doing, ladies?" Branson asks, throwing an arm over

a shoulder of each. Lily and Tabby both smile up and lean into him. They shower him with *good-games*, for which he thanks them humbly and brushes off the compliments.

"Hey, you guys played a great game tonight," Branson says to me and Trip, deflecting the attention. He knows they played poorly tonight, win or not. "What'd you end up with, Matt?"

"Eighteen, I think."

"That's badass, man. I don't think I ever got close to that when I played JV."

Tabby melts into Branson. So humble. So complimentary. So perfect.

"We're heading to Valentino's," Branson says. "You coming along, or do you have to get home?" He's talking to Tabby now, and just like that, it's like they're the only two people in the lobby. I assume *we* includes Lighty and Leppo, and probably a bunch of Lily's friends—maybe half the student section, for all I know—but it definitely does not include me.

"I'd love to go," Tabby says, smiling up at him from under his arm. "I'll text my dad. He won't mind."

"What do you two studs have planned for this evening?" he says, looking at Trip and me.

For once, Trip will not revel in my embarrassment, because it is directly linked to his own: *Matt and I are gonna play some video games and have a sleepover at my house! It's gonna be super cool!!! My mom's gonna make root beer floats, too!*

Before we can think of something cool to say instead, Lighty calls from the lobby entrance, standing with Leppo, their gym bags slung over their shoulders, ready to go. They all turn to leave, one last nod from Branson, a quick wave from Lily and Tabby.

None of them look back.

■ ■ ■

"So seriously, dude. How does that happen?"

I down the last glob from the bottom of the glass of my second root beer float and shake my head. We're sprawled out at opposite ends of the giant sectional in Trip's basement, pizza boxes on the coffee table in front of us, Xbox controllers on our laps. Trip continues. "How do you go lights-out, eighteen points in three quarters, then botch a layup, get your shit swatted, and airball a three? It's like your body was suddenly taken over by the spirit of some squirrelly-ass twelve-year-old."

"Well, seeing as most people mistake you for a squirrelly-ass twelve-year-old, I suppose that's a valid question."

"Touché. And go fuck yourself."

"Hi, Mrs. Fogle," I say, waving. Trip jerks around, sees no one, and exhales. His mom would literally wash his mouth out with soap—I've seen her do it.

I laugh and start flipping through the characters on the TV screen, preparing for battle. Trip picks up a spent pizza crust from the box and backhands me with it on my arm.

"Oww! Son of a bitch!" I rub my arm where his pizza crust has already left a pink welt.

"Sorry. Spasm."

This is what we do after most games—well, minus the pizza-crust pistol-whipping: eat pizza and drink root beer floats in Trip's basement. We rehash every single moment of our game, first usually with Trip's mom and dad, then again after they head back upstairs.

"And right as the girls came in, too," Trip says, resuming what I hoped was a dead conversation as we select new players for our next round of battle, Trip some scantily clad demon-girl wielding twin swords, me some hulking mutant with a bull's head and a battle-ax.

"Thank you, Trip. I remember."

"If you're trying to impress the ladies," Trip continues, "I will tell you, squirrelly twelve-year-old is not terribly effective."

"As evidenced by your reputation with the ladies?"

"That is correct. And, Matthew," Trip says amid a fury of taps on his controller, "I just made you my bitch."

On the screen, his demon-girl flips into the air over another empty swing from my dude's battle-ax and lands on his shoulders. In one quick motion, she scissor-cuts my poor bastard's head off, reaches down into his gaping neck-stump, pulls out his still-beating heart, and eats it.

Sums things up nicely.

CHAPTER NINETEEN

'TWAS THE WEEK BEFORE CHRISTMAS

School is dragging its way to break, but at least the torture of the weeks following Thanksgiving relents in the last week before Christmas.

Still no reach-backs in science, but Tabby does at least turn around and look at me again. And she says bye to me as she and Branson walk away, shoulder to shoulder down the hall. So that's nice.

Mr. Ellis kicks off our week of gift writing by sharing this strange little poem called "Sentimental Moment or Why Did the Baguette Cross the Road?" After a deep breath, he reads aloud:

> *Don't fill up on bread*
> *I say absentmindedly*
> *The servings here are huge*
>
> *My son, whose hair may be*
> *receding a bit, says*
> *Did you really just*
> *say that to me?*
>
> *What he doesn't know*
> *is that when we're walking*

together, when we get
to the curb
I sometimes start to reach
for his hand.

He stares at us all for a moment, expectantly, as he often does after reading something out loud, then goes into a long, emotional rant about parenthood, and responsibility, and how some things will stay the same no matter how old you are. And after another deep breath, he tells us how when he first read this poem a couple of years ago, he immediately thought of his own father, printed a copy, and gave it to him. A few months later, he found it taped to the wall next to his dad's workbench. His voice gets a little wobbly at that last part, and suddenly we all seem to have great interest in our desks or the floor or the side walls.

I try to imagine what Dad would do if I wrote him a poem for Christmas. I could probably get Mom to cry, but I think it would make Dad highly uncomfortable. I'm going to stick with my original plan for him: an Admiral Ackbar action figure from *Star Wars*—in fact, *that* might make him cry.

I could play it safe and do my gift of writing for Gramma. Zoom in on her sugar cookies and sweet tea. I could maybe do one for Murray, too, to go with the new stuffed animal I got him. Or perhaps one on behalf of Bernard?

Wow. Really, M-Dub? *Three* poems?

Damn you, Ellis. Damn you and your Poetry Jedi mind tricks.

■ ■ ■

The last two games are pretty much the same, though I don't quite go into full-on f-bomb-charley-horse meltdown mode when Tabby and crew show up for the varsity games. Instead, I more or less stop doing anything that could cause such a meltdown: no shooting, no layups unless I'm truly wide-open and it would be too awkward and embarrassing *not* to take it, which nearly causes meltdown anyway. Basically, I get to play a little over two quarters the way I know I can play, and two quarters like a scared little kid—granted, a fundamentally sound, pass-first, defensive-minded little kid.

Overall, the games still go pretty well, but I think Trip's catching on to the fact that I take almost no shots after the first half, even wide-open shots—especially since this means I'm giving up solid would-be assists from him. The man takes pride in his assists.

When I finally board the bus after school on Friday, Miss Edna is all smiles.

"Hi, Matt! I was hoping you'd be on today. Merry Christmas!" She hands me a bag stuffed full of homemade Christmas cookies and holiday Reese's, a candy cane taped to the outside. "Make sure you grab a drink from the cooler," she says, motioning with her thumb to the seat behind her.

"Thanks, Miss Edna."

At least two cases of Little Hugs are on ice in the cooler. I grab a blue one and walk down the aisle to my seat near the back.

Seriously. Greatest bus ever. Even without Tabby.

I flop down into my seat, jam a thumb through the foil, and

take the first glorious swig of Little Hug. I pull my iPod from my coat and flip through songs, thinking about tonight's game and what awaits me over Christmas break: sleep, basketball—though there's no holiday tournament for JV, so I'll get a little break there—and at least one much-needed turkey- and stuffing-induced coma.

Before I get my earbuds in and tear into my cookies, though, I see Miss Edna jump out of her seat and throw her arms in the air. A second later, Tabby appears, coming up the steps. Her wide smile matches Miss Edna's, and as soon as she reaches the top step, Miss Edna wraps her in a huge hug. It's been probably two months since Tabby's ridden the bus, after barely missing a day in over nine years. I guess I'm not the only one who's missed her.

Tabby talks with Miss Edna for a moment, both of them laughing, Tabby looking a little sheepish, and once, Miss Edna even glances at me. When a line starts to form behind Tabby, Miss Edna gives her one last squeeze on her shoulders and hands her a bag of holiday goodies. Tabby grabs her own Little Hug from the cooler—green, it's always been green—and looks up. For a moment I think she's going to stay at the front and catch up with Miss Edna some more; she's still smiling and laughing at something Miss Edna's saying, but her smile disappears when she catches my eye. Her eyes drop to the floor for a second, and when she looks back, a smaller one returns.

Now it's my turn to avoid eye contact. I take another long swig of blue Hug, my eyes glued to the ceiling, then make a show of looking down into my cookie bag, as though much depends upon which shape I choose: Star with green sugar? Boot with chocolate sprinkles? Naked snowman? But when I feel her standing next to me in the aisle, I automatically slide in against the window.

"Hey."

"Hey," I say through a mouthful of sprinkled boot.

We sit in awkward silence before I come through with my conversational Jedi skills.

"I think it's really shameful, you know." Tabby looks at me, startled. "The way you're using Miss Edna, only showing up for cookies and Little Hugs. Shameful."

She punches my arm, clearly relieved.

I rub my shoulder and smile. I've never been so happy to be punched. And because I can't allow that happiness to go on for too long, I say, "No Liam today?" with the faintest hope that she's here because they broke up—or, better yet, that she *chose* to ride the bus to be with me. Her face tells me it's neither.

"He said he had some last-minute shopping to do and that I wasn't allowed to come along." She can't even contain her smile as she says it.

"Oh?" I say, trying my best to play along. "Someone special to shop for?"

She punches me again, lighter this time. She's still smiling when her phone buzzes. I don't need to look to see who it is, but there's a pic of an empty passenger seat and a frowning emoji.

Sigh.

In my mind, I throw my arm around Tabby and take a Christmas cookie/Little Hug selfie—*ridin' the cheese with M-Dubz 2day, muthafuckaz!!!* Instead, I leave Tabby to her texting—put my earbuds in, stuff a naked snowman in my mouth, and stare out the window.

I mean, isn't this what I wanted? Just to be next to her again?

I jump when Tabby pulls the earbud from my left ear. Without a word, she puts it in her right and takes my iPod from my hand. A moment later, "Seaweed Song" comes on, a Passion Pit song that we used to listen to all the time last year. She leans her head on the seat behind her and closes her eyes. I turn back to the window and watch the same houses pass by, the familiar favorites decked out with lights and decorations waiting to be lit for the night.

Yeah. I did want this back.

Tabby flips through songs the rest of the way home, some old songs we used to listen to all the time, others seemingly chosen at random. We don't talk. A few times I see her typing in her phone, and I wonder how she can share two different experiences at the same time with such ease, texting with him and sharing music with me. But maybe I'm just having a different experience.

When we get to our stop, Miss Edna gives Tabby one more squeeze from her seat and makes us each take another Little Hug.

We're greeted by snow flurries and a gust of December air when we step off onto our street. I pull up my hood, and as the bus drives away, we both pause for a moment and watch our breath. Without a word, Tabby hands me her second green Hug. I punch my thumb through the foil and hand it back to her, then do the same with my own. My hands are already freezing.

We walk mostly in silence, munching on cookies.

"Murray's probably losing his mind right now," I say, looking up into the gray afternoon, tiny flakes prickling my face.

"Awww, I miss my Murray. I haven't seen him in a while."

I nod, take my last sip of blue Hug, and watch the flurries float down around us.

We continue in silence for the rest of the short walk down our street until we reach the circle.

"Matt, are we okay?"

"What? Yeah. Yeah, of course we're okay." Which feels stupid, pretending like I don't know what she could be talking about. But Tabby seems to accept it. She smiles and nods without looking up at me.

"Good luck at your game tonight, Matt."

"Thanks."

I'm about to say more, but she's already turning toward her house, looking down at her phone.

It's okay.

I have a pretty good idea how this night will go, anyway.

CHAPTER TWENTY

GRAVY MAKES EVERYTHING BETTER, PART II

"Mom, is it inappropriate to have stuffing and gravy for breakfast?" I say, eyeing the Christmas Day leftovers in the fridge.

"It might be more inappropriate to call it breakfast at eleven-thirty," Mom says from the kitchen table, where she and Murray sift through pieces of his new deep-ocean puzzle. He got it for Christmas at Gramma and Grampa's house yesterday, where I did, in fact, make Gramma cry with my mad poetry skillz. At least, I assume it was the poem that made her cry and not the movie I got for her.

Dad wanted to get them a Blu-ray player to try to force them into the twenty-first century, so I tried to do my part for the cause: I found a Blu-ray of the old original *Muppet Movie* that we used to watch together on VHS whenever I slept over at their house as a kid. And since that generally coincided with mass consumption of fresh-baked sugar cookies and sweet tea, I could even work a line in about it in her poem.

In all, I wrote three poems as gifts—which shall not be revealed to Trip under any circumstances—not including the dumb little rhyme I stuck in the box with Grampa's gift. I found a pair of suspenders online lined with turkey silhouettes. No tears, but he did belly-laugh at the much-more-appropriate bulge/indulge rhyme I ripped off from Trip. And he had those bad boys hooked up to his signature sweatpants before he opened another gift.

"I'll heat up some gravy for you," Mom says, kissing Murray on top of the head as she gets up from the table. Murray absently rubs the top of his head without looking up from his puzzle.

"You're rubbing it in," I say, but he doesn't hear me. They've got the border of the puzzle finished, covering nearly the entire table, and once Murray's locked in on something, it's hard to shake his focus. Kind of impressive, really.

When my near-mixing-bowl portion of stuffing and gravy is ready, I carry it and a glass of milk to my room. Breakfast of champions.

I set my goods on my desk and wake my laptop. Once I've got my music started, I settle into a busy day of gaming, YouTube, and *SportsCenter*. And probably more gravy. But before I finish off my first bowl of stuffing, my instant messenger dings to life on the screen.

TabithaHut: Merry Xmas, Matty.

TabithaHut: Can I come over? I have presents.

I look over at the huge gift bag on the floor at the end of my bed, white envelope sticking out of the top.

M-Dub: Me too.

M-Dub: And since when do you have to ask?

M-Dub: ;)

We both know since when, I think. But I'm still pretending nothing's wrong. And, really, I *do* wish she still felt like she could show up unannounced.

A few minutes later, as I'm pacing my room, taking erratic shots at the Nerf hoop, the doorbell rings downstairs. I hear the door open and Mom's excited greeting, followed closely by

Murray tearing in from the kitchen, yelling Tabby's name. Apparently the one thing that can break his focus.

When I come down the steps, Mom's still got Tabby locked in a hug, despite the shopping bag of presents hanging from Tabby's hand.

"We missed you yesterday, sweetie," Mom says, her hands still on Tabby's shoulders, keeping her at arm's length, as though she's afraid she'll escape. I know the feeling.

Tabby's wearing the earflap hat and an oversize Gettysburg College hoodie I've never seen before.

"Yeah, I missed you guys, too."

It was maybe the first Christmas Tabby *didn't* come over in the evening, though no one mentioned it last night.

"Liam wanted to take me to his grandma's house," Tabby explains. "He must have told her my dad was going in to work last night like he always does, and she insisted I come to her house for dessert. I didn't have the heart to tell her it wasn't a big deal."

"Well, that was sweet of her," Mom says. She pulls Tabby into the living room, Mom peppering her with small-talk questions about Liam's grandma and what they do for Christmas and how her Christmas morning was with her dad. Murray interrupts every other word to show Tabby each one of his presents.

I sit down on the bottom step and watch as he blurs past me to the tree in the den downstairs, flying back up a second later with a new gift, which he piles next to Tabby on the couch like he's presenting gifts to the altar.

On about his fifth trip, Mom stops him and says, "Murray, bring up the gifts for Tabby, okay? There should be three with her name on them behind the tree. Can you do that?"

His eyes light up, and he takes off again. He returns a moment later, his arms full of wrapped boxes, this time with Dad in tow.

"Hey, Tabby's here!" he says, the same way he says it every time she's here, and sits down in his easy chair next to the couch. Murray drops the presents on Tabby's lap and sits down on the floor directly in front of her.

"Thank you, Murray! Are these all from you?"

"Mm-hmm," he replies, nodding his head and smiling at her. She looks over at me for the first time, sitting on the bottom step, and smiles.

"You guys didn't have to do this," she says.

"Oh, stop it, Tabby," Mom says. "Just open them."

Tabby opens the first two boxes and gushes over the sweaters Mom picked out for her. In the third box is an extra-long scarf that Mom must have crocheted to go with the earflap hat, and a pair of socks with chili peppers on them.

"Those are from me!" Murray says, pointing when Tabby holds the socks in front of her.

"These are perfect, Murray! Thank you!"

Murray beams, bouncing in his seat on the floor.

"I brought presents for you guys, too," Tabby says, reaching for the bag by her feet.

Both of my parents hug her after opening their gift—a pound of coffee from my dad's favorite coffee shop and two oversize mugs. She smiles at me again as Murray reaches into his small gift bag, squealing as he pulls out a bald eagle Webkinz. Murray jumps up and flies his eagle to each one of us for a closer look, then, when he lands back in his spot on the floor, points to the one present left next to Tabby.

"Whose is that?"

Tabby pauses, and before she answers, Dad scoops Murray up off the ground.

"C'mon, bud, let's go make some coffee," he says, Murray hanging over his shoulder laughing. Mom busies herself with the wrapping paper on the floor.

Tabby looks over at me, and I nod for her to follow me up the steps. We've never really gotten gifts for each other before, but I guess we both felt it was warranted this year.

My heart starts pounding as Tabby sits down on my bed. I swing my door partway closed behind her and pick up the Nerf ball from the floor.

"I just got you something small," Tabby says, holding an oddly shaped present.

"I like the sweatshirt," I say, indicating her Gettysburg College hoodie. She looks down at it and beams, putting my present back on the bed next to her.

"Liam got it for me," she says. She looks up, and the happiness on her face kills me. "He just got accepted. He was so excited to tell me!"

"Liam's going to Gettysburg?" I say. That doesn't sound right. I know I've heard him in the locker room, talking about this small school in North Carolina he got into. He's even talked about playing basketball for them. Division III. He's met the coach.

I don't say any of this to Tabby. But I must look confused, because she says, "What?" and I can't read her expression, but it's not the same happy face she had a moment ago.

"N-nothing," I stammer. "No, that's awesome. Gettysburg's a great school. And it's, like, less than a half hour from here."

Tabby stares down at the front of the sweatshirt again. Her smile has returned.

Just like that, I feel like I'm losing my shit all over again. I look up at the door, at the divot left by my notebook a month ago, and for once, I decide to get off this fucking roller coaster before it starts. Just be normal for once.

"So what'd you get me?" I say, lobbing my Nerf ball at the hoop on my door and forcing a smile. "A Webkinz?"

"Here," she says, coming back from the little world she was lost in, and hands me the present. "It's nothing, really. It's kind of stupid."

I take the oddly shaped package, wrapped in Sunday comics. It's light, kind of soft. I put it up to my ear and shake it.

"Underwear?"

"Open it already."

Faking happy feels better than stewing angry. Joking with Tabby, it actually just feels like happy.

I tear open the paper and pull out a pair of black gloves.

"Batting gloves?"

"They're receiving gloves," she says, grinning. "Grippy." She's enjoying the look on my face. "Now when you're shooting baskets in your driveway in the middle of winter, I don't have to watch you stick your hands in your armpits."

I laugh—for real—and shake my head, feeling my face grow hot.

"Kind of a selfish gift, really," she says.

I pull them on, reach under my bed for my basketball, and sit down beside her on the bed.

"You're right. Grippy," I say. I shoot the ball into the air a few times to test them out for her. "Thank you."

"All right, now where's my present?" she says. "What'd you get me?"

"Underwear."

At which, of course, she punches me in the arm. I put my basketball on the bed next to me and reach around the end of my bed for Tabby's gift.

The bag is pretty big, and there's some definite heft to it when I slide it along the floor in front of her.

"A lot of underwear," I say when I see her eyes widen. But as soon as she picks up the bag, she breaks into a huge smile. The sound is unmistakable—especially to Tabby.

"Oh my god, this is all Nerds?" she says, gaping at the strain on the handles of the bag as she lifts it up to her lap.

"Yup. Merry Christmas."

There are two cases in that bag. Twelve large boxes of Rainbow Nerds per case. A shit-ton of Nerds. So no matter what happens, every time she reaches for another handful, every time she gets another hankering, she'll think of me.

Either that, or she gets diabetes, and she'll end up thinking of me every time she pricks her finger to check her blood sugar. But that's the risk you take when you try to harness the power of the Nerds.

For Tabby, I'm rolling the dice.

She pulls one case from the bag, turns it over and over in her hands in reverence. She pulls back the perforated cardboard, revealing twelve brightly colored boxes. She runs her fingers along the perfect row of boxes, an odd grin glued to her face.

"Whoa."

"Yeah."

"I almost don't want to eat them, it's so beautiful," she says, after which she pulls out the first in the row and tears it open.

"Oh, I forgot the card!" she says after crunching her first mouthful.

"Don't worry about that," I say. "It's just a card." I had resisted the urge to swipe the envelope right before I slid the bag over to her, but now I really wish I hadn't. I stand up as she opens the envelope and busy myself with taking off my gloves, straightening my empty stuffing bowl on my desk, picking up my Nerf ball from the floor.

I turn and see Tabby smiling at the picture she's pulled from the envelope. It's of the two of us sitting on the couch in the den, popcorn bag between us, flashing our biggest, cheesiest smiles for the camera. We're probably about ten in the picture, somewhere around the start of fifth grade. The year of Rebecca Gaskins.

"Where did you get this?"

"It was in a photo album Mom made for me a couple of years ago. Thought you'd like it."

She laughs and puts her hand to her mouth. She flips it over and looks at the back, and I take a shot at the Nerf rim across the room. It's only a couple of lines, but I can't watch her read what I wrote:

> *You helped me get*
> *my first girlfriend.*
>
> *I hope you'll be*
> *there for the last.*

I left out the lines that continued in my head, about how I hope *she'll* be the last. I'm sure she knows by this point, anyway, but is it really fair to profess my undying love—now that she's clearly fallen for someone who seems just as crazy about her? I've ruined enough already.

I go to pick up the Nerf ball again without looking at her.

But before I step across the room in front of her, Tabby stands and wraps her arms around me. I tense for a moment, but then relent and wrap my arms around her, resting my chin on top of her head.

"I love you, Matty."

I close my eyes and squeeze her tighter.

"I love you, too."

I know we're saying two different things, that her words don't mean the same as mine. But it feels good to hear it. I thought I'd fucked things up too much to ever hear them in *any* context.

"We *are* okay, right?"

I nod, my chin still on her head, and as much as I want to stand here and keep holding on, I let her go. And for the first time in forever, we just sit and talk about our year.

"I missed this," Tabby says after a while. "I don't know what happened."

"Yeah. Sorry for being such a douche."

She shakes her head and holds up a finger, the universal sign for Tabby-lecture. "Listen," she says through another mouthful of Nerds, "that's bullshit. If you're gonna say something derogatory, it had better not involve the female anatomy in any way. *You're* the idiot—use your own body parts."

I shake my head and smile. "Noted. Sorry for being a dick."

"More of an asshole, actually."

"Got it."

"Wait, I forgot that I'm the asshole," she says, and hands me her box of Nerds. "You're my dingleberry."

■ ■ ■

Tabby stays for dinner, which, to her delight, is leftovers from yesterday. She hadn't gotten her holiday stuffing fix yet, so she was thrilled when she saw Mom in the kitchen, heating up yet another batch of gravy. If there's a gravy-consumption threshold for when your blood actually congeals, we haven't reached it. But we have to be getting damn close.

Mom and Dad are thrilled to have her. Mom can actually talk casually with Tabby about Branson over dinner, and I learn more about them than I ever expected or cared to. Their increasingly regular trips through the McDonald's drive-through after school for milk shakes. Branson's plans to major in communications next year (my specialty). Tabby's misadventures attempting to make whoopie pies with Branson's grandmother. It's hard to listen to, but it puts Tabby at ease and lets me shut up for a while.

Murray is beside himself. Candy Land is brought out before the dishes are cleared from the table, and on my second consecutive game of pulling Plumpy down the homestretch, Tabby is introduced to the inner dark of Mr. Mint, candy cane lumberjack, much to Murray's—and Tabby's—delight.

Despite her getting regular texts from Branson, it's everything I've been missing since October.

It makes it almost bearable when, after a final round of thanks and hugs, his black Accord is outside to pick her up.

"That was nice," Mom says, sitting down across from me at the table, where I'm staring at Candy Land, mindlessly reading the character stories on the inside of the box. She sips reheated coffee from her new mug and continues. "Tabby and this Liam boy seem to be pretty serious."

I nod. They do indeed seem pretty serious.

"This hasn't been easy for you." It's not a question. If she knows the full extent, she doesn't say. Thank God. "At least he sounds like a nice guy."

"Yeah. He's a great guy," I say, without any expression, turning the blue Candy Land kid over and over in my hand. "Top athlete. Top student. Senior. He's the best."

"Would you rather her first serious boyfriend be someone who *isn't* nice?"

I look up at her finally. "Of course not, Mom. What kind of friend do you think I am?"

Images flash in my brain—of Lighty following Tabby in the hall. Or Corey Sheridan. Branson *is* different—that's what makes this so hard.

"Matthew, sweetie, I think you're a wonderful friend. The kind of friend Tabby would clearly hate to lose."

"Clearly," I say, though I know she's right. But I just want to whine about it—for lack of any other reasonable solution—and if you can't be whiny to your mother, who can you be whiny to?

Mom sets her mug down and sighs.

"So maybe you don't want to hear my advice, but listen for a minute anyway."

I go back to fiddling with the Candy Land tokens, pretending to be disinterested. But honestly, at this point, I'd love some advice. Mom's always had the same scary inside-my-brain thing that Tabby has—or maybe I'm not the deep, unsolvable mystery I seem to think I am.

"If Tabby's important to you—*really* important to you—be

her friend. You two have a history together, *stories* together, that you're going to remember and talk about and tell others for the rest of your lives. Those stories don't have to end because she has a boyfriend. It doesn't take them away."

The air feels sharp in my nose. My eyes squeeze closed to keep the tears from spilling over. I can't look up at Mom.

"Listen, Matthew. Tabby's fifteen, just like you, and this is her first real boyfriend. Do you know how many people end up with their first boyfriend or girlfriend? Almost zero. And the ones who do are kind of weird anyway."

She pauses. I know she's smiling at me, but I still can't look up.

"I know it's harder because it's Tabby, and she's a girl. But, you know—mistahs before sistahs. Bros before hoes."

"Wow, Mom," I say, shaking my head. "Please never say *bros before hoes* to me ever again."

She laughs.

"Just be her friend, Matty. Don't stop being her friend."

"I know, Mom. I won't."

"And, you know, I can't say what's going to happen down the road, or what either of you are going to want in your lives. But remember, the best relationships are based on friendship. Your father? That grown man who is right now probably playing with Admiral Ackbar in the den? He's my best friend."

"God, that's kinda sad."

Mom laughs again. "Just be her friend."

CHAPTER TWENTY-ONE

HAPPY NEW YEAR

Unfortunately, water soaks right through my new gloves. But maybe I'm an idiot for shooting foul shots in the freezing drizzle (frizzle?) at eight-thirty in the morning.

What better way to start the New Year, right?

I'm sure Mr. Hodgson is saying the same thing right now.

It is ass cold out here this morning, but I need to get my shit together, and that starts here on the driveway. No way anyone else is out on New Year's morning putting time in.

Granted, no one else probably fell asleep at ten-thirty on New Year's Eve while watching *Star Wars: Episode III* on the couch with their dad. But still.

So when Tabby's dad's truck backs out of their driveway a little after nine, she finds *this guy* standing in the frizzle like a dumbass, with his hands up his shirt, pressed inside his armpits.

Tabby and her dad laugh at me from inside the truck. I pull both of my black-gloved hands from my shirt and wave like a moron. Tabby waves back with a box of Nerds in her hand.

Not a bad start, really.

Tabby and her dad are headed up to her grandma's nursing

home a couple of hours away to have pork and sauerkraut with her (for good luck!). It's really the only extended family Tabby has, and they hardly ever see her. From what Tabby's told me over the years, she's not a very nice woman.

"Last year she thought I was my mom—who she hasn't seen in, like, fifteen years—and kept making comments about my clothes over dinner. Nothing like having your grandma call you a slut in a room full of old people. But at least the pork and sauerkraut is gross!"

Tabby told me that one yesterday when she stopped by. She really had a hard time pulling herself away from our *Star Wars* marathon. And I used every bit of the Force I could muster to get her to stay, but the power of the Dark Accord was too strong.

Mom asked me this morning if I'd made my New Year's resolution yet. I told her it's to get a tattoo on my butt cheek of half a heart, like those friendship necklaces, and Trip was going to get the other half—we're still arguing over who gets the *Best* butt cheek and who gets the *Friends* cheek. Each has its own issues in isolation. I feel like there's a poem in there somewhere.

But as I pull these soaking receiving gloves off my pruney, half-frozen hands, it does seem like a valid question—the resolution question, not the butt-cheek question.

The two things I want most haven't changed: I still want to play varsity, and I still wish it were *my* varsity jacket hanging off Tabby's arms in the stands, that it was me she locked eyes with like I was the only other person in the gym.

But wishing these things doesn't make them so. And

constantly wishing and pining has kind of made me an asshole, I think.

So here's what we're gonna do—my resolutions:

1. Practice hard. Play hard. Turn off my stupid brain. The last one is easier said than done, but it's got to happen. I've got less than half a season left, and that means Branson and Lighty have less than half a season left before their varsity careers are over. If I want to have any chance of stepping into their place next year as a sophomore, I'm going to have to turn my brain off and go. I can't wish Tabby and company were watching me and pissing my pants that they're watching me at the same time. I'm not out here freezing my nuts off so I can stop playing anytime anyone shows up to watch. I want to run with Trip the way we do at the Y.

   Work my ass off. Play hard. No need to think.

2. Be Tabby's friend. Turn off my stupid brain.

Again, easier said than done.

It's still going to ache every time I see them together, and I don't necessarily want to stand there and see them off every morning when she hops into his car and gives him a kiss. But Mom's right: she hasn't written me out of her life, and there's no way I'm writing her out of mine. I still love that girl.

God, I love that girl.

And just like on the court, Branson's high school career is almost over. Next year—no rides to school. No hugs in the hallway.

No postgame gatherings at Valentino's. In a few short months, Tabby and Branson have gone from curiosity, gossip fodder— *A senior dating a freshman? Is that even legal?*—to Franklin's most endearing couple. Branson's senior friends love her, his sister and sophomore friends love her, everybody in a school of twelve hundred kids seems to know who she is now.

There's nothing I can do about that.

But in a few short months, it could just as easily fade away. When it does, I'll still be here. To make her laugh. Get jacked in the arm. Watch *Star Wars*. Get lectured. Supply her with Nerds.

Be her friend.

I take one last shot before heading back inside.

Buckets.

CHAPTER TWENTY-TWO

WELCOME BACK

The gods shine upon me this morning, dropping the temperatures far enough overnight to turn the roads into an icy mess—at least, enough of a mess to grant us a two-hour delay for our first day back.

That means an extra hour of sleep, an extra bowl of Cinnamon Toast Crunch, and a few extra minutes for foul shots in the driveway before Miss Edna pulls up at the end of the street.

I'm at twelve in a row (fifty-seven out of sixty-two) when Branson pulls into the circle to get Tabby. He doesn't flash his usual peace sign as he passes this morning, but whatever. Not gonna think about it.

He idles in front of her house for a few minutes before finally getting out and walking up to her door. After ringing the bell and knocking, he looks at his phone, tries to call her, and, after no response, finally looks over at me. He jogs—*jogs*—across her frozen front lawn and across the circle to the edge of my driveway.

"Wainwright, have you heard from Tabby?" he says, one hand still holding his phone, the other running over the top of his short crop of hair.

"Not since she left yesterday," I say, maybe a little tickled that I might know something he doesn't. I can still be an asshole on the inside, right? "She went up to see her grandmother for New Year's. Some nursing home, like an hour or so from here." Then, feeling particularly douchey—sorry, *dicky*—I add, "They go up to see her every New Year's."

"I know," he says, oblivious to my attempts to be an asshole, which actually just makes me feel like an asshole—I thought we were going to *stop* thinking, here, bud? "I talked to her when she got there yesterday. But I haven't heard from her since."

He really looks worried, and panic starts to form deep in my gut.

"I've been texting and calling since last night, and she won't answer. Did they come home last night?"

"I have no idea."

Fuck. I have no idea.

"Here, let's check the garage, see if her dad's truck is parked in there. They might just be zonked after a full day of having an old woman call Tabby a slut."

"What?"

Score.

"Sorry. Old joke," I say. "C'mon."

He follows me back across the circle in silence. My brain is working extra hard to not think. To not go where Liam's is going. It's not working very well. I can tell her dad's truck is not in there before we're even up to the windows.

"Shit," Liam says, running his hand over his head again. He punches his phone and holds it to his ear, his breath coming out in puffs that rise up over his panicked face, staring out over the circle. I hear Tabby's voice mail come on before he ends the call.

"Shit, shit, shit," he says to himself, like he's forgotten I'm standing here.

"Dude, Liam, it's okay," I say automatically, trying to get him to calm down. I've never seen him like this—unraveled—and it's freaking me out, too. "Her dad may have gone back to work already. He works crazy hours," I say.

He looks back up at her house, at her window, without responding. I can't tell what he's thinking, but he looks like he could climb up the side of the house right now and break through her window.

But we both know she's not in there.

"They probably got a hotel up there last night instead of trying to drive home in this," I say, but I'm not even sure he hears me.

This late in the morning, the sun glistens off the thin layer of ice encasing every tree branch in the circle. A wave of panic rushes through me, from my stomach out, and I feel like I have to sit down, but I force it away. Because everything's fine.

I hear my bus drive off at the end of the street.

Fucking everything is fine.

"I don't understand why she isn't responding," Liam says, both hands white-knuckling the steering wheel.

I've reiterated my hotel theory three times on the short ride to school. I can't think of anything else to say beyond, "I'm sure it's fine," because I'm sure it's fine.

I get some strange looks from the other seniors in the parking lot when I step out of the passenger side of the black Accord. Liam doesn't notice.

■ ■ ■

We're in the middle of sharing our gifts-of-writing success stories in Mr. Ellis's class when the announcement comes over the loudspeaker:

"Pardon the interruption ... Teachers, please check your emails for some important information. Thank you."

My classmates buzz around me while Mr. Ellis walks over to his desk and leans over to read his email. Normally, that's the unofficial *holy-shit-we're-getting-out-early* announcement. But that seems pretty unlikely, given we already had a two-hour delay this morning and the sunshine outside right now is nearly blinding, reflecting off the melting ice and puddles.

I don't look around at anyone, not even Trip. In my head, I'm still trying to convince Liam that everything's fine. More than twelve hundred kids in this school, and teachers get tons of "important emails" every day. Bus delays. Lunch menu changes. Meeting cancellations. Meeting reschedulings. All very important.

I watch Mr. Ellis read his email. After what seems like an impossibly long time, he gasps, puts a hand over his mouth. He crouches down behind his desk chair and continues staring at the screen. Then, without a word, he gets up and walks out of the room.

It's fine.

Everything's fine.

He comes back in from the hallway and gently closes his door. I refuse to look up from my desk, because everything's fine, and who needs to hear an "important" announcement about an entrée change in the cafeteria? Like I care if we're having hot dogs instead of chicken potpie.

Everything's fine.

"Gang, I need to share something with you."

His voice is a hoarse whisper—he struggles to even make it past *gang*.

The man must really love himself some potpie.

I close my eyes.

I really just want to go home and shoot some hoops in the driveway.

"Sorry. Let me just try to read this to you first."

I bet I can hit fifty straight from the line.

"'Students and staff: Late Sunday night, Tabitha Laughlin passed away in an automobile accident. Tabby was a freshman and a good friend to many of us here at Franklin High School. She will be greatly missed. Guidance counselors and crisis services will be on hand today for anyone who needs some support. Please do not hesitate to let teachers know when you feel you need to talk to someone.'"

It took Mr. Ellis two tries to get the name out. And when he finishes, tears are streaming down his cheeks. I can actually see one drop from the bottom of his jaw to the floor.

After the initial shock, people openly sob around the room, horrible choking gasps that don't even sound real. Trip stares straight at me, his face frozen.

I stare down at my writing folder on top of my desk. I didn't get to share how well my gifts of writing went. I made Gramma cry. A tear slipped off her face, too. Murray made me read his out loud three times in a row and every day of break after that. Three gift poems in all.

It's okay. I didn't really want to admit to everyone I'd written that many poems on my own, anyway, you know?

Everything's fine.

The hallway is a mess of huddled groups and animated faces crying. It echoes off the lockers: *Liam Branson. Liam's girlfriend. That freshman.* Occasionally just *Tabby.* I pass a particularly large, concern-stricken group huddled around an open locker, and I realize it's Liam's. I automatically think to tell him again that it's okay. Everything's fine.

Everything's fine.

It's the same in the cafeteria. I hear Liam's name five times for every one time I hear Tabby's. More crying. More arms around people's shoulders. I eat my hot dog in silence. It's just a hot dog. It's not that big of a deal.

Everything's fine.

I get called to the office at the end of lunch. Mom's sobbing when I walk through the door. She immediately wraps me up in her arms, Murray clinging to her leg. He looks up at me, confused. I don't know what to tell him, but I can't stop the tears from streaming down my face. Mom keeps talking and crying and talking and crying, even as our car pulls out of the still-full parking lot. But I'm not hearing a word she's saying.

It seems my brain has finally stopped working.

CHAPTER TWENTY-THREE

THAT DIRECTOR NO LONGER WORKS HERE

The gods must have decided to shine their light upon me again this morning, because when I open my eyes, my clock says it's 9:18. I'm buried under my covers in just my boxers, but I don't remember getting into bed last night.

For a moment, I wonder if I'm getting a do-over. Like it's Groundhog Day, and yesterday has been erased. But when I cross the hall to the bathroom, I hear Mom crying in the kitchen. No erasing. No reset button. No Groundhog Day.

My movie is shit.

Mom and Dad are both in the kitchen, huddled close over their oversize coffee mugs at the kitchen table. Their heads touch, and Mom clutches a tissue with a trembling hand. Dad's eyes are closed.

"Why aren't I at school?"

They both stand at the sound of my voice, and Mom rushes over to wrap me in another hug. Dad's eyes are red and puffy, like he's had one of his sneezing fits after mowing the lawn, and I have to look away.

Outside the window over the sink, the morning sun sparkles off the icicles still hanging from the swing set in the backyard.

"Why aren't I at school?" I ask again. "Is there another delay or something?"

"Oh, sweetie," Mom replies, stepping back, holding me at arm's length. "You don't have to go in today. You can stay home."

"We have a game tonight."

"Matt, it's okay. You can miss one game. Stay home and relax today."

Dad moves toward us, nodding his puffy head and trying to smile. I look at the clock on the stove. 9:26. I think I've gotta be in school by ten to be eligible to play.

"It's okay," I say, pulling away and retreating to the stairs.

"Matthew, I really think you should—" Dad puts his arm around her, and she stares up at him, pleading.

I should have time for a quick shower. "I want to go to school. I'm fine."

The team bus ride to Catholic is silent. Forty-five minutes to prop my knees up on the seat in front of me, blast my music, and play out game scenarios in my head.

Branson's not on the bus. He never came into school today, I guess, and Coach Langley doesn't say a word about it when he takes roll before we leave. Trip nudges me once on the way there, asks if I'm doing okay, and I nod without looking up.

A few times, when I lose focus or start to doze, I see flashes of Tabby at the gym doors in an oversize varsity jacket, or in the truck with her dad, waving a box of Nerds, but I force them away. Focus on game scenarios, shooting free throws in the strange yellow lighting of Catholic's gym. Catholic doesn't give a shit if we're sad.

In the JV game, I knock down a three from the corner with thirty-eight seconds left to play, extending our lead to five, meaning Catholic's point guard has to rush, gets sloppy, and Trip picks him. He kicks it to me, and instead of driving in for the easy layup, I pull up and knock down another three from the side, because fuck you.

Game fucking over.

Twenty-six points.

Trip nearly knocks me on my ass when the buzzer sounds, he's so jacked up, and right now, it's perfect. Right now, nothing matters. Just Trip and DeAndre Miller, and knowing this private-school douche cannot stop me.

The varsity team is getting waxed. Catholic's stud forward, Tyson Avery, the guy Branson would have matched up against, is going off even more than I did. They look lost out there.

Sitting with Trip in the stands back in the dress clothes we have to wear for away games, watching this mess, it does nothing to slow the adrenaline still burning inside from our win.

There's a part of me, way in the back of my brain, that wants to be able to say that the game was for Tabby. That as the buzzer sounded, I could have pointed to the rafters and dropped to my knees, sobbing. The final, dramatic scene in my shitty movie.

But fuck that part of my stupid brain.

The realistic part knows it wasn't for Tabby at all. It was just a game. Five guys trying to put a leather ball through a metal circle more times than the other five guys. Just a game where I played my best because I could finally turn off my stupid brain.

So really, movie brain, I played better because Tabby wasn't here. This good feeling I have sitting here? This adrenaline, this contentment? It couldn't have happened with Tabby in those stands.

And I feel good.

How fucking twisted is that?

CHAPTER TWENTY-FOUR

STICK TO THE PLAN

Mom has me sleep in again, still thinking I need a day away from everything. But there's no way I'm missing practice or games.

"I think you'd feel better if—"

Nope.

Practice hard. Play hard. Turn off my brain.

No reason to change that part of the plan.

That does mean, though, that by the time Mom drops me off with notes for the office asking them to keep a special eye on me, I've been missing my first few classes the last couple of days, since our first day back. So when I show up in Mrs. Shepler's class, I'm shocked at how normal everything seems. It's a Thursday. Everything continues to run exactly as before, like Tabby played no part in making this system work. She's simply off the ride. Research papers are still due on Monday. Quiz on Friday. Practice and games continue as scheduled.

Nothing stops.

Except Tabby.

The only hiccup is when Mrs. Shepler hands back our Thursday review packets. When Rebecca Gaskins turns around to pass the last packets to Evan and me, I can see she's holding three packets, that Shepler sent the usual number back without thinking. And I can see that *Rebecca* sees it's three packets for just Evan and me. She can't look up at us when she hands me all three.

I drop one in front of Evan, hold two blank packets. Do I raise my hand, tell Mrs. Shepler we have an extra—let it hang in the air who the extra would be for? For a moment, my brain automatically thinks—just like Shepler's automatically counted out the normal number—that I'll give it to Tabby on the bus.

And that's when my brain turns back on. Holding a stupid fucking biology packet that's never going to be completed. No grade will be entered. It won't affect her average, won't ever be made up, but it doesn't matter because there's nowhere for her stupid report card to go anyway. No reason to report a numerical representation of her understanding of meiosis versus mitosis. Seventy-two percent? Doesn't matter. Ninety-eight percent? Awesome job. Still doesn't fucking matter. Her cells don't do that anymore; no study of living things because she's not a living thing. Her name just disappears from the roster while the rest of us are expected to complete our assignments like normal. For us, they still matter.

Everything keeps going, except Tabby.

And for the first time, my brain pushes to her last seconds, trying to see the exact moment the world kept moving without her.

They said it was instant, that she wouldn't have felt a thing. But how do they know? If time's relative—if two hours of trick-or-treating with Tabby can feel like two minutes while a forty-minute science class, or twenty seconds in front of Corey Sheridan with tears threatening, drags on for an eternity—what's it mean to die instantly?

Did she have time to see the headlights? To realize they weren't swerving, to scream out and grab her father's arm?

Were her final seconds nothing but pure animal panic? And then nothing?

How long does it take for the body to shut down? Do those nanoseconds, her last on earth, stretch out into infinity?

What were her last words? Was she talking about Liam? Were they laughing about how awful the pork and sauerkraut was?

The official report was that an SUV lost control on a patch of ice coming off a turn, hit Tabby's dad's pickup head-on. Died instantly. Felt no pain. Probably never saw it coming.

There's not even anyone to blame. The other driver wasn't speeding, wasn't drunk, didn't fall asleep at the wheel. Just bad driving conditions and terrible timing. The driver—who walked away with a broken collarbone and a mild concussion—was so devastated and so guilt-ridden by what happened that he asked to make a huge donation to the family. When he found out there was really no family left to support, he offered to take care of the funeral costs. How can you hate him?

I'm still holding the two blank packets in my hands when I realize Mrs. Shepler is next to me. Talking to me.

"—you can get your notes from your lab partner before you start on your packet."

I must nod or give some signal of comprehension because she walks away to her desk, never noticing the extra packet in my hands.

I glance at Evan, who's pretending to look through his notebook for these essential notes, though by the flushing in his usually pale face and the way he won't look up at me, I can tell he hasn't taken a single note since before Christmas.

I shove both packets into my book bag and walk out.

Fuck this place.

CHAPTER TWENTY-FIVE

GOD SUCKS AT THIS

Two caskets sit at the front of the church, the top half of each lid open so that the bodies are only visible from the chest up. The line to see the bodies snakes all the way to the back doors of the church, where I stand against the wall. Separate from the line. I'm not ready yet.

The only family to receive is Grandma in her wheelchair, who looks more confused than in mourning, and Tabby's dad's brother and his son, neither of whom I've ever seen before. The uncle has a hand resting on top of the wheelchair, his son slightly behind him. They look pained, like they're trying to figure out the appropriate expression and response for each *I'm sorry for your loss* they receive, as if the loss isn't really that traumatic for them, which I suppose it isn't.

I've never seen the woman sitting alone at the far left side of the second row before, so I can only guess that it's Tabby's mother. Her hair a mess of red pulled back in a ponytail, she methodically chews at each of her cuticles, one after another and back again. She stares straight ahead, speaks to no one, like she's in a trance. A few people glance at her as they pass, but nothing more.

Liam Branson sits up front with Lily, their family around

them. He looks like he hasn't stopped crying for days. Maybe he hasn't. The line is packed with students, 99 percent of which couldn't tell you jack shit about Tabby, beyond the fact that *she was really nice* and that *she was Liam's girlfriend* and *ohmigod, they made the* best *couple.* Naturally, every one of them stops to pay Liam their respects, like after two months he's a fucking family member.

Sprinkled in among the mourning teenagers are some of Tabby's dad's friends and coworkers—tough-looking men who look as bewildered and out of place as Tabby's senile grandmother. Some of Tabby's teachers—who must have left school early with half the student body—are here, including Mr. Ellis, shoulder to shoulder with Mrs. Shepler. I recognize a math teacher. Mrs. Dolan, the art teacher. Miss Edna.

And of course my family.

Mom and Dad sit up front as well, by the right-hand aisle, the viewing line directly in front of them. Gramma and Grampa sit behind them. When we first walked in, and I saw all these people, the two caskets up front, I told Mom, "I can't." She nodded, rubbed my arm, and moved slowly to the front, two hands clasped around Dad's.

Murray stands next to me in the back, staring straight ahead, one hand lightly holding onto the bottom of my jacket, like he doesn't know he's doing it. I don't know how much he understands of what's happening, or what's going through his head. But he decided, like me, that he didn't want to go up front.

He looks up once and says, "Matty, when are we going home?"

I sit my hand on top of his head, try my best to meet his eyes. "I don't know, buddy. Soon." Which he accepts without another word.

I watch all these people giving clueless, ambivalent family members—not to mention the family of a kid who's known Tabby less than half a year—their deepest sympathies. No one stops to give condolences to my family. Not one.

So I nearly lose it when Mr. Holowitz—he of OTM ≠ OTM fame—walks by and squeezes my arm. He used to call us Frick and Frack when we walked into his classroom together each morning. He looks like he wants to say something to me, his hand still around my elbow, but he can't get any words out, and I'm frozen. He gives me one more knowing look and moves on, but when Miss Edna puts a hand on my shoulder a moment later, the other clutching a balled-up tissue over her mouth, I'm about to break. Of the hundreds of people in this church, they're the first to recognize the connection I have to Tabby, and I can't breathe.

I can't go up there. That's not Tabby. I have a glimpse of red hair from back here, but I know that's not her.

Tabby would lecture me for not sitting with my family, for judging Branson and his legion of fake mourners. They give him a hug, wipe their eyes, and check their phones as soon as they walk out the door. Slap down a crying emoji with angel wings and find out where everyone's meeting up afterward.

But there's no lecture.

I should go up there and say goodbye, but who am I saying goodbye to? She's already gone. Her insides were emptied out days ago, stagnant blood pulled from her veins. If she scraped her elbows and fell asleep against me, it'd be embalming fluid soaking into my shirt while the Ewoks help thwart the Imperial Stormtroopers, the stench of formaldehyde making the last of the popcorn inedible.

That's not Tabby.

With pews starting to fill up and the viewing line still snaking back to the exits, Grampa stands, sidesteps to the end of his pew in the second row. When there's the slightest break in the line of teenagers waiting to view the bodies, he steps forward in front of them to Tabby. No one looks twice.

He rests a hand on the closed half of the lid and looks down at her. I can't see if he says anything, but he stays that way for a minute. He nods once and turns to find Murray and me in the back, bypassing Tabby's family and the Bransons.

I drop my head when he gives me a pursed smile coming back up the aisle, the first hot tears slipping to the corners of my mouth. Murray leans in and wraps his arms around Grampa's leg, Grampa's arm draped over his shoulder, gently scratching Murray's back. I'd do anything to still be able to sink into Grampa like that.

We stay that way until the line dwindles, the pastor making sympathetic gestures to the last of the viewers, and then sit down with Grampa in the last row. As the viewing spills into the funeral service, the pastor steps to the front of the church, behind the caskets, and begins to speak.

His voice is kind and reassuring. But after a few opening prayers and a brief welcome, his words are empty. There are no eulogies. He didn't know Tabby or her dad personally. After a few more numbing hymns, he speaks in infuriatingly generic terms about "the mystery of God's love" and I think, *Yeah, this is a pretty big fucking mystery.*

What bullshit.

What utter fucking bullshit.

How can anybody sit here, look at what remains of such a

beautiful, perfect human being, and honestly think that a patch of ice on a dark road in Nowhere, Pennsylvania, a luxury SUV, and blunt-force trauma are part of some greater plan for the universe? That there was a divine reason for Tabby's lungs to be impaled by her own shattered ribs?

What kind of fucked-up plan is that?

Why are people not burning this fucking place to the ground?

"C'mon, let's get out of here for a few minutes." Grampa's hand is on my shoulder, and I can feel that he's shaking, too. As the pastor fills the air with more empty words, the three of us file out the back into the bright afternoon. We sit down on a bench outside the church, find clusters of teens and adults, checking phones, looking spent and bored.

I don't know how long we sit on that bench in the cool sunshine, no trace of the ice and snow that ended it all a few days ago. Everything keeps moving. But when I hear the organ music start up again, I know the funeral is probably almost over.

A couple of minutes later, the doors open, and Tabby's and her dad's caskets come out, carried by a combination of her dad's coworkers and employees of the funeral home. The caskets are loaded into two separate hearses, parked side by side. The lids are closed, and it hits me that they'll never be opened again. I'll never see Tabby's face ever again, and I can't rewind a few minutes to when it was open and I could have had one last look at her—even if it's not really her—and I hate myself for it. I close my eyes and rest my head in my hands, trying to focus on breathing, in and out of my lungs, as everyone else spills out of the church around me.

Tabby, waving her box of Nerds as she and her dad drive

away, flashes over and over in my head, this grainy clip losing a little of its impact with every loop. The last time I saw her.

"We should head to the car," Dad says softly over us. "The procession is going to leave soon."

"Why don't I take Murray home," Grampa says. "I think we've had enough."

I follow Grampa and Murray and climb into the backseat of Grampa's car without a word. Mom and Dad don't say anything about it—just head to their car, Dad's arm around Mom's shoulder.

I think I've had enough, too.

CHAPTER TWENTY-SIX

WAKE, PART I

Grampa's on the couch in the den when I come down from changing out of dress clothes into sweats. His tie's off, his dress shirt untucked and unbuttoned, his belly pressing against his thin undershirt as he flips through channels. He stops on a replay of last night's Wizards game, sighs, and tosses the remote down on the couch next to him. He looks over the back of the couch when he hears me behind him.

"Murray okay?"

I nod. "In his room."

Grampa must have told him to change into pj's, but he only got as far as undressing; when I walked past his room, he was playing with his stuffed animals in his underwear. I could hear him talking to them in different voices, carrying on conversations between animals, but I didn't stick around to hear what may have been playing out.

Grampa pats the seat next to him, and I sink into the cushion and lean into him, his arm around my shoulder. He smells like old-man aftershave and breath mints. It's overpowering and completely welcome. We watch an entire quarter in silence. I'm grateful for his Jedi-like ability to know when we don't need to talk, that it doesn't help to ask if I'm okay.

I think we're both dozing, because when we hear the door open in the kitchen, they're finishing the halftime report on the TV. We look at each other with bleary eyes. He gives my knee a squeeze and stands.

When we get into the kitchen, Mom and Gramma are wrapped in a hug. Dad stands behind them holding two huge bags of Chinese food. Grampa kisses Gramma and Mom each on top of their heads.

"Matt, why don't you get some plates and forks and set the table," Grampa says, relieving Dad of the food bags and carrying them to the dining room table.

I nod and move toward the cupboard, but not before Mom brings me in for another hug, pulling my head down next to hers.

"I'm so sorry, Matthew," she says, squeezing me, her tear-soaked cheek pressing against the side of my head. She's the first person to actually say that to me, and the air burns in my nose as I try to breathe.

She squeezes for what feels like another five minutes before saying, "The graves are in a beautiful spot. I'll have to show you, when you're ready."

Which for some reason makes me suddenly furious, and I have no idea why. I force a nod and break away from her embrace to grab a stack of plates from the cupboard behind her, after which, thankfully, she heads upstairs to find Murray. I'm hoping it takes her a while because I don't think I can deal with another hug at the moment. My inner–movie director has me standing at the grave site holding fresh-picked daisies—Tabby's favorite—in the rain, like always, and I want to punch him in his stupid fucking face. I don't know what Tabby's favorite flowers are—were—if she even ever had any. Who the fuck under fifty years old has a favorite flower?

I set out the plates while Gramma puts the takeout boxes in the middle of the table and Grampa busies himself with making a pyramid of egg rolls on a big plate. Gramma keeps touching me when I get near her—little affectionate squeezes on my elbow, or a hand on the small of my back—and I know she's fighting hard not to hug me, too, so I head back into the kitchen to pour water for everyone. When I come back, Mom's carrying Murray to the table in his pj's.

We eat in awkward, terrible silence. But what the hell is there to say? *The funeral was really sad, but Chinatown fucking killed this moo shu tonight!*

Gramma's the one to break the silence a few minutes later, and as soon as she starts, I'm wishing for the scrapes of silverware on dishes again.

"I remember the first time we met Tabby. I bet she wasn't two yet, and you were already babysitting her full-time by then."

Mom nods, her face frozen between a smile and a sob.

"We stopped by one day after lunch. I remember I pulled Matty up on the couch with me to read a book. What's that book he used to love, with the chubby little cat and dog?"

Hondo & Fabian.

"*Hondo and Fabian,*" Mom says, smiling and pressing her napkin to the corner of her eyes.

"That's right, *Hondo and Fabian.* I sat down with little Matty to read *Hondo and Fabian,* and that little girl—didn't know me from Adam—climbed right up on that couch next to me, all ready to read."

"I remember that," Mom says.

"Two of them laughing and pointing at that cat—doesn't it mess with the toilet paper or something?"

I liked the turkey sandwich page even more.

"Next time we came, Grampa'd gone out and bought another copy for Tabby to take home with her."

"Remember she brought it with her the first time they both stayed over at our house?" Grampa says, setting his napkin on his empty plate and leaning back in his chair. "Probably about first grade, I think. They talked us into letting them stay up late to watch a movie, and I let them watch some old kids' movie, ended up scaring the bejeezus out of them."

The NeverEnding Story. That was a weird-ass movie. I remember that one.

"They ended up piling blankets and couch cushions and pillows into our room to sleep on the floor at the end of our bed. Then we couldn't get the little boogers to stop talking to us or whispering to each other and get to sleep."

Dad laughs now. "God, you were a sucker for her," he says, smiling and shaking his head at Grampa. "I was never allowed to do that kind of stuff as a kid."

"Eh, you weren't that cute of a kid," Grampa says, winking at me. I look down at my plate, start peeling the wrapper off a half-eaten egg roll.

"I remember the first day Steve brought her over here," Mom starts, her voice thick, unsteady. "She was only a few months old. Crystal had been gone a week, but she was gone for good. In fact, today's the first time I've seen her since they moved in—almost fifteen years."

"We felt stupid, we hadn't even introduced ourselves yet," Dad says with a humorless chuckle, steering Mom back to her story. I've heard this one, too, and I just want it to stop.

"Nope, but he came across the circle with this beautiful, screaming, furious baby in his arms—he looked like he was about to lose it when we opened our door. We invited him in. I remember I was holding Matt when he came in, and I took that little girl out of his arms and held you both. You just stared at her."

I know she's talking to me, but I'm still focused on dismantling the egg roll on my plate.

"She screamed for a few more seconds, and then stopped and stared back at you. Just like that, she's smiling and yelling baby gibberish and smiling some more. And you stared at her. I could feel you wriggle when she yelled to you, but you just watched her. From the first day, you were the quiet one, following her lead."

She reaches across the table and squeezes my hand, and my lungs immediately stop working, again. I reach for the lo mein with my other hand, and she lets go so I can dump another pile onto my plate. It doesn't taste like anything. Just weight in my mouth and a reason to look down as Mom continues.

"Steve had already missed a week of work, and he didn't know if Crystal was coming back, or what kind of shape she'd be in if she did, and he just sat there and told us everything that day. How Crystal had done really well through most of the pregnancy, and how he thought buying the house up here would change things for them."

Mom trails off, thinking. They've never talked much about Tabby's mom—at least not with me—and Tabby never said much, either. She wondered sometimes, and we'd search the Internet, and play the what-if game. But it was always just her and her dad, and that was fine. She was happy.

"I remember how desperate he was," Mom starts again. "He had no one else to help them."

"Thought you'd lost your mind," Grampa says, a humorless laugh to match Dad's. "Just had your first child of your own, barely settled into this house, and you get involved with a drug-addict mom and a desperate dad working swing shift in a factory."

"Best decision we ever made," Mom says, and she can do nothing to stop the tears from flowing down her face now. She doesn't even try.

My brain tries to imagine what would have happened if my parents had said no. That it was too much for them. That they were sorry and they felt for them and all that, but they couldn't manage that kind of new commitment in their young lives.

Would she have been my best friend? Would we have ever shared Little Hugs on the bus? Would we have shared a secret love of Ewoks and a blatant love of Nerds?

I try to imagine *not* knowing these things, just knowing her as the girl across the street, someone your parents wave to out of neighborly obligation.

She wouldn't have been Tabby. And I wouldn't be me.

But now, there is no Tabby.

And I hate being me.

When I look up from my plate, they're all looking at me. I don't know if they think it's my turn to share, or if I've been staring at my plate too long, or if I've got a huge snot bubble coming out my nose, or what. I blow my nose in my napkin to be sure.

This is some kind of therapy for them—some clinical step in the grieving process we're supposed to go through, where we remember the dead so that they live on in our hearts, or some shit like that. But I can't do it. All these people can follow the steps, and say goodbye, and laugh and tell stories, and remember without hating themselves. What the fuck is wrong with me?

I can't. I don't want to remember Tabby. I want to go throw on *Return of the Jedi* with a big-ass bowl of popcorn and a box of Nerds and veg out on the couch with my friend. It feels like it's been so long, and it's not that much to ask, and everyone could stop fucking crying.

"I remember trick or treat," Murray says, beaming at his chance to join the storytelling. "Me and Matt were eagles, and Tabby went, too. And I got so much candy. And Tabby said she'd give me *three* Reesie cups for *one* little box of Nerds, 'cause Reesie cups are my favorite." He holds up three fingers with his left hand, one with his right, smiling for the first time today, like this fucking therapy session is working for him, wiping away his sadness and ensuring she lives on in his tiny little heart, and it hits me that by the time he's our age—*my* age—he'll barely remember her, and I just need him to stop fucking talking.

Instead, he does a fake-sounding laugh and keeps going.

"I told her she's too old to trick-or-treat, and she didn't have a costume, and so she didn't even *have* any Reesie cups. But I gave her some of my Nerds anyway." He does his fake laugh again, like he's a grown-up telling a story, and I can't stand it. I don't even know if it's true, or if he's just making it up as he goes, or if his four-year-old brain knows the difference. I just know I can't deal with any more of this.

So when Mom reaches over and runs her hand through his

curls and says, "She was a pretty special friend, huh," I have to get up and leave the table.

I hit every other stair up to my room and close the door behind me. Put my music on and collapse onto my bed. My fingers brush against my basketball under my bed, and I automatically scoop it up and roll over onto my back. I shoot the ball toward the ceiling with my right hand, focusing on the backspin, over and over until the burning in my forearm locks into a full-on cramp, and I switch to my left.

My brain needs to turn off again for a while, but when the fuck has my brain ever done what it's supposed to do? All their perfect memories flash through my head, their cherished first moments with our Tabby. I can see the divot still in my door without looking at it, and my brain slows down to show me replays of essentially telling Tabby to fuck off on one of the craziest, most confusing days of her life. Because *I* couldn't handle it.

And I see her lying in the street, Corey Sheridan pedaling away on his bike.

And I can see her stretching and not reaching back in science.

Air-balling shots and throwing temper tantrums on the court when she wasn't really there to see me.

Every time I've been a worthless-cock-loser-fucking asshole, and now she's fucking *gone*.

I sit up and fire my ball at my door, as hard as I can at that fucking divot. It slams off the door and rolls to a stop under my desk, and now it's a divot inside a dent. Stupid inside of stupid.

All these fantasies about finding each other—about realizing our childhood friendship was really love in its infant form—all of these stupid daydreams come flooding through my stupid brain.

And what of her fantasies? What happened to them? Where did they go? I realize I don't even know what Tabby's are. Were. And that only makes it worse, because it's like it's always been all about me. Stupid, selfish me.

"Matt? Are you okay?" Mom says from the other side of the door. The knob turns slowly.

"I'm fine!" I yell, too loud. Then, "Please don't come in."

It's silent for a moment, and I can hear Dad's voice speaking softly to Mom. I don't know what he says, but Mom sniffs again and then releases the knob, and the two of them walk slowly back down the steps.

I pull my laptop off my desk because I just want to see her. I lean my back against the wall and pull up Tabby's page. I'm met by literally thousands of messages, saying goodbyes, and sending prayers, shitty song lyrics and angel emojis, and I see myself standing in the back of the church, unwilling to go up and say goodbye, climbing into the car headed away from the cemetery instead of following the procession and paying my final respects.

What would Tabby say if she could somehow know?

All these people can follow the steps, and say goodbye, and laugh and tell stories, and *remember* without hating themselves. What the fuck is wrong with me?

Tabby could probably tell me.

CHAPTER TWENTY-SEVEN

MY FIVE SENSES AREN'T INTERESTED TODAY

"Two things you need to know about writing memoir: First, memoir zooms in on one specific moment. Second, memoir tries to figure out why that moment matters in the big picture of your life. How that moment's helped shape who you are—or, in your case, who you're becoming."

I'm waiting for Ilca to interject, to put an end to wherever this terrible idea is going, but for once, the old hag bookcase is silent.

This is the new unit Mr. Ellis told us he's so pumped to start. He paces while he talks, his hands gesturing wildly. I'm not sure why we can't keep doing poetry.

Yes, that was a real thing my brain said to myself.

"Guys, this is one of my absolute favorite genres to write, because memories are so important, you know? I think it's our memories that make us who we are—those moments that, for whatever reason, big or small, stick in our brains, that make up *our stories*." He pauses, grins. "So our first job is to try to figure out what some of those moments might be."

Nope. Not interested.

Mr. Ellis rushes around as he talks, first handing back big pieces of colored construction paper, then slamming down plastic bins of markers on random desks throughout the room. He thrives on the confused looks he gets, passing out the paraphernalia of an elementary art class.

I don't really care. I'm trying to think of a new persona I could try in a poem. Maybe a garbage man? A sprinkled donut? A lobster in those tanks at the grocery store?

"Now remember our first key is zooming in on specific *moments*. Single *moments*," he says, holding up one finger. "So not *How me and my family go to the beach every year and it's super fun*, but *That one time at Ocean City when I was six and my favorite sand shovel got pulled out by a wave and my mom swam up and down the beach for a half hour and still couldn't find it, and it still haunts me to this day*." He gets it all out in one breath, then inhales deeply and continues. "Or, instead of *My trip to Hersheypark*, zoom in on *That one time at Hersheypark when my brother dared me to eat four corn dogs before getting on the sooperdooperLooper, and I puked it up on his girlfriend in the seat behind me*."

People groan and laugh around me.

"See what I'm talking about? Moments. *Your* moments."

Maybe I could try one from the point of view of a ride operator at an amusement park. That would work.

"All right, so here's where we're gonna start—just a little exercise to get some strong, sensory memories flowing."

Or maybe a sketchy carnival ride operator. That might be even better.

"Strictly from memory, I want you to draw a map of your neighborhood as a kid, including all the important neighborhood landmarks you remember—home base for hide-and-seek, your buddy's pool, that old dude's porch that you ding-dong-ditched every other week—all of it."

He shows us his own map, drawn on yellow construction paper, and talks us through some highlights, and my chest tightens, my brain flashing through images of my neighborhood—the circle, my driveway, the old sandbox in Tabby's backyard—and Tabby's in all of them.

"All right, you've got fifteen minutes to sketch out your neighborhood. Grab markers as you need them. Go."

Fuck. I stare at my big orange sheet, and I can see where the outlines should go without drawing a thing—the circle, the houses, mailboxes and driveways, swing sets. Tabby's part of all of them.

Next to me, Trip's engrossed in his map, purple marker cap in his teeth as he draws. He's loving this. Like everybody else.

I look back down at my paper and start doodling out my carny ride operator, covering my paper as best I can while I sketch in a stupid-looking gap-toothed grin. A wifebeater and a hairy belly that sticks out from the bottom, a trucker hat that reads "I ♥ Little Boys." I give him a huge corn dog in one hand while the other grasps a lever on a box next to him—his on/off switch for his carnival ride, the Twirl-N-Ralph.

It's maybe ten times more fucking stupid than it sounds, but who cares?

I grab a handful of markers from a nearby desk and set about coloring this bad boy in, hovering close over my desk again.

I'm finishing the lettering on the TWIRL-N-RALPH sign when Mr. Ellis tells us our drawing time is up. I turn my guy facedown on my desk.

"All right, gang, next step. Time to really start zooming in."

I think I'm going to name my dude Maurice. Maurice Lester.

"I want you to look over your maps and mark five spots."

Friends call him Mo.

"Five spots where you have especially strong, vivid sensory memories. Moments that—if you close your eyes—you can still see or hear or feel or smell or even taste clearly."

Mo Lester. I probably won't be able to read this one to Murray when it's done.

"Once you have your five spots, I'd like you to write at least a paragraph for each one, zooming in on those sensory details you still remember. It's to brainstorm ideas you might use for a more in-depth memoir, so keep it to a paragraph and focus on sensory details. The last few minutes are yours to write. Have these ready to go tomorrow, all right?"

Some people have started pouring memories onto their paper before Mr. Ellis has finished talking. Sensory details coming out their asses, apparently.

I jot the title at the top of the flip side of my orange paper: "The Ballad of Maurice J. Lester, Carnival Ride Operator."

This may be my best poem yet.

CHAPTER TWENTY-EIGHT

THE JV SQUAD STRIKES BACK

Devin Heiner twists his ankle during a rebounding drill and is sitting on the sidelines, looking all too happy to be getting his ankle wrapped by Monica Dunlap, our student trainer, who's holding an ice pack to his foot and laughing at some story he's telling her.

It's not a huge loss.

Instead of subbing me in for Devin, Coach Langley slides me out to the three-spot in his place and tells Tyler Forry, one of the senior varsity backup big men, to change his jersey around and fill in down low for me.

And suddenly shit gets real. Trip's at the top of the key, the ball against his hip, taking stock of his new cast before checking the ball back to Elijah Leppo, and the intensity ratchets up a notch.

Now we have DeAndre Miller and Tyler both down low, and while neither is nearly as good as Lighty, neither one has any problems banging around with Lighty on the blocks. Tyler is essentially a clone of DeAndre Miller, just a year older—not very skilled, but huge nonetheless and willing to work hard. Plus the added benefit that he's clearly pissed about his sudden demotion—even if only temporary—to the JV squad, and he's more likely to bang harder than he is to pout. I've held my own against Lighty in scrimmages, but he's never really had to worry about being put on his ass from a box-out.

And moving outside to the wing means I'm finally matched up against Branson.

Heartbroken Branson.

Whom the entire school mourns for as though he's the one who died.

As though he's the one who's lost everything.

When Coach gives the green light, Trip checks the ball back to Leppo.

And we go.

For almost an hour, we go.

At first, I forget how fast Branson is, and he knocks down a jumper on their first possession—one fast dribble to his left and a quick pull-up from the baseline—and my head nearly explodes.

He will not take any more away from me.

He makes a few baskets, but none without my hand in his face, and after a few minutes, he's missing a lot more shots than he's making. And every time—the second the ball leaves his hands and clears my outstretched fingertips—I've got my back slammed into him, boxing him out, relishing watching his shot bounce off the front rim and hearing him start to swear under his breath when Coach yells for him to follow his shot.

When I knock down two straight jumpers on the next two possessions, I can tell he's starting to get pissed. DeAndre and Tyler are both setting brutal, borderline illegal screens for me, both seeming to relish the chance to stick it to the varsity starters for once. Plus it helps that Trip, after each of my baskets, knows to give *them* the props for it, calling them out and smacking them on the ass on the way back up the court—made better by the fact that those asses are nearly eye level with Trip.

When it happens the third time and I bury another jumper from the elbow, Coach finally blows his whistle and stops us. I assume he's going to get on Tyler for sticking his elbows out on the screen, but instead, Coach yells, "Liam! You've got to do a better job slipping those screens!" After which, Coach grabs my jersey and pulls me back down to the block to demonstrate: Tyler jogs down to set another screen on Coach—much narrower than the ones he's been setting, I notice—and I start to move to go off Tyler's screen. As soon as I move, Coach drives his bony elbow into my sternum and doesn't let me anywhere near Tyler's shoulder, and I'm stuck looping out around him. Trip completes the demo by attempting to pass it to me, even though Coach is clearly between me and the ball, and Trip would get benched immediately if he made that pass during a game. Coach easily swats the pass away and returns to the sideline.

"Gotta fight through," he says again. "Trip, take the ball out top. Again."

I refuse to go back to being practice dummy. This feels too good.

So when Tyler Forry barrels down to the block again, elbows out, I can sense Branson ready to nail me in the chest, ready to use me to get back into Coach's good graces. I take one step out—and see Branson's elbow coming up—before cutting underneath and popping into the middle of the lane. Dirty, but Trip seemed to already know exactly what I was going to do: he swings a perfect bounce pass around Elijah Leppo and hits me right as I get to the foul line, and I've buried another short jumper before Branson can begin to recover.

I expect the whistle again, but Coach's face is expressionless as we run up the court.

Branson's face is bright red, and he's breathing heavily when I meet him out on the wing on defense at the other end of the court.

"What the fuck was that?" he says.

"Fuck you."

For a second, he's stunned—looks at me, blinks a few times—then sets his jaw and the intensity goes up yet another notch.

He comes into the block, and I'm ready for a back screen from Lighty, but instead Branson gets me in the chest with his shoulder—hard—and cuts back out, where Elijah gets him the ball. I'm back out on him, my hand already up, before he can get off an open shot. Instead, he pump-fakes and does another lightning-fast dribble to his left, and my head's about to explode again, because I *will not* concede another open shot to this fucker. As he's about to blow by me, I'm barely able to catch him with my hip, and I shove him in the direction he's heading, sending him and the ball sprawling out of bounds. It's an obvious foul, but hopefully not an obvious flagrant foul.

As Branson pops up to his feet and slaps the ball in his hands, Coach blows the whistle.

"All right, men. Bring it in. Nice work."

My heart is pounding so hard I can hear it inside my head—only partly from how hard we've been running—and I can't focus on anything Coach is saying during our end-of-practice huddle. Though I'm getting the impression he was pleased with the intensity of our scrimmage. And oblivious to the fact that Branson's probably thirty seconds from removing my head from my body.

Well, fuck him. He can have it.

Branson won't look at me. He won't look at anyone, actually. He's fuming, staring only at the floor in front of him or the door to leave. When our huddle breaks, he heads straight to the locker room without a word to anyone.

By the time Trip and I make it to the locker room after gathering up all the balls, Branson's already on his way out. In fact, he almost knocks me down when he comes out the door, still wearing his sweat-soaked practice jersey, his bag and coat slung over his shoulder. Despite plowing straight through us, he doesn't look up.

Fuck him.

As Trip and I watch him stalk away, I catch sight of something familiar. Tabby's earflap hat—the one Mom crocheted—is tied to the strap of his gym bag.

I've heard people say that something feels like being stabbed in the heart, but this feels like it's literally happening—like something sharp is pressing down on my chest, and it won't allow me to take a breath. He runs his hand over the light blue pom-pom and visibly exhales before he pushes through the door to the parking lot.

I don't know why it hurts so much more than seeing his arm over Tabby's shoulder or her locking eyes with him from the stands, but right now, I hate him so much.

I hate his heartbreak.

I hate all the heartbreak for him.

I hate him holding her hat, like it only has special meaning to him, like he fucking owns it all because he's the shattered boyfriend.

Hate.

Him.

"Matt, you coming?"

I manage a nod and follow Trip into the locker room.

CHAPTER TWENTY-NINE

THE NEW (SHITTY) NORMAL

You know, if we're not going to do any actual science, you'd think she could at least make a new fucking seating chart every now and then. Shuffle the fucking deck chairs on this sinking piece of shit.

Rebecca Gaskins has made it to about the third slide of notes every day this week before disappearing to the bathroom for twenty-plus minutes, leaving both seats empty at the lab table in front of Evan and me. And when Mrs. Shepler hands back the wrong number of packets again today, Rebecca again sticks me with the extra and raises her hand to go see the guidance counselor, and I again have the impulse to save it so I can give it to Tabby later, and decide *fuck all of this* and pull out a book.

I decided to reread *Part-Time Indian,* and Mrs. Shepler's PowerPoint marathons have been the perfect opportunity. I don't feel like staring at an empty seat and imagining what used to occupy that space, and, really, RNA replication can suck my ass.

Evan clears his throat once and thumbs through his empty notebook, glancing nervously at me. Guess what, buddy boy? My notebook's also empty. So you can suck my ass, too.

■ ■ ■

English isn't much better. We've done 180,000 fucking activities "mining for meaningful moments," and we're finally ready to "zoom in on one" and start writing these stupid things. None of which I've done, nor plan to do. Some of us have barely hit puberty—how many significant moments could we have? And why would we want to pinpoint the moments that have made us these half-formed pieces of shit?

I'm reading *Part-Time Indian* when Mr. Ellis comes back to my desk and stands over me.

"Matt, you haven't started any of your three leads yet. What's up?"

"I wanted to see how Alexie sets up his basketball scenes," I lie.

"So you're zooming in on a basketball memory?"

I nod. I don't even have my writing folder out of my book bag.

"Nice."

Even if I did, he'd only find Carny Mo, two more persona poems, and an ode to Internet pornography.

He stares at me a second, like he's about to say more, and nods again, a pained smile on his face. When he walks away, I go back to reading.

Devin Heiner is loving life on the sidelines. It's been a week since he turned his ankle—a "severe sprain" according to Devin's doctor—and he's still using crutches to get around.

Coach was apparently so pleased with our scrimmage last week that he's called for the same matchups every practice since then. It earned Tyler a few minutes of action during the last varsity game, so he's a little less indignant about being relegated to the JV squad during practice runs.

As soon as Leppo brings the ball up the court to start the scrimmage and I meet Branson out on the wing, the intensity picks up right where we left off before, reigniting, like Coach is turning the dial on a gas stove.

We don't say a word to each other—to anyone, really—but I make sure to say *fuck you* with every box-out, every hand in his face, every shot I hit, every foul I commit when he gets by me. In turn, he gets faster, quicker every time down the court, hits more and more shots despite my defense, and never looks at me afterward. In fact, despite playing with more intensity every day, he never shows any emotion at all.

At the end of practice, he's out the door before half the team has gotten their shoes off in the locker room. He doesn't change. Doesn't shower. Just grabs his bag, checks for Tabby's hat, and storms out.

It's everything I imagined at the beginning of the season, isn't it? Like it was fate. Branson takes his game to another level because I work his ass off in practice. Right where I hoped I'd be.

Fate can suck my ass, too.

At home after practice, Mom heats up dinner for me, giving me a long look when she hands me my plate. Dad starts to say something, too, but stops when I hit the stairs up to my room.

Murray's been spending a lot more time in his room lately, too, playing with his stuffed animals, so I haven't had to deal with any Candy Land, thank God.

He's in there now as I pass his open door, sitting on his knees on the floor with Bernard, a few random teddy bears, and Chaz, the bald eagle Webkinz Tabby got him for Christmas.

When my door is closed behind me, I set my dinner plate and glass of milk on my desk.

Before I can stop myself, Tabby's page is up in front of me. I don't need to do this, but there she is. I know what's on here. I check it every night. Her last post, early in the morning on New Year's Day, with a grinning, thumbs-up selfie: *Happy New Year! Don't forget to eat your pork and sauerkraut today! It's good luck—no matter what your digestive tract says!* ;)

Below that, a handful of generic replies throughout the day, then nothing until the first RIP post on Tuesday, from some girl I don't know, probably from the bathroom right after the announcement, getting off on being the first to broadcast her sorrow. Like there's special consideration for those closest to the dead.

Shortly after her post, the stream of RIPs and farewells begins, literally more than a thousand of them. I've read them all. None from me, but I've read them all.

The comments have slowed down now, the newest one from late last night—a kid from Eastern Adams who clearly knows Branson more than he knew Tabby.

Is this really it? It's been eleven days since the accident. Can this really be it? Happy New Year, a thousand online farewells, and then nothing?

I start typing my first comment, something that feels more like me and Tabby.

My New Year's resolution: be less of a douche—JK!

Wow, you're a douche. I hold backspace to clear it, then try again.

Nerds becoming dangerously overpopulated without their natural predator. Please come back!

Seriously? You're a douche and a fucking moron.

I miss you.

My finger's on the button to post, and I feel the burning in my nose again. I take in a jagged breath, hold down backspace again, and scroll all the way up to the top, go back to Tabby's last post for the millionth time.

Happy New Year . . .

I just stare at it, like it's important. But fuck, it's just Instagram. A meaningless couple of thumb strokes on her phone, probably while waiting for her dad to find his keys so they can go.

And then what? I try to imagine everything that happened after. From Tabby's thumbs punching the screen of her phone to that girl in the bathroom thumbing R-I-P and scrolling for the appropriate emoji. What were the moments that existed in between?

Tabby saw me for the last time, waving goodbye with a box of Nerds.

She rode two hours in the car with her dad.

She ate nursing-home pork and sauerkraut with an angry old woman who probably called her a slut.

She got back in the car and was driven home.

But she didn't make it home.

Somewhere between those two posts, while the rest of us were playing Xbox or deciding which new outfit we'd wear for the first day back, Tabby didn't make it home. Her story stopped on a dark, icy road, without any meaning or closure or resolution of any kind. Like the pages of the book were ripped out mid-chapter, page 62, and just thrown away.

But what was on that last page?

I spent that day shooting baskets and working out my plans for the future—how my varsity basketball career would unfold and how I'd fit into Tabby's life. Did she do the same? While she was staring out the window at the passing trees, or listening to the sounds of old people chewing, was she figuring out her plans for the future? Was she picturing where she'd be this time next year?

Was I in those plans?

The shame and the hatred wash over me as soon as I think it, but I can't keep my brain from going where it's going. Fucking asshole.

In the car, in those last moments, was she thinking about me?

You fucking asshole loser. And then what? Would that make her last page a little nicer? Would you feel a little better if you knew she died thinking of you?

I swear to God, if you answer yes, I'll fucking kill you.

I exit out when I hear Mom coming up the steps. She probably thinks I'm looking at porn when she opens the door and sees the blank screen and my burning face.

That's probably better.

"Matty? You doing okay?" she says, touching my shoulder before clearing away my plate and empty glass.

"Yeah. Just tired from practice," I say without looking up at her. I can feel her eyes on me. I reach for my book bag and stand, facing away from her. "I'm going to read and go to bed."

I pretend to root through my bag and finally pull out *Part-*

Time Indian. She's still looking at me, like she wants to say more. Like this would be a good time for another therapy session.

Instead, she says, "Make sure you brush your teeth."

Right.

So when I wake up and face this shit again tomorrow, at least I won't suffer from gingivitis.

CHAPTER THIRTY

IT'S CALLED A WORKING LUNCH

"Matt, have a seat."

I set my tray down on a desk in the front row, drop my book bag next to it, and sit down to eat my chicken patty sandwich.

"So, Matt, I need you to help me out here. You've been one of my best students this year—maybe one of my best ever. You're into the books we've read, your writing is brilliant—my God, your poems . . .

"So I don't understand what's happened with your memoir." He pauses, waits for some kind of response. I chew my chicken patty without looking up. It tastes like paprika and cartilage, drowned in ranch. Mom would have a panic attack. Mr. Ellis continues.

"The rough draft was due on Monday, and I still haven't gotten it from you." He pauses again. "I mean, I thought you were zooming in on a basketball memory. And I'm pumped to see it, but I haven't actually *seen* any of it yet. Do you have it? Can I take a look?"

"I threw it away. I didn't like it."

"Don't throw your writing away, Matt. You know that—it's all useful." He pretends my lost work is a tragedy, but we both know I'm lying.

He takes a deep breath, lets it out slowly.

"Look, Matt. I can't let you skip the assignment and take a zero. It's my class policy. And you're too good to do that to yourself. Is there something else you want to talk about?"

"No." Same old shit. "I just don't know what to write."

Mr. Ellis stands and comes around the front of his desk, jumping at the chance to steer this back to the writing. "Well why didn't you say so? I can help you with that. That's why I'm here!" As if I said, *I don't know what to write because I haven't been able to pin down the perfect topic yet,* when what I'm really saying is *I don't know what to write because this is pointless and it physically hurts my brain to have to play along and fake it with some stupid memory.*

"Okay. Here's what I need you to do." He pulls a sheet of paper from a pile next to him and sets it in front of me. "It's just a simple template for thinking about your memoir. I use these with my students who struggle with writing in general and need a little help laying out their ideas. This should be pretty easy for you, but I want to see what you come up with."

I look down at the worksheet in front of me.

MEMOIR: FINDING THE MOMENTS THAT MATTER

1. NAME IT: What's one of your biggest moments?

2. SHOW: Let the reader *see* it, *hear* it, *feel* it . . .

3. REFLECT: What did you learn or take away from this moment?

I read over this assignment, seething.

"Think it over while—"

"Can I take this home with me? I'll finish it tonight."

"Matt, you're two weeks behind on this already. I'm not sure you've done *any* of the parts yet." He gives me a knowing look, which pisses me off, because he doesn't know anything, beyond the fact that I don't want to do this stupid assignment. Which, in Teacherland, I guess is the only information that really matters. "I'm happy to work with you, give you whatever help you need. But I can't let you skip the assignment. That's my policy."

Wow. I do not give a flying fuck about your policy.

There's no policy for seniors dating freshmen, or for terrible things happening to good people for no reason. But for this, there's a fucking policy.

"Finish your lunch first, then give it a try." He touches the worksheet on my desk. "I'll write you a pass to your next class if you need it."

He goes back and sits behind his desk and busies himself with papers, decidedly leaving me to my thoughts and my writing.

This was the one place—the *one* place—where I got to feel normal. Where I got to laugh and feel smart. Where my brain could think and create and function outside of its normal bullshit.

I don't want to think about who I am right now. I don't want to sit and ponder the moments that have made me this way, that *have made me who I am today.*

I don't want to *be* who I am today.

My half-empty tray sits on the desk beside me, and I'm staring at this stupid paper, these stupid questions. Mr. Ellis looks up at the clock on the wall behind him, then back at me. He lets out a deep breath and goes back to the papers on his desk.

You know what? Fine. Fuck you.

MEMOIR: FINDING THE MOMENTS THAT MATTER

1. NAME IT: What's one of your biggest moments?
   When I lost my friend

2. SHOW: Let the reader *see* it, *hear* it, *feel* it . . .
   When the SUV hit their car, I imagine her chest was crushed and blood exploded from her mouth and nose as she died.

3. REFLECT: What did you learn or take away from this moment?
   I learned that life makes no fucking sense, much like this assignment.

   The End. By Matthew James Wainwright.

The bell rings as I'm writing. When I finish, Mr. Ellis is outside his door, greeting his next class as they trickle in from the hallway.

I grab my bag, leave the tray, throw my paper on his desk, and walk out.

CHAPTER THIRTY-ONE

LET'S JUST GET ON THE BUS ALREADY

That afternoon, Dad drops me off outside the gym for the bus ride to Eastern Adams, one of our last away games of the season.

Coach Wise stands outside the team bus, directing people away.

"Team meeting in the locker room before we go. Head inside, Matt."

Most of the team is already there when I walk into the locker room, sitting silently on the benches, all looking uncomfortable in their dress shirts and ties. I sit down next to Trip in the back, furrow my brows in question. He shrugs in response, and we sit in silence while the last few players trickle in.

Devin Heiner hobbles in last, followed by Coach Wise, who leans against the locker room door.

Damn, did someone else die?

Instinctively, I think of Branson and quickly scan the room, my legs and arms tingling—but, no, he's right there in the front row, his head bowed, Lighty and Leppo on either side of him. Right where he's supposed to be.

Finally, Coach Langley comes out of his office, looks at Coach Wise, who nods that everyone's here.

Coach Langley looks as uncomfortable as the rest of us, sitting here waiting to find out why we're not already on the bus to Eastern Adams.

He unwraps a stick of gum and chews on it violently, pulls out a folded piece of paper, looks at it, folds it back up, and puts it back in his pocket.

"Men, you've listened to me talk about adversity all season. *Overcoming* adversity. And you should be proud—very proud—of the way you've done that, the way you've overcome adversity as a team. At the end of practice, when your legs are burning and you can't imagine one more sprint, you reach down and hit one more opportunity under thirty seconds.

"You show up, early in the morning the day after Thanksgiving, when all your friends are either shopping or sleeping, running off every ounce of turkey you put in you the day before. After a tough loss at Catholic, you came back, you worked hard, you refocused, and you won your next three games. Even on JV—Devin goes down in practice, and his teammates step up. Everybody stepped up, JV and varsity, and we've had the best practices we've had all season. And, believe me, that shows up in games."

I don't know where Coach is going with this, or why we're here listening to it right now. But it does feel good.

"Adversity," he says again with emphasis, slapping his rolled-up game notes in his palm.

Coach runs a hand through his thinning hair then, looking down at the floor, like he's suddenly run out of words and can't remember why we're here. He pulls out another stick of gum and adds it to the first—though the first very well could have disintegrated by now beneath the power of his jaw.

What the hell—

"I've known Liam Branson a long time," he says, quieter, his voice rumbling out of him. He reaches forward and rests his hand on Liam's bowed head. Liam's shoulders quake silently.

No fucking way.

"He's played for me on varsity since he was a sophomore. And I've watched him play, in camps and youth leagues, since he was ten."

Coach takes his hand off Liam's head, and it bows even lower. Next to him, Leppo rests a fist on Liam's shoulder.

I don't want to hear this shit.

"It's rare to see a young man play with so much heart, to see him work so hard for his teammates, no matter the circumstances. But, gentlemen, we play basketball. We play a *game*. It's the best game I know, and I believe you learn things about each other, and about life, that you can't anywhere else. But it's a game. With made-up rules we all agree to follow, and if you lose, you can play another game."

He pauses and takes a deep breath. *Just stop already.*

"Liam's suffered a loss that's not so easy to come back from. Battling adversity that most grown men *can't* overcome. Men, this is where our game can mean something more. When you pull together for your teammate when he needs you most.

"I'm proud of all the things you've accomplished so far this season—and I'll be proud to be your coach no matter what happens the rest of the way. But these last few games, men, these last few games we play for Liam."

The locker room is silent, the entire team—JV and varsity— nodding their heads with such solemn agreement that I want to puke.

The fuck if I'm playing for *Liam* and his great loss.

Coach nods then at Lighty and steps back. Lighty stands and faces the rest of us and pulls his open gym bag onto the bench in front of him.

"Bring it in."

The whole team huddles around them, and I end up stuck behind Branson, still slumped over on the bench, rubbing his face in his hands as the rest of the team looks at him with fire in their eyes, ready to overcome the shit out of some adversity, apparently.

I'm ready to just get on the bus. But it looks like Lighty isn't through stoking this fire for his friend.

"The seniors decided we wanted to do something to show our support. To show everyone that we're united for Liam." He holds out a fist for Liam, who taps it lightly without looking up. "So I got these to wear on our arms for the rest of the season."

He takes a plastic Nike bag out of his gym bag, reaches in, and pulls out a handful of light blue armbands.

The laugh escapes my mouth before I can stop it, and while I'm screaming *You're fucking kidding me* in my head, I'm not a hundred percent clear whether it reaches my lips as well.

Lighty looks like he's about to kill me, but it's Branson, who's shown no emotion in weeks but now has tears streaming down his face, who stands and drills me in the face.

An explosion of white, and I'm out.

"Don't get me wrong, Matt. There will be consequences for his actions," Coach Langley says, standing over me on the locker room bench, my head in my hands, just like Liam a short while ago. Only I'm holding an ice pack to my left eye, which has already swollen shut, and Coach is not nearly as sympathetic to my suffering in this moment.

He waits until the locker room door closes behind Monica the trainer before he continues. We're the only ones here: the rest of the team got on the bus while I was laid out on the floor, and it pulled away while Coach and Monica helped me up and sat me on this bench.

"But right now we need to discuss *your* actions and *your* consequences."

I get the whole "seeing stars" thing now, but that makes it sound a hell of a lot more mystical than it really is.

"Matt, you've done an admirable job this season, performing at the level you have as a freshman. The way you've stepped up in Devin's absence in practice, going head-on with a player much better than you currently are. And I don't say that as an insult, Matt—Liam Branson is one of the top players in the county. Maybe the best player I've ever coached—"

"Yeah, I've heard this already," I say into my hands. I don't look up at Coach, but I hear him breathing, feel the tension roiling off him. I don't mean for it to sound the way it does, but, shit, there's probably only one way that can sound.

"I cannot begin to wrap my brain around what you found funny or off-putting or whatever your issue was with what your teammates did here tonight—what you found so trivial in supporting a teammate when he's gone through hell." He stops, and I can almost feel Coach holding back. "But I will tell you, Matt, it is the most disappointing thing I've ever seen in a locker room."

He takes a moment to compose himself. "Grab your stuff and head outside. Your dad should be here in about five minutes."

The locker room door closes, and I'm alone. I pull the ice

pack off my face and press my finger into the numb swelling over my left eye. My chin sinks lower into my chest, my eyes resting on this stupid-ass light-saber tie. I pull it loose, the two sides dangling, and my face burns at the ridiculousness of it. My mind flashes to Corey Sheridan, and I feel like a stupid little kid again, standing in front of him, feeling the burning in the back of my eyes and nose. I dig my fingers into my hair and squeeze my good eye closed.

What does this mean? Am I off the team?

Why? Because I don't feel sorry for goddam Liam Branson? Because I don't want to work my ass off in his name? Because I don't want every shot I hit—every three I knock down, every opponent I shut down on D—to be dedicated to the Liam-Branson-Is-Going-Through-a-Lot Fund?

Because *I* got punched in the face?

Fuck him. Fuck all of them.

CHAPTER THIRTY-TWO

MR. MINT IS MORE OF A MONSTER THAN WE ORIGINALLY THOUGHT

Coach must have told Dad what happened, because he doesn't say a word when I get in the car. No *How's your day?* or *What happened to your eye?* No Dave Matthews playing, either. He waits silently until I strap in, raises his hand to Coach Langley through the window, and pulls away.

It remains silent the whole ride home—just muffled road noise and the steady airflow from the heater. The sky's already dark. One stupid house still has its Christmas lights on, hanging loose around darkened windows, and for some reason, it infuriates me. I want to jump out of this car and tear them from this lazy asshole's house.

We turn onto our street. The trees blur past in the dark, my one good eye unfocused out the window, but I know the houses by heart. The Hollingers'. The Stambaughs'. The Weavers'. The Hodgsons'.

Tabby's.

Dad backs into our driveway, his headlights shining on a PUBLIC SALE/AUCTION sign in front of Tabby's that wasn't there this morning. Dad stares at it for a moment before backing into the garage, but he doesn't say a word. He's out of the car the second the engine's off.

I wait in the car, staring out across the dark street as the garage door closes. I wait for the garage light to turn off, and when my eyes adjust to the dark, the silhouette of the sign becomes visible again through the grimy garage door window.

Sometime soon, cars will slow down through the circle, read the sign, and see something totally different from what I'm seeing.

New family. New home.

They'll see happiness and potential.

Three bedrooms, two baths.

A half-finished basement that smells a little musty, but with some work . . .

I see one more part of me that's gone.

Mom's waiting inside the door when I come in from the garage. Just the sight of her—the look of concern on her face—makes my eyes start to burn again.

She reaches up to touch my swollen-closed eye.

"It's fine," I say, brushing past her.

I shut my door as soon as I'm inside my room, drop all my shit on the floor.

Now what?

Fucking shit, now what?

The team's probably dressed, getting ready to run out for warm-ups, and I'm here, and I don't know what the fuck I'm supposed to do.

There's nothing left.

I lie down on my bed, try to pull my blankets over me and will myself into sleep, but my eye is throbbing, my body can't relax—like my lungs have forgotten how to breathe on their own and every breath is a conscious effort—and my brain is like some shitty old TV that gets only two fuzzy channels, and it flips back and forth between one showing an unfamiliar starting five walking out onto the court for the JV game, and the other a dark house with a FOR SALE sign posted out front.

I hate them both.

I grab my ball from the floor and wait for the familiar burn while I focus on the rotation of the ball. Why the fuck am I doing this? I'm not sure if I'm even on the team, or if I'll ever be welcomed back. The look on Branson's face when he decked me; the look on Coach's face afterward in the locker room.

I switch to my left hand, my right cramped and burning on the bed beside me, and my brain switches back to the house. Is all their stuff still in there, right where it belonged, right where they left it? All the things that make up a life, and no one's coming to get it.

Are dishes still in the sink? A cereal bowl and spoon dried cloudy? Dregs of coffee, cold at the bottom of the pot? A load of laundry, cold and wrinkled, still in the dryer? All that stuff just sitting inside that dark house. Stuff that, less than a month ago, had a purpose.

Now what?

It's like it's all been left on pause, but no one's coming back to finish the movie. Their screen went black.

I'm about to switch hands again when my door creaks open.

"I'm fine," I say. "Please leave me alone."

It opens farther, followed by shuffling feet. Murray.

"Can you play Candy Land with me?"

The ball rests on my palm for a moment, suspended in front

of my face, then I start shooting again without taking my eyes off the rotation.

"Not right now, Murray."

"Please, Matt?" He takes another step closer.

"Not now. Please get out."

"Pleeease?" he says, closer, his voice getting whiny. I can't deal with this shit.

"Get out."

"You never play with me—"

"Murray—"

"Why can't you just—"

"Murray!"

"Pleeeease, Matty—"

"MURRAY! GET! THE FUCK! OUT!"

The ball flies across the room and crashes into my dresser, sticks of deodorant and shit tumbling off the top.

Murray jumps at the sudden outburst and drops the Candy Land box. Tears are in his eyes before he runs out of the room, his own door slamming shut a second later.

Why can't he just listen the first goddam time?

I get up to get my ball, shove the door closed again. My foot sends the half-open Candy Land box under my bed, cards scattering over the floor—Plumpy faceup on top—before I drop on my back and start shooting again.

The door opens again a minute later, and this time I know without looking that it's Mom, probably just come from Murray's room, who I'm sure is fine, but I'm sure I'll have to hear about this anyway.

I fucking asked him nicely.

Can't somebody else play fucking Candy Land for once?

Tabby would've played, asshole.

Mom's standing there, looking around my room. She bends down and picks a stick of deodorant off the floor, fits the cracked cap back on, and places it on the dresser.

I keep shooting.

"Matthew, look at me."

Her voice comes out calmer than I expected, but I'm not going to look at her. I stay on my bed, watching the perfect back-spin of shot after shot toward my ceiling.

"You know, Matty, everyone's the star of their own movie."

I catch the ball and shift my eyes—only my eyes—to Mom for the first time.

"Really, Mom? What the hell is that supposed to mean?" I shake my head and let out a disgusted sigh, looking back up at the ceiling and shooting again. "I don't need this shit now, too."

But before the next shot even lands in my hand, Mom snatches it out of the air and pins it down onto my chest, hard. She's much quicker than she looks.

"What it means, Matthew"—her voice shakes and her eyes brim with tears—"is that you're not the only one hurting. It's like everyone's supposed to know how much *you're* hurting—and I know you are, Matthew, I do—but not just that you're hurting, that you're hurting the most. That your pain is worse than everyone else's. That they couldn't possibly understand the depths of your pain.

"Because how could they, Matthew? They haven't lived your life. They're not the star of your movie—you are. They're in their own movies, and while you're walking around hating the world for not understanding your pain, they're hurting, too."

Mom sighs and sits down on the edge of the desk chair next to me.

"I keep trying to remind myself this every day as I watch you treat everyone around you worse and worse. And part of me wants to shake you, but I know you're hurting. I know—"

She pauses, looks at me, and takes my silence as an invitation to keep going.

"It's like you think everyone is faking their pain but you. Or that you're the only one who really deserves to suffer over Tabby—the only one with the right to hurt as much as you do."

I hate her, because I *do* believe that. Why shouldn't I believe that?

"I don't mean to say to just get over it. My God, Matthew, *I'm* not over it. I watched her as a *baby,* Matthew. I was there when she learned to walk—it was in our living room. I was there when she got on that bus to kindergarten. When—" She stops, chokes on her words. Then, quieter, "I'll never be over it."

She's right. I don't need for her to be right. I need . . . fuck, I don't know what I need.

Mom's composed herself, regains her course.

"Murray lost a sister, Matthew, same as you. And when he finally reaches out for a little comfort—a simple game with his big brother—you tell him to fuck off."

I've never heard Mom say that before—using my words. It sounds ugly and all wrong.

I'm ugly. All wrong.

"And even Liam, Matthew." She touches my eye now. I don't move. "*Especially* Liam Branson. Enough is enough now. You're not fighting over her anymore. You're both allowed to hurt over

Tabby, just like the rest of us. He's not to blame here. *No one's* to blame. He fell in love with an amazing girl. And his heart is broken now, too. Not just yours. I'm not telling you to get over it," she repeats. "I'm asking you to stop hating the rest of us for it." She looks at the door, then back to me. "And if you can't do that yet, fake it."

She stands, looks at the door again, and her jaw clenches. "Murray's—we're all—hurting enough. We don't need you to add to it. Just fake it."

Mom's lecture fluctuates between sorrow, sympathy, and utter contempt.

I flip from feeling sorry to hating her in equal measure.

"Are you done?" I say.

Her lips purse for a second, but she lets out a long breath, nods, and walks out, closing the door silently behind her.

CHAPTER THIRTY-THREE

HOW MUCH WOOD CAN AN ASSHOLE CHOP . . .

My alarm goes off way too early the next morning for Saturday practice, and I crawl out of bed even though I'm not sure it applies to me anymore.

I get in the shower and stand with my face under the showerhead, hot water stinging my eye, which looks more like an overripe plum stuck to my eye socket. I want it to melt away, along with everything else from last night. Mom never came back in—nor did anyone else—and I was awake past one, flipping through Instagram posts, yearbooks, photo albums, until every image started to lose its meaning.

Around midnight, I got the brilliant idea to call her phone, to see if I could still hear her voice. I don't know where her phone might be, if it actually rang out there somewhere—cutting through the silence in that empty house, maybe—but her voice mail picked up after the first ring.

The first time nearly stopped my heart. Her voice—*Tabby's* voice—right there in my ear, recorded long before any of this. Before high school. Before Branson.

I dialed and redialed for the next hour, her voice bringing some spark of life back to the pictures, and I tried to consume them all at once, like it could somehow get me closer to the real thing. But every time after that first call, just like the photos, the effect got a little weaker, until her voice didn't mean anything anymore, like when you say the same word over and over until it sounds like gibberish and your brain can't connect any meaning to the sound.

Her voice mail turned into a meaningless string of sounds. Not Tabby anymore.

You wanted two things more than anything.

You lost them both.

What the fuck do you want now?

To go back.

A new list forms in my head while the steam fills the room around me.

PEOPLE I'VE ESSENTIALLY TOLD TO FUCK OFF
IN THE PAST TWENTY-FOUR HOURS:

1. Mrs. Shepler
2. Evan Walko
3. Mr. Ellis
4. Branson
5. Coach
6. Okay, basically the entire team
7. Murray
8. Mom

Pretty impressive run, there, M-Dub.

When I come back to my room in my towel, I find an overstuffed duffel bag on my bed. Mom must have done this while I was in the shower, but why? My first thought, honestly, is military school. But that seems pretty quick to organize overnight.

I fight the urge to throw the duffel into the wall across the hallway—start revisiting my list—and crawl back between my sheets. Instead, I throw on sweats and go downstairs to find that Grampa's car is parked out front, even though it's barely six in the morning.

So not military school.

But I am still being sent away.

Grampa's in the kitchen with Mom and Dad, the three of them huddled around the table drinking coffee.

"There he is," Grampa says with a smile when I walk in.

Mom looks pained, but smiles.

Dad doesn't look up from his coffee at all.

"Grampa?" Murray calls in a sleepy voice from the steps behind me.

"Hey, how's my Murray?" Grampa calls back, winking at me, like this is all totally normal. Just a normal January predawn Saturday breakfast visit.

Murray tears past me into the kitchen in his pj's, Chaz the eagle tucked under his arm, and goes straight to Grampa at the table.

"What are you doing here, Grampa?" Murray says, sinking into his side for a hug.

"Thought I'd bring you a little something for breakfast," he says, sliding a box of powdered donuts in front of Murray.

"Are you staying?" he asks, powdered sugar already coating his lips after one bite.

"Just for breakfast. Then me and Matty have to get out of here."

Murray looks up at me, visibly wary of me for maybe the first time in his life.

"Oh" is all he says before squeezing Chaz tighter and climbing into Grampa's lap, reaching for another powdered donut.

Looks like I'm leaving soon.

"I need help with some things before this big snowstorm they're calling for," he says in way of explanation ten minutes into the drive to his house.

I nod and force a smile. He hasn't mentioned my eye, so I'm guessing he knows at least part of the story. Which is fine. I don't know what I'd tell him if he asked. I replay it in my head—laughing at Branson, at Lighty, at the whole team in their little moment of unity; getting drilled in the face by a guy in tears; the whole team grabbing their stuff and walking out to board the bus, ignoring my body laid out on the locker room floor; Coach's palpable disgust. How the hell do you explain that to your grandfather?

The sun's barely up, buried behind a wall of slate-gray clouds, and my body sinks into the couch-like passenger seat of Grampa's white boat of a car. My brain's a scrambled mess, and I don't know if I'm missed at practice right now or not, but it does feel good to be driving away.

Like he's reading my mind, he says, "Sometimes it's good to step out of your own life for a while. Call a time-out."

He reaches over and bumps my leg, then turns the volume up a little on his old-school R & B station, and we stay like that for the rest of the hour's drive to their house.

"Let's see if we can't get Gramma to make us some pancakes," Grampa says, climbing out of the car.

Gramma and Grampa's house sits roughly in the middle of nowhere, a long, low one-story house off a back-country road surrounded by woods and cornfields, a good twenty minutes from the nearest town. From the edge of their driveway, you can look out over a few sloping hills and catch a glimpse of the lake in the nearby state park. With the steel cloud cover and freezing temperatures, though, I can't find it in the distance.

"But let's not mention the donuts," he whispers as I pass by him through the front door.

Gramma envelops me in a hug, a spatula in one hand. She holds my face with the other, runs a thumb down my temple around my swollen eye.

"That was easy," Grampa says, walking in the door behind me and clapping me on the shoulder.

I put my bag in the spare bedroom where I always sleep, then start setting the table in the kitchen while Gramma tends to the griddle. Because that's what you do at Gramma's. You can suck at being a human in your daily life, but at Gramma's you set the table without being asked.

After an obscene stack of chocolate chip pancakes and an equally absurd pile of bacon, I start to feel somewhat human again. Bloated, but human. Gramma and Grampa asked questions about basketball and school while we ate, which felt weird at first, but they spoke as though neither one was permanently ruined. Which maybe means they don't know what's happened in the past couple of days, but still.

"All right," Grampa says, pushing back from the table. "We've got work to do."

"You make sure Matty does it," Gramma warns, clearing plates. "You're too old to be swinging that thing around."

"Ahhh." He waves her off—though we both know he'll listen—and I follow him out to the backyard.

Half of Grampa's backyard butts up against a farmer's field—right now the jagged black remains of cornstalks sticking out of the frozen earth—while the other half borders woods that run along the edge of the cornfield until the treeline disappears over the next hill a few hundred yards away. Just out from the woods in the yard sits a humongous, ancient tree stump, leveled off about two feet above the ground. Grampa uses it to split wood for the fireplace.

A truckload of cut logs covers the ground behind the stump.

"That's a big ax," I say, admiring the red-handled behemoth that sits in the center of the stump, like the lumberjack equivalent of the sword in the stone (Canadian release only).

"That is a big ax," Grampa confirms. "A maul, actually. Wider head. Better for splitting."

"Noted."

We stand for a moment, admiring the maul in a haze of testosterone, before Grampa snaps us both out of it, clapping and rubbing his hands together.

"All right, this storm tonight is supposed to dump a good foot of snow on us, and we're about out of wood for the fireplace. I've been a little slow on my chopping this year," he adds, sliding the maul off the edge of the stump, and I catch a twinge of shame in his voice. Suddenly, I'm ready to chop the shit out of this wood.

Grampa walks around behind the stump and lifts a log from the pile—with seemingly a lot less effort than his momentary shame would indicate—and places it in the center of the stump.

"Grab Cass, here," he says, nodding to the maul.

"Cass?"

"That's what I call her," he replies. "Your Gramma had an aunt Cass. Not a very nice woman. Wide face—wide everything, really—and would cut you down in a heartbeat."

"Fitting," I say, grabbing Cass by the handle and lugging her to the ground next to me.

"Lucky you never met her."

He's about to dive into a story—likely one Gramma wouldn't appreciate him sharing with me—but stops himself.

"You remember how to do this?" he asks. He taught me when I was about twelve, with a much smaller ax and less-than-fruitful results. That's also the last time I held an ax.

"I think so," I say.

"Legs apart. Swing straight down. Let the ax do the work once it's dropping."

"Got it."

"And don't take your leg off," he adds. "Gramma will kill me."

"Thanks for the vote of confidence."

He laughs and rests both his hands on my shoulders.

"You'll be okay."

And I know by the way he says it that he's talking about more than splitting wood.

I nod and feel my eyes burn. My voice has suddenly stopped working, but Grampa's already headed for the garage behind me.

I attempt to obliterate the first log, but the first few swings rattle my entire skeleton, my arms stinging numb before I figure out what he meant by *Let the ax do the work.* It's not unlike *Turn your stupid brain off,* but it's a little easier to manage with the maul.

It's not long before I'm sweating, despite the subfreezing temperatures and the gray, sunless sky, and I've got my coat on the ground behind me and my sweatshirt sleeves pushed up.

Even playing nonstop basketball, my muscles are not prepared for this—I can feel the strain in my back and shoulders before I'm finished with the first log. But the burn feels good, and I start to find a rhythm.

My mind is a blur. The better I get at splitting wood—the more my downswings go slicing through the wood and into the stump with a satisfying, jarring thump—the more my brain opens up, flashing through random, incoherent clips of shitty moments.

Corey Sheridan leaning over his handlebars.

Shoving extra science packets to the bottom of my book bag.

Tabby waving as she hops into the black Accord.

Air-balling threes.

Crying on the bench in youth league.

Lighty singing *cockmonster* to a grinning Branson in the locker room.

Standing in the back of the church, too far away to see her.

Lighty draping a heavy arm over a sinking Branson.

Watching closed caskets lifted into the back of hearses.

Tabby's face reading my stupid do list.

Murray's face at the table this morning.

No order. No logic. Just a different snapshot with every swing, some repeating, some not even real, creating this incoherent montage of shit, and I keep swinging.

"Christ almighty, kid," Grampa says, pulling up behind me with a wheelbarrow. "Pace yourself. Take a breather."

He slowly fills the wheelbarrow with split logs, pats me again on the shoulder before wheeling the load to a low stack outside the back door, before disappearing into the garage.

And I start again.

Grampa returns and loads the wheelbarrow I don't know how many times, all without a word. But by late afternoon—the wide pile by the back door now stacked four feet high and two rows deep, the light already fading—the first heavy snowflakes start falling from the sky. They're so big you can hear them land, a thin layer coating the backyard within minutes.

"Good timing," Grampa says, placing the last of the wood on the top of the pile. "Thank you, Matty."

I take the wheelbarrow to the garage for him and meet him back inside.

My sweats are drenched, and even though I don't feel it, my limbs are ice-cold, and it finally hits me how exhausted I am.

"Why don't you go take a warm shower?" Gramma calls from the kitchen. "We'll have dinner in a little bit."

■　■　■

That evening, after a long shower and three of Gramma's bacon grilled cheeses, I'm sprawled out on an old easy chair in the living room next to the fire. Gramma's on the sofa, absorbed in one of her historical romance novels we like to tease her about. Grampa's on his giant La-Z-Boy, fooling with a crossword puzzle, a muted basketball game playing on the TV.

I watch mindlessly, occasionally staring out the window behind me at the falling snow, as the day finally catches up with me.

I'm miles away from everything else in my life. My hands are covered in blisters, my muscles are screaming, my eye is throbbing, and I can barely lift my arms—and it actually feels okay.

CHAPTER THIRTY-FOUR

WAKE, PART II

How the hell does Grampa live out here and not own a snow-blower?

The storm dumped at least a foot. When I woke up this morning in bed—I barely remember climbing in last night—it was after eleven and still going. The first shock, though, was attempting to stand up. I was *literally* sore from head to toe, including a number of places I didn't know *could* get that sore.

The third big shock—number two was Grampa sheepishly revealing the lack-of-snowblower situation while I was having cereal—is attempting to lift the first giant shovelful of snow from the driveway. My arms and back scream in protest, promptly give out, and I dump the shovelful back into the block it had sliced out of the drift.

Okay.

The snow's tapered to flurries now, and I find their mailbox poking up out of the snow at the end of the driveway a few hundred feet away.

The physical punishment ended up being a good thing yesterday, right?

I attack the snow again, ignoring the pain, and within a few minutes, I've got a small strip of driveway carved out along the garage, and the soreness has given way to a general burning all over.

Within an hour, the last flurries have stopped, and the sun is fighting through the remaining clouds, reflecting blinding white off the thick blanket that covers everything but the quarter of Grampa's driveway I have cleared, and it's breathtaking.

I miss home.

I miss Tabby.

I miss before.

I've fucked so much up since Tabby died, and I just want to go back, handle it all differently.

Murray must be loving this. He must've shit when he woke up this morning and saw *this*. He'd have been in my room before eight, shaking me awake and demanding I get up and see before bugging Mom to let us outside.

At least, he would have before yesterday.

Fuck.

I go back to attacking the snow, launching each shovelful as far as I can into the yard.

Tabby would've loved this, too.

She would have been out her front door as soon as she saw Murray and me out there, grinning as she waded through the shin-deep snow across the circle, eating fresh handfuls the whole way, and flopping down on her back as soon as she reached us to make a snow angel, which Murray would immediately copy, laughing next to her.

I miss her.

Tears stream down my face, and I keep shoveling.

■ ■ ■

If I could sit around that table again with my family after Tabby's funeral, I'd put that fucking egg roll down and tell them how I remember the forts we used to build in the snowdrifts after the plows came through the circle. We'd spend half the day planning and digging, tunnels connecting different chambers loaded with premade snowballs, just in case of an attack.

Then I'd tell them how we fell in love with *Return of the Jedi*, especially—despite Dad's eye-rolling—the Ewoks, and how Tabby could do a frighteningly good Jabba impersonation.

I'd tell them about how, the summer we were ten, I hit a lightning bug with a Wiffle ball bat and laughed and mock-ooohed at how it stayed lit and arced through the air, dead and glowing. And then how Tabby took the bat out of my hands and hit me in the arm with it full force, the same way she'd slam Corey Sheridan a couple of years later. I never ever hit a lightning bug after that.

I'd tell them how much I miss my friend.

God, how the fuck can she be gone?

The sun hangs low in the sky, and I'm not sure how long I've been standing at the end of the driveway, staring into it, or how long I've been crying, but when I turn around, Grampa's sitting in a lawn chair inside the garage, a steaming mug in his hands, an empty lawn chair next to him.

I drag my body back up the driveway to the garage.

"How ya feel?" Grampa asks.

"Okay."

He pats the chair next to him and produces another steaming mug from the floor beside him and hands it to me.

"Gramma made hot chocolate for you."

I take my sopping gloves off and wrap my fingers around the mug, then suck a few molten marshmallows off the top.

"Thank you, Matty. It would've taken me three days to do all this. And a lot of Bengay."

I smile, which takes about all the energy I have left at the moment. "Anytime, Grampa."

"You're a good kid," he says, shaking my knee with his hand. I feel like a six-year-old, but right now, that doesn't feel too bad.

We sit silently in our lawn chairs, like we're lounging on the beach staring out into the waves instead of sitting in a freezing garage, our breaths visible, staring at an asphalt ribbon cut into a sheet of white.

I don't know how or why I feel okay right now. Grampa's a fucking Jedi.

I take another swig of hot chocolate, rest my mug on my stomach, and let out a long sigh. Grampa does the same.

"Grampa, did I ever tell you about the time Tabby hit me with a Wiffle ball bat?"

CHAPTER THIRTY-FIVE

GRAMPA'S STORY

Day of chopping. Day of shoveling. Blisters on top of blisters. Grampa laughs when I stagger out of bed at noon, standing shakily in the kitchen like an eighty-year-old dementia patient.

"You kinda look like you pooped your pants," he says, watching me wobble, half hunched over, to the fridge.

"I might have," I say. "I can't really tell."

"Sometimes I can't, either."

So today I rest.

On Tuesday, there's still no mention of leaving, or missing school or practice. The roads were plowed yesterday, but otherwise I have no idea if school got canceled, or if I'm just AWOL. I do miss home, but part of me is scared that I'm missing a version of home that doesn't exist anymore—that if I go home, I'll find myself pulled right back into the spiral of shit Grampa lifted me out of. Tabby's still gone. Basketball's still fucked. I still hurt Murray and who knows who else. Still the same asshole. So maybe I'm better off here.

Sometime after breakfast—well, my breakfast, anyway—

Grampa asks if I'd mind taking a ride with him, just as I've come out of the bathroom.

"Uh, sure."

He nods and turns back down the hallway to the kitchen, grabs his keys off the counter and two bottles of root beer from the fridge.

Right. He means now.

This is my fourth day, and we still haven't talked about why I'm here—no mention of what happened to my eye, or how my parents had me shipped off without telling me, or any part of how my life is clearly coming apart at the seams. I suspect this "ride" is the time for that conversation.

But it doesn't come.

So far, thirty minutes in, it really is just a ride. We cruise along Pennsylvania country two-lanes I don't recognize, other than that they don't lead back home. We travel through hamlets and little stoplight towns I've never heard of, and I swear, it seems like Grampa is getting tenser the longer we go, like *he's* the one who suddenly doesn't want to talk about anything, tapping his thumbs against the steering wheel even though the radio is too low to hear.

After nearly an hour, sitting at a stoplight in a little town called Newville, I break this bizarre silence.

"So where are we headed, Grampa?" I say, forcing a laugh.

He turns to me and smiles, his eyes wet.

"Sorry, bud," he says, his voice strained. "We're almost there."

What the hell?

Is he taking me to the crash site? What the fuck?

My heart goes haywire in my chest, and, even though we're

sitting in the middle of a town, I look all around us for the sharp turn where it happened.

But right outside of Newville, as we're about to drive back into snow-blanketed fields, we pull into the parking lot of a small redbrick church sitting alone in a copse of leafless trees.

"Just a quick stop," he says, turning off the engine, staring into the trees behind the church, and I can't help thinking, *On the way to what?* We've driven an hour into nowhere, in silence, to an empty old church on a Tuesday morning, and Grampa's suddenly not Grampa out here. What the hell are we doing?

He gets out of the car after another silent stretch, and I follow him to the end of the shoveled walkway behind the church. Beyond the cluster of leafless trees, penned in from the surrounding fields by an old wrought-iron fence, weathered headstones stick up out of the snow.

Grampa still seems like he's on another planet. He turns to me and looks like he's about to finally start talking, but stops. His eyes are still glassy and he gives me another difficult smile, pulls his hand over his mouth, and pats me on the side of my arm before walking right into the snow, sinking in past his ankles.

There's an open archway into the cemetery about a hundred feet away, beneath the last of the trees, but that path hasn't been shoveled. Just Grampa making his own with his boots. I follow.

I don't understand, but I follow.

Are his parents buried here, my great-grandparents? Why the hell would he bring me an hour up here in the snow on a Tuesday morning for this?

He passes beneath the archway and into the cemetery, breaking new snow with each step. The sun is bright, but the air is frigid, and he has his hands deep in his coat pockets. I'm looking around at everything as we walk—names on headstones, a pair of cardinals landing on the fence and flying off again, the coil of chimney smoke from a farmhouse in the distance—but his focus seems set on a point in the back right of the cemetery.

About three-quarters of the way along what I assume is the main path, Grampa turns down a row to the right, passes ten or more headstones without acknowledgment, then stops between two of matching gray granite.

I come up next to him, shoulder to shoulder. On the left:

ELIZABETH MARIE STAUB WAINWRIGHT
6/12/1941—10/10/1963

On the right:

LAURA ELIZABETH WAINWRIGHT
9/30/1961—10/10/1963

"That was my first wife, Beth," he says, indicating the grave on the left.

I look at him, confused, but he steps forward to the headstone and brushes snow off the top. He rests both hands on top and bows his head, and I still don't get what the hell is going on, but I feel like I'm intruding standing here, seeing something I'm not meant to see.

I piece together what I can, watching Grampa. A twenty-two-year-old wife—not Gramma, obviously. A two-year-old girl—not my dad, obviously. I'm trying to figure out the math, with my dad, with me, when Grampa takes a deep breath, runs his hands over the top of the headstone, and moves to the headstone next to it.

Laura Elizabeth Wainwright.

A little girl.

He does the same as at the first—brushing off the snow, resting his hands, bowing his head—but for this one, he lowers himself to his knees, almost like he's trying to get eye level with a little kid. And then, after a couple of minutes, the snow soaking into his knees, I see him reach into his coat pocket and pull out a little bag, and I watch him place what appear to be white mini-marshmallows—three of them—on top of the headstone.

He pushes himself back to his feet, brushing snow from his pants. He faces me again, one hand still resting on the headstone.

"This was my first child. Laura."

He looks back down at the items he placed on the grave.

"She loved marshmallows," he explains, looking almost embarrassed, reaching out and squeezing one between his fingers. "Little turkey ate a whole bag of them once. Pulled them out of the drawer when we weren't watching."

He laughs to himself, then looks back up, sheepish, and steps back to where I'm standing.

"It's kind of stupid," he says quietly. "She'd be in her fifties now."

I have no idea what to say to this, other than "I'm pretty sure I'll still like marshmallows in my fifties."

And Grampa wraps me in a huge, tight hug, and suddenly I'm crying—like, tears-running-off-my-chin, getting-snot-on-Grampa's-coat crying, and I don't even know why.

"I meant to tell you on the way up here," he says after a

minute, his voice thick. "But I couldn't seem to get the words out. Know what I mean?"

I nod into his shoulder.

I know what he means.

"They were on their way home from Beth's grandmother's," Grampa says, both hands around his mug of coffee in the booth across from me.

Sun streams through the windows of the Newville Diner, thawing us from our time in the cemetery.

"How old were you?"

"Twenty-three. Not all that much older than you, really, crazy as that seems. One of my first years of teaching. Fifth graders. It didn't go very well." Grampa shakes his head, remembering. "I just hated everyone after the accident. My two girls were gone, but I still had to get up in front of a roomful of ten- and eleven-year-olds every day and pretend like I cared about them learning long division or parts of speech."

I sip at my soda and wait for him to continue.

"I got meaner and meaner. It seemed like all these little shits, they were so wrapped up in their kid drama—who pushed who, who liked him or her—when I'd had my whole family ripped away from me for no reason. And I hated them for it." He shakes his head again, ashamed. "Ten-year-olds."

My mind flashes to Mr. Holowitz. Our Frick-and-Frack year. First girlfriends. All good memories now.

"Those were the days when we paddled kids in school," Grampa continues, staring into his coffee mug. "By Christmas, a kid was getting it about every day. Usually the same ones."

This is almost impossible to picture. My grandpa, the friendliest, kindest man I know, being mean to *anyone* just doesn't compute. And kids? Forget it.

I pick at my fries while he talks, rapt. But he barely touches his food at all—keeps his hands wrapped around his coffee mug and continues.

"David Flickinger—I'll never forget his name—was one of the toughest, nastiest, neediest kids I ever had. And the meaner I got, the more he pushed back. One day, he was really struggling—we both were struggling. I think he'd already gotten paddled early that morning, and he was flat-out mad, and every time I turned around to write on the board, he'd flip me the bird. And, you know, kids are kids—they started laughing at this, and it must've egged him on to take it to another level. I hadn't caught him yet, but I knew he was doing *something* behind me. So I decided to take an extra-long time writing on the board, you know, really give him some time to get carried away with himself."

The story's almost funny, but Grampa does not enjoy telling it.

"When I whipped around to catch him, he was standing on his chair, pants down, shaking his little ass at me, both middle fingers in the air."

I laugh. I can't help it.

"I broke the paddle," he says through a humorless smile. "Little booger didn't even cry."

"Do you know whatever happened to that kid?"

"Jail," he says, expressionless. "I know he had a whole world of baggage with him, and you make your own choices as an adult, but I also know that I own a little piece of that one. I never hit a kid after that. I shouldn't have been allowed to step foot in a classroom after that."

This from the man who spent another forty years in education, who went on to be an elementary school principal who was adored by everyone, according to Dad.

"When my principal—who was actually a very nice man—confronted me about it after getting a call from that boy's horrible mother, I may have suggested an inappropriate act he could go handle alone."

"And you didn't get fired?"

"Another teacher stepped in. A friend of mine down the hall who knew what was going on. I don't know how she convinced him, but she started checking in on me after that, every day. And at first I was just as awful to her, too, but she kept showing up, kept talking, kept helping, kept waiting for me to pull my head out of my ass."

He smiles finally. "Over fifty years later, she's still waiting."

"Wait, seriously? Gramma?"

"Pretty nice ending, huh?"

"Wow. Yeah."

He looks down into his mug again, says quieter, smile gone, "Pretty nice ending. Look, Matty, I don't talk about this much. It doesn't do me any good. I've got a beautiful life—a lifetime with your Gramma, your dad and mom, you, Murray . . ."

It's crazy to think about—this whole life and family that predates Gramma and all of us, all of this. Is this what will happen with me? Will all this just be a life that predates my real one someday? Will Tabby matter that little? I mean, watching Grampa in the cemetery, it clearly still matters to him, but it's like this part of him that's buried, this part of him that no one else will ever know about. Is that really all I get to take from Tabby? A sad memory to bury while I start a different life?

Grampa again seems to read my mind.

"You can say it," he says.

I pick up another fry and put it back down. "So what's the point? I mean, is there no reason for anything that happens? Just deal with it and move on?"

"Seems that way, doesn't it?" That's not the answer I was expecting. He takes his glasses off and sets them down next to his coffee cup, stares at them for a moment. "I don't know what the point of all this is, Matt. There are times—like with Beth and Laura, with Tabby—where there can't possibly be a point. Others, it's like the stars have lined themselves up just for you. I spent a lot of years trying to make those two fit together somehow." He looks right at me now. "I'm not sure they ever do. I decided, however long I get, if I can spend time with the people I love, I don't really care what the point is. If there's a God—and I'm pretty skeptical, myself—I figure he can fill me in when my time comes. Otherwise, I want to spend my time with the people I love."

"I miss her," I say.

"Me too."

"And I know you found Gramma, and everything turned out well—I mean, I'm glad I'm here—but I don't want her to be a memory. I don't want her death to be the shitty part of my happy movie."

"Yeah," he says, "I understand. Like I said, Matty, I have a beautiful life—a perfect family that maybe I love and appreciate even more fiercely because of what happened, and I know I wouldn't change a thing. I wouldn't change a *thing*. But sometimes, as awful as this sounds, I hate myself for it.

"I twist it all around in my mind, and it's like I'm saying I'd let my girls die all over again if I had the choice, because everything's turned out great for me. Like I'd kiss my little girl one last time and send her off. And I know that's stupid—of course I didn't choose for it to happen that way—but I guess that's how guilt works. It sneaks up on you sometimes," he says, staring out the window, back toward the cemetery. "That's usually when I make a trip up here."

The waitress comes by to ask if we're finished, which pulls Grampa back. She leaves the check on the table for us and clears the table, Grampa's plate still untouched.

"I'm sorry for dumping all this on you, Matty," he says, staring blankly at the check. "This was all supposed to help somehow, but I've totally lost why."

"It does," I say, and I mean it. Because (1) it *does* help. Maybe not how he intended, but it almost feels good to see that it still hurts all these years later, even if he does have a beautiful life. That he's still just as pissed at the universe. And (2) seeing as reason number one makes no fucking sense, I'm almost relieved to know that it's not just *my* brain that's a jumbled, masochistic mess. Maybe it's genetic.

(You're welcome, future Wainwrights!)

"Your eye's looking better," Grampa says in the car, a few minutes from the house.

We've talked most of the way back from Newville. About loving Tabby still, and losing her, and how to move forward without hating myself for it.

"Should soon be able to see well enough to get your shot back. Sounds like you had a pretty good season."

Had a pretty good season, I think. We still haven't acknowledged the fact that the team's wrapping up the season right now without me. Trip's running the floor whether I'm there or not, and I wonder if I'm as easy to replace as Devin Heiner. Shit, it's just JV. Not like anybody's even printing our records in the paper.

"I don't think it matters anymore, Grampa." I look at my reflection in the side mirror, my left eye still a little swollen, though the plum has turned a sickly yellow around the edges.

"Why is that? You don't want to play anymore?" he asks.

I turn and look at him, making sure if he's serious. "I'm pretty sure I'm off the team," I say.

"For getting punched in the face?"

"For getting myself punched in the face."

"By that Branson boy?"

I nod.

"The one who'd been seeing Tabby?"

I nod again.

"Matty. You made a bad decision. In the middle of the worst time in your life. That's all. I don't think you're done for good."

"Coach Lang—"

"I've known Coach Langley a long time, Matthew. He was one of my students—after I was done being an asshole," he adds. "You'll be fine. You don't get judged solely by your worst moments."

I keep picturing the look on Coach's face, the disgust in his voice in the locker room, and I can't imagine walking back in there.

"You'll be fine," Grampa says. "You've got a lot of work to do. But you had a lot of work to do before any of this, too, right?"

I nod. I planned to work my ass off to make varsity next year.

"So keep doing it. Don't kill yourself over what's happened this season. Believe me, Langley knows all about hurt. He understands. Play hard. Be good to your teammates. And be good to yourself, Matty."

I manage an okay, my chest tight again as we pull into the driveway.

It's amazing: that's pretty much the same advice I've tried giving myself—play hard, turn off your brain—but it sounds so much better coming from Grampa.

CHAPTER THIRTY-SIX

GRAVY MAKES EVERYTHING BETTER, PART III

I don't recognize the cars in front of Tabby's house when we pull into the circle, nearly two weeks after Grampa picked me up, and his words from that morning finally hit home.

Sometimes you have to step out of your own life for a while. Call a time-out.

The sign is gone. A green hatchback sits in the driveway, its hatch open. The garage door is up as well, and two little kids—maybe smaller than Murray—are inside playing with empty boxes. A young woman steps out of the garage and waves to me before pulling more boxes from the car and disappearing back inside.

"You okay?" Grampa asks, setting my bag on the ground and squeezing his arm around my shoulder.

"Yeah," I say, grabbing my bag.

After our trip to Newville, I stayed with Gramma and Grampa for another week, helping Gramma clean out the attic, splitting more wood, having daily talks with Grampa at various diners, eating anything and everything Gramma put in front of me, even writing a bit—at their encouragement—in yellow-edged notebooks that we found in Gramma's stash of old classroom supplies, one of which had R2-D2 and C-3PO on the cover. Which will not be revealed to Trip under any circumstances.

It really was a time-out.

It's not like any of my problems took care of themselves while I was gone—the problems were with *me*, and they're right where I left them. But my head is in a better place to deal with them now.

I had to step out of my life for a while.

So I will not shove those two children aside and storm into their house to make sure they aren't messing up Tabby's room, because that's completely insane, right?

Right.

Good talk.

I am overwhelmed by the unmistakable force that is Mom's gravy as soon as I step foot inside the house behind Gramma and Grampa, and I immediately feel tears in my eyes.

Seriously, who cries over gravy?

Get ahold of yourself, M-Dub—you're losing your shit already.

Mom wraps me in a hug immediately, telling me how much she's missed me, and Dad's close behind her, teary-eyed and chewing discreetly, clearly having snuck a hunk of stuffing the moment Mom left the kitchen.

Murray's already in Grampa's arms, cutting glances at me, Bernard and Chaz both tucked under his arm. When Mom releases me, I walk over to them.

"Hey, buddy. I missed you," I say, leaning in to give him a

light head butt. He reaches out and wraps his little arms around my neck, a stuffed animal in each hand. I breathe in deeply and more tears stream down my face.

Honestly, this gravy is a menace.

Murray is attached to me during dinner. His chair literally touches mine. He sits on his knees to eat, wriggling, jabbering through mouthfuls of food—despite Mom's repeated admonishments—about everything he's done over the past two weeks, from building snowmen to making animal documentaries to even meeting the new neighbors, which breaks my heart all over again, knowing Tabby's already fading for him.

After he's excused from the table, I get a chance to just listen to the grown-ups talk about nothing and slow my brain down a little. I'm about to reach for a third helping of stuffing when Murray appears again in the doorway from the living room, Candy Land in his hands, Bernard and Chaz perched on top of the lid.

I notice Mom pause mid-conversation, just for a moment, glancing at Murray, and then me. I drop the serving spoon back into the tray.

"I was just thinking that," I say to Murray, and follow him into the living room.

Instead of our usual one-on-one Candy Land bout, Murray sets out a token for Bernard, as well as one for Chaz, who, after his first card, I decide has a pompous, regal voice, but with intermittent squawks he can't seem to control.

"Oh, excuse me, my good man, but I believe this double-

purple permits me to—*SQUAWK!*—travel the Gumdrop Pass—
SQUAWK!"

"Right-o, guv-nah!"

It's a lot to keep up with, but Murray's loving it.

And wouldn't you know it, even with four players, I still pull that motherfucker Plumpy, coming down the home stretch.

Murray cackles with delight.

Kid's a shark.

CHAPTER THIRTY-SEVEN

I'M READY FOR SOME SERIOUS SCIENCE PACKETS

I stay home the next day, Friday, my last day being AWOL. But Mom drives me into school after dismissal to get makeup work from my teachers and turn in my basketball gear.

She pulls up in front of the school and parks along the curb.

"I'll wait in the car," she says, opening her book. "Take your time."

I decide to take care of basketball first.

I find Coach Langley in the locker room office, chatting with two of the wrestling coaches. The rest of the team turned in their uniforms and practice jerseys yesterday, two days after our last game. The season's officially over. My stomach drops and my whole body feels numb, but I force myself to knock.

"Hey, Matt. Come on in."

I pull my stack of jerseys out of my bag and hand them over, half expecting him to rip them out of my hands. But he tosses them on separate piles stacked against the wall and checks my name off on a clipboard on his desk.

Without looking up, he says, "Open gyms start up in two weeks."

"I'll be there."

"Better be," he says.

I nod and go, wondering what the hell just happened.

So. (1) Grampa is, in fact, a Jedi. (2) I am going to work my ever-loving ass off.

On to the teachers.

After an alarming hug and a stack of study guides from Mrs. Shepler, my book bag is loaded down, and I have one last stop. Mr. Ellis.

Even more than with Coach, I am dreading having to face Mr. Ellis. The last time I saw him, he was confronting me about a major assignment I refused to do. Then when he tried to help, I essentially told him his assignments were pointless and to shove it up his ass. And this to my hands-down favorite teacher of all time. Nice.

Like I said, calling a time-out didn't make my shit disappear. Maybe now, though, I can handle his disappointment *without* telling him to fuck off.

When I turn the corner to his hallway, though, I freeze. Mr. Ellis is sitting on the floor outside his room, staring into an open locker. I know whose it is.

Mr. Ellis does a double take when he sees me and gets to his feet, one hand on the locker door like I've caught him in the middle of something embarrassing and he can't decide whether to close the locker.

"Matt," he says, looking into the locker again, then back at me. "I'm sorry. I didn't realize you were coming in today." He puts a hand on my shoulder when I reach him, then quickly pulls it away.

Tabby's locker is mostly empty, tidy, her textbooks and binders stacked on the bottom, a couple of random items on the top shelf, the rest probably cleaned out by Tabby before she left for Christmas break.

"I was finally getting around to cleaning it out," he says quietly in explanation. "Haven't been able to get myself to do it, and no one's asked for the books yet."

I stare, breathless.

"I loved that girl," he says, and I look at him, stunned, but he's still staring into the open locker. "She was in my homeroom. And my last-period class. What an awesome human being."

I can't respond to this—I feel like I might have to sit down on the floor, too, my eyes burning.

He reaches into the top of the locker, picks up a hairbrush and sets it back down. He reaches in farther, then chuckles, and pulls out an empty box of Nerds, smiling and shaking his head with tears in his eyes.

I don't know what the dying-animal noise is that escapes my mouth, but it startles Mr. Ellis. I reach for the empty box, and now I do sit, dropping to my knees on the floor.

I don't want to cry in front of this man. I really don't. I'm supposed to have my shit together now. Time-out, and all. But here I am, on the floor of an empty hallway, sobbing into a tiny, empty candy box like a freaking lunatic.

Mr. Ellis helps me to my feet and pulls me into a hug. Not how this was supposed to go.

"I'm so sorry, Matt. I didn't know."

I force myself under control, clutching the empty box. "No. Sorry. It's okay," I stammer, wiping at my eyes.

He leads me into his empty classroom and sits down in a student desk in the front. He pulls out the chair next to him for me to sit, and I do, taking deep breaths but not letting go of the box.

"So you two were pretty close, huh?"

I nod. "She was my neighbor." I shake my head—that sounds stupid. "We grew up together," I try again. "She was one of my closest friends. My first friend." Which still doesn't sound quite right—not enough. How do I explain what Tabby was?

"I'm so sorry, Matt," he says again when we've both calmed down a bit. "I had no idea. Your memoir—I never meant for you to have to—"

"No, it's okay," I say. "You shouldn't be apologizing. I'm the one who was a jerk. I'm sorry I wrote what I did—for not writing at all before that. I'm sorry I've treated you the way I have in class."

"No, don't worry about it, Matt. I understand now."

We go on deflecting each other's apologies for a few minutes before I finally pull myself together.

I rub my eyes again. "Okay, I didn't actually come here to cry all over you," I say. "I wanted to get any makeup work from the past two weeks. Besides the memoir. I'm coming back on Monday."

Mr. Ellis smiles and shakes his head. "You're good, Matt. Let's start fresh on Monday. And please don't worry about the memoir. I'm just excited to have you back in class. We've missed you."

I don't know that I buy all that, but it feels good, nonetheless. And I do miss being in here. Trip, and Mr. Ellis, and feeling normal, and funny, and halfway intelligent again.

"Thanks, Mr. Ellis."

"Oh, hey," Mr. Ellis says as I stand up to leave. "I don't know if you've heard, or seen any of the posters." He nods to one hanging inside his classroom door. "But the students and staff have organized a dance-a-thon. For Tabby. It's tomorrow, all day."

I walk to the poster and read.

TABBI-THON—1st Annual Memorial Dance-a-thon in Memory of Tabitha Laughlin

The text is imposed over a black-and-white image of the student section from one of the basketball games, Tabby in the center, face painted, hair braided, huge varsity jacket draped over her raised arms.

"The school's set up a scholarship in Tabby's name, so all the money raised will go to getting it started. I'm hoping we can do it every year."

I nod, still looking at the poster, again unable to get any words to come out.

"It should be pretty emotional, but fun. I think a lot of us need that."

"Cool" is the best I can manage to choke out, still staring at Tabby's image—one that broke my heart before but obliterates it now.

"Hope I see you there, then, Matt. And thank you for coming in."

"Thanks," I say, forcing a smile without meeting his eyes. I give a small wave with the hand still clutching the Nerds box and walk out.

It's a good thing.

It is. I know it is.

But knowing it doesn't stop these waves of resentment. Of jealousy.

But it's okay. It is.

Other people loved her, too. And I'm sure they are hurting, and this is a good thing they're doing in her name. It's good. Had it been for someone else, Tabby would have loved it. And talked about it, and raised money for it, and badgered me about it, and danced her heart out the entire time. Of course other people loved her.

I've been so obsessed with wanting her influence all to myself, I've missed how far-reaching her effect really is.

Not like she lives on in our hearts, or some made-up shit like that—I pass more and more posters in the halls on my way out, and looking at her picture doesn't make her feel *alive in my heart*. If anything, she feels even more acutely *gone*.

She's gone.

She doesn't *live on* in anyone's heart.

But she's left an indelible mark on mine. A lasting effect on everything I do.

Good work, brain. That made perfect sense.

Mom's exactly where I left her, the car idling along the curb in front of the school.

I throw my bags in the backseat—book bag heavier than before, gym bag lighter—and climb in the front.

"Everything okay?"

"Yeah. Everything's fine."

And, all things considering, it kinda is.

CHAPTER THIRTY-EIGHT

TWELVE HOURS OF AWKWARD STEP-SLIDES IS NOT ACCEPTABLE

The Y gym is empty when I walk in at nine the next morning, which is exactly what I'd been hoping for when Dad dropped me off.

Even though I got up with the alarm I set for the Tabbi-thon this morning, I knew before I fell asleep last night that there was no way I could go. It's too much to handle. It really is awesome, and I'm sure it will be a huge, tear-soaked success, but I don't think I can survive twelve hours of feeling like an outsider at an event for someone I knew better than anyone. Still too much resentment. Too much jealousy. Too much potential for galactic meltdown.

Plus dancing.

I do feel guilty. I can hear Tabby's lecture in my head, her telling me to get over myself, that it's for something actually important, while punching me in the arm. But it's too much still.

And, really, it's not like every one of her lectures was successful. There's a reason they happened with such frequency.

So I'm here.

I take a deep breath and jog to the nearest basket for an easy layup. It's the first shot I've taken in over two weeks. I know, big deal. But that's the longest I've gone without shooting since Dad put up the driveway hoop in fourth grade.

I go straight into my driveway shootaround routine, and it immediately feels right, like my brain clicks into place again. I have nine months until next season starts, and I am determined to follow Grampa's advice: *Play hard. Be good to your teammates. And be good to yourself.* Onc and thrcc I can start now.

I lock into a rhythm and run through my entire routine three times in a little over an hour, and move on to free throws. For the first time in a while, as I hit shot after shot, my brain can look forward and not see only shit. It's not what I imagined a few months ago, but it's okay. Some of it's even good.

I'm over a hundred free throws in when Branson walks through the door, alone.

Shit.

I keep shooting without any acknowledgment, like maybe I don't recognize him in this crowd of two, or maybe I'm too laser-focused on my game to notice. I brick two straight, though, naturally, before I'm back in a rhythm.

And the weirdest thing, without a word, Branson slides in under the basket to rebound for me, feeding me at the line shot after shot, which, I'll admit, is more nerve-racking than any end-of-game scenario I could have concocted on my own. What the hell is he doing here? Why is he not at the Tabbi-thon?

But I just keep shooting.

And Branson keeps rebounding.

Finally, after a stretch where I hit ten in a row, Branson rests the ball on his hip and looks at me.

"Wainwright, do you have any idea how fucking jealous I am

of you?" Like we're in the middle of some argument and not actually shooting baskets in an empty gym in utter silence.

I stare at him, confused, unable to speak. Is he serious?

"She talked about you all the time," he continues, again like we're mid-conversation. "Every story she had involved you somehow."

Again, I have nothing to say to this. I never imagined Tabby telling Branson our stories—I'm not sure I even imagined anything beyond them staring longingly at each other, or making out, or everything else my shitty brain refused to shut off. Not sharing goofy memories of childhood, and laughing together. Being friends.

A new wave of jealousy hits me, which is stupid, but I also realize that, for the first time, I really do feel sorry for him. For his loss.

"I'm sorry," I say quietly.

He slings the ball underhand back to me at the foul line. "Why would you be sorry for that? You were friends."

I realize he doesn't understand what I'm sorry for, that we're on two different trains of thought, but I'm again at a loss.

"Look," he says. "I know you loved her. It wasn't that hard to tell." I pretend to focus on dribbling. "But I loved her, too. I really did."

He says it like he's trying to convince me, like he needs me to understand this point.

"I'm sorry about the locker room," he says, looking at the floor. "For weeks, I don't know, it was like you didn't think I had any right to be upset. Like I was some kind of fraud for being crushed over her. And it made me crazy. I mean, I can't help that

I didn't know her as a kid. But, fucking-A, Wainwright, I still really loved her. And when you laughed at it, I don't know, I lost my mind. I'm sorry."

"It's okay," I say. "It was well deserved."

And he looks up, relieved almost. I can't believe he's been torturing himself over what *I* think. He had Tabby—why would he give a fuck what *I* think?

But I mattered to Tabby. I did.

And Tabby mattered to him.

"Why aren't you at the dance-athon?" I ask, taking another shot, trying to steer us out of this.

"I was there," he says. "For about an hour, at the beginning, but I had to get out of there. I couldn't handle watching all those people who didn't even know her crying and gushing about her."

"Yeah," I say. "Yeah. I know what you mean."

This is weird. But after a few more shots, he holds the ball again and says, "So are we good?"

I look at him. He really needs us to be good. It's crazy, but he really needs it. Liam Branson, senior stud athlete, heartbroken heartthrob of Franklin High—he needs *us* to be okay. I don't hate him. I really don't.

"We're good," I say.

And no, shitty movie director, he doesn't wrap me in an emotional, tear-soaked bro-hug at the foul line, the ball dropping meaningfully between our feet on the floor, our shared love of Tabby bringing us together in our loss. (You're still fired, by the way.)

Instead, Branson nods and, after my next shot, takes one of his own. We rebound for each other then, feeding it back after makes. Once his shot's warmed up, he says, "One-on-one?" and proceeds to whoop my ass for the next hour.

Which seems fair, I guess. And honestly, the last thing I want is for him to go easy. If I plan on taking his spot next year, I've got to be able to hang at this level.

He praises and encourages me after every shot I make, like he's coaching me up, and I think, *He really is this nice.* Dammit.

After our fifth game to twenty-one, we're both hanging on to our shorts, our shirts soaked through.

"So are you really going to Gettysburg next year?"

He drops his head, maybe catching his breath, then stands up straight.

"I haven't decided yet," he says. "I *was* going to. Before . . ." He pauses to wipe sweat from his face with his shirt. "But now I'm not sure. The coach at Guilford—this D-three school in North Carolina I was going to go to—he still wants me. He called again the other day."

"That's awesome," I say. "I can't imagine playing college."

"Me neither," he says. "That's always been my goal." He takes another deep breath and scoops the ball up off the floor, sinks a lazy jumper. "Anyway, I've still got time to decide."

"You should do it," I say. And, for once, for the right reasons.

He nods.

"I think I'm headed out," he says. "You want a ride home?"

"No, thanks; my mom's coming soon, I think."

"All right, man." He nods again, holds out his fist. "I'll see you later."

"Later," I say. And he's gone.

"So how did the last three games go?" I ask, sucking down a root beer float in Trip's basement later that evening.

"Eh, not great. We beat Eastern Adams because they suck. Lost by eight to Central, by twelve to Spring Garden."

"Damn."

"Yeah. Heiner somehow reinjured his ankle against Central." He throws air quotes around *reinjured.* "So thanks for being there, asshole."

I laugh. He doesn't ask about where I was or what I was doing for the past two weeks, for which I'm grateful.

After a few more rounds of bloodbath on his Xbox, we stand to gather our trash and glasses to take upstairs and reload on snacks. I'm about to tell Trip about Branson at the Y, but instead I ask, "Did you go to the Tabbi-thon today?"

He's gathering up an empty pizza box, but pauses and sits it back on the coffee table. He looks at me, stone-faced.

"Why, yes, Matt. I went to a twelve-hour dance-athon by myself. In fact, it's still going. I'm there right now, doing an awkward step-slide behind a group of upperclassmen in a dark corner of the gym." He starts step-sliding while he talks, his arms going into awkward, arrhythmic clapping motions, his face dead serious. "I'm having the time of my life."

I start laughing then, hard, and with that stupid look on his face, I can't stop. And suddenly—either because I still need to be in time-out or because I need to get a restraining order against this jaded movie director in my brain—I'm crying, just as hard, and I grab Trip in a hug.

"Right," he says, over my shoulder. "Because this is what happens when I dance."

I squeeze my eyes closed and laugh-cry more, unable to pull my shit together and break this terrible, awkward embrace.

"Would this be an inappropriate time to grab your ass?" he

says, and I let him go, more laughing than crying now, and because I seem to have lost all control of my brain functions, the words spurt out.

"I loved her, Trip."

Trip stares at me for a minute, then shakes his head.

"Listen, dumbass," he says. "Is there some reason you think you're smarter than me? That maybe you're so deep and mysterious that no one could understand what's in your head? Or do you think that I'm a complete fucking moron?"

He shakes his head again in disgust and picks up the empty pizza box.

"You've followed the girl around relentlessly since I've known you."

"I know. I just—"

The insides of my nostrils suddenly burn, and I have to turn my head away.

"Holy shit, was that you?"

"Yes. Yes it was."

"Seriously? You farted now? What is this, our tree scene?"

"Yes, Matt. It is our tree scene."

"Dear God, Trip, that is pungent."

"That's what you get," he says, and walks past me up the steps.

CHAPTER THIRTY-NINE

I STILL THINK "MINING FOR MEMORIES" SOUNDS STUPID

It takes all of two periods for school to feel normal again on Monday.

I expected everyone to point and stare in the halls, but no one does. I expected to feel lost at first, trying to pick up where we are in all my classes, but I don't. Routine takes over, and everything's fine. Just like after Tabby died, nothing's really any different. Quizzes were given. Papers were due. Whatever. Everyone else kept living.

The only class I'm still anxious about is English. I was up late last night writing. Mr. Ellis is different—I don't want to slip back into the current unnoticed.

I meet Trip at the corner of the English hall, and after he punches my arm in greeting, we walk together to Mr. Ellis's class.

Mr. Ellis is waiting outside his door like always, chatting up his students. He says welcome back to Trip as he walks in ahead of me into the classroom, but for me, he clamps his hands on my shoulders and gives them a shake, that goofy-ass smile on his face, and lets me continue on without a word.

"Welcome back, gang!" he says right after the bell, pulling his door closed behind him. "New unit today. Kickin' it old-school with a little Shakespeare."

"About time you follow the curriculum," Ilca mutters, her growl deep and resentful.

"Ilca loves Shakespeare," Mr. Ellis whispers behind his hand. "Especially the tragedies." He claps his hands together, excited. "All right, so we're going to read *Romeo and Juliet* together—and I know you probably already know the gist of the story, but I'm pumped to hear your thoughts as we get going. I want to keep you guys writing, though, so we may try our hands at sonnets, too—a little challenge for the poets in the room." He looks right at me as he says this, smiling.

It's good to be back.

At the end of class, while everyone's packing up, I flip open my writing folder and pull out a couple of typed pages.

"I'll be there in a second," I say to Trip. "Just have to turn in some makeup work."

When Trip leaves, I take a deep breath and scrawl a note across the top.

> *Mr. Ellis,*
> > *It's not exactly a memoir, but I hope this works.*
> > *Thanks for being awesome.*
> > > > > > *Matt*

I pack up the rest of my stuff, drop the paper on Mr. Ellis's desk, and go to find Trip in the hall.

■ ■ ■

IN DEFENSE OF YOLO

Let's be honest. Fifty years from now, YOLO will undoubtedly be seen as the dumbest contribution our generation offered up to the world.

You think I can chug this entire two-liter of Mountain Dew? YOLO!

You think I should go meet this guy I met online in the mall parking lot? YOLO!

You think anyone's ever tried to have sex with a porcupine? YOLO!

But, at its core, there's some basic truth to it. We only live once.

I lost my friend. She knew me better than anyone else in my life—from my favorite lunch after morning kindergarten, to my first girlfriend in fifth grade, to the worst things I've ever done. I loved her. And now it's like a part of me—a part of these memories—is gone. An icy road and an SUV, and YOLO has never been more devastatingly true.

Tabby's "once" is over.

I know this sounds like it's headed for another "seize the day" message, but I don't buy that. Because if I could go back, if I could spend more time with Tabby, would I change anything? Would I "seize the opportunity" and devise more forward ways to get her to choose me?

No.

Professing my love, or kissing her, or whatever romantic movie climax I secretly hoped for probably wouldn't have changed her feelings for the other guy.

But you know what? I'd give anything to go back, microwave another bag of popcorn, and slip in *Return of the Jedi* with my friend.

Sure, it's great to seize the day, live life to the fullest, all that jazz. But I think what matters even more is appreciating the moments we get. Noticing that, as you hand your friend yet another box of Nerds, that *this moment* is perfect. That any given moment might be.

Because at any given moment, you can lose what you love.

At any given moment, your whole world can change.

You can be spared by a friend.

You can learn other people's stories.

Your buddy can drop a fart that curls linoleum.

At any given moment, you can miss your friend so bad that your eyes burn and you have to put down your pen.

But that doesn't mean you won't pick it up again.

ACKNOWLEDGMENTS

So, so much to be thankful for.

To Laura Crockett, my dream agent, who never thought she would like a book about basketball—or one with so much swearing. You do nothing but put good into this world. Thanks for letting me be part of that.

To Erin Clarke, my absurdly talented editor, for loving Matt's story and for making it so much better. This whole process has been a joy, and I am fortunate to have you, and the entire brilliant team at Knopf, on my side.

To Keith and Seth—friends, colleagues, early readers—for giving me the exact feedback, exactly when I needed it. Keith, you're more of a mentor than you could ever know—as a teacher, a writer, a human being. Thank you. Seth, your incredible hard work and dedication push me to be better. I can't wait for the world to read your books.

To my students. I'd never be a writer if I hadn't first become a teacher. It just wouldn't have happened. I have so many amazing students who have listened to pieces of this story as it came together—who offered valuable feedback and enthusiasm in the earliest stages. It would be impossible (and probably illegal) to name them all. But if you're reading this, you know who you are. You're my true first readers.

To Mom and Dad, for raising me to love laughter and to love stories, for crying when you read this (multiple times!) and again when we got the news, for every early-morning breakfast. Everything comes back to you.

To my girls, Maddie and Mabel. I am blown away.

And finally, to Dawn. You, my love, are the Nerds.